Charmed

THE WARREN WITCHES

More titles in the

THE WARREN WITCHES

A Collection of Original Short Stories
Based on the Hit TV Series Created by
Constance M. Burge

SIMON & SCHUSTER

Many thanks to Phyllis Ungerleider for her immense help with this book.

First published in Great Britain in 2005 by Simon & Schuster UK Ltd.
Africa House, 64–78 Kingsway, London WC2B 6AH
A Viacom Company.

Originally published in 2005 by Simon Spotlight Entertainment,
an imprint of Simon & Schuster Children's Division, New York.

A CIP catalogue record for this book is available from the British Library upon request.

ISBN 141690123X

1 3 5 7 9 10 8 6 4 2

Printed by Cox & Wyman Ltd, Reading, Berks

Table of Contents

Old Friend

Laura J. Burns

"But the sign says two for five dollars."

Paige Matthews stopped short in the middle of the grocery aisle, sending a honeydew melon flying from her cart. She bent to retrieve it, but her attention was on the voice she'd just heard. It sounded familiar.

"And if they're two for five dollars, they can't be four fifty-nine each." The woman's voice rose in annoyance. Paige glanced around. She was alone in the produce aisle. The argument must be taking place one aisle over.

"Why don't you just buy two?"

"I don't need two!"

Paige shoved the grocery cart forward, maneuvering it around the corner and into the bread aisle. "Emily!" she called as she ran. "Emily Griffin! Is that you?"

The petite blond girl arguing with the teenage clerk turned around, eyes widening when she caught sight of Paige.

Paige's mouth dropped open. The girl *looked* like her old college friend. Same perky upturned nose, same smattering of freckles on her cheeks, same big blue eyes. But Paige and Emily had graduated years ago, and Paige hadn't seen her since. Was it possible that after all this time, Emily could still look *exactly* the same? "Em?" she said. "I can't believe it's you."

Emily's face broke into a smile. "Paige the Rage!" She threw her arms around Paige. "It's been forever since I've seen you!"

Paige looked her friend up and down. "You look incredible," she said honestly. "I want to know your secret."

"Oh, please." Emily rolled her eyes. "You're still a million times hotter than me and you know it. So what's up? How are you? Tell me everything."

"Well . . ." Paige had no idea where to start. Since college she'd had a career as a social worker, found out that she had two long-lost half sisters, Piper and Phoebe Halliwell, and discovered that she herself was a witch. Well, half a witch. And half a Whitelighter. "That's a long story," she said. "Let's talk about you."

"Um, do you want the pasta or not?" the clerk interrupted, holding out the fresh ravioli he and Emily had been bickering over.

"Oh!" Emily said. "I totally forgot. I only want one—I live alone, so I'm not going to eat two whole packages. But I'm not paying that price."

The kid rolled his eyes.

"Forget the pasta," Paige said. "Come home and have dinner with me. We can catch up while I cook."

"Well . . ." Emily glanced at her watch.

"Or I'll get my sister to cook," Paige rushed on, imagining Piper's incredible homemade alfredo sauce. "She's a real chef."

Emily's eyebrows drew together. "Your *sister*?"

Paige nodded. "Piper Halliwell. She owns a club, P3, but she used to work as a chef. Best cook ever. I mean it." She waved the salesclerk away and took Emily by the arm, pulling her toward the checkout counters. "She'll make you pasta from scratch."

"Piper Halliwell," Emily repeated. "Um, since when do you have a sister? Did I miss something?"

"You missed *everything*," Paige said. "You went AWOL after college. A ton of stuff has happened, but I could never find you to tell you about it."

Emily bit her lip. "Yeah, I was away for a while," she said vaguely. "So I missed you getting a sister?"

"A half sister," Paige replied. "Well, two half sisters, Piper and Phoebe Halliwell."

"Phoebe—'Ask Phoebe'?" Emily cried. "The advice columnist?"

"Yup. I'm so unglamorous compared to them," Paige joked. "But they're completely cool and I want you to meet them." She began dumping items from her cart onto the conveyer belt at the cashier station. "Seriously, Em, I have a lot to tell you. Come have dinner at the Manor."

"The Manor?" Emily burst out laughing. "You sound like a soap-opera star."

"I live like one, too!" Paige joked. "Halliwell Manor—it's an old Victorian. It's gorgeous."

"You moved in with your new sisters?" Emily asked. "Wow. So you're really close to them, huh?"

Saving the world from evil together is a great bonding tool, Paige thought. "They're my best friends in the world," she said aloud. "So what do you say?"

"A big beautiful house and a real chef cooking me dinner? You've convinced me," Emily answered. "Dinner at the Manor it is."

"I can't believe you live here, Paige," Emily murmured, gazing around the dining room.

"It's a lot better than the itty-bitty apartment I used to live in,"

Paige agreed. "Which you never visited me at, by the way. What happened to you after graduation? It's like you just fell off the face of the earth."

"Oh, you know . . ." Emily kept looking around the room as she spoke. "I went to Africa with the Peace Corps."

"No way!" Phoebe cried, coming in from the kitchen with a huge bowl of spinach salad. "That's so impressive. I always wanted to join the Peace Corps."

"Why didn't you?" Emily asked.

Phoebe shot Paige an "oops" look. "Um . . . our family is really tight-knit," she said. "My grams didn't want me to go so far away from my sisters."

Because we need the Power of Three to keep the world safe from evil, Paige finished the sentence in her head. "We all stick close to home," she said aloud. "But Phoebe manages to help people here even if she's not in the Peace Corps."

Phoebe smiled at her.

"Yeah, you write that advice column," Emily said. "I always read it."

"That's what I like to hear," Phoebe joked. "But that's boring compared to Africa. Tell us about it."

"Can I get anyone salad?" Emily reached for the bowl.

"Me!" Paige said, sticking her plate out for Emily to serve her.

"Mushroom ravioli coming up in five minutes," Piper reported as she came into the dining room carrying her son, Wyatt.

"I thought Leo was watching him," Phoebe said. She held out her arms for her nephew.

"He had to go," Piper replied.

Paige bit her lip. Piper's husband was their Whitelighter, but he also had other witches to protect. He must've had to orb off to help someone. "That's okay, Wyatt can hang with us while you cook," she told Piper.

"I have a few minutes to sit," Piper said. "And I heard you guys talking about Africa. Sounds interesting. Which country were you in, Emily?"

"Oh. I was in Zambia," Emily said. "Ever since college. I'm only back for a visit, so I won't be around for long," she added, glancing at Paige.

"Well, keep in touch this time," Paige told her. "I missed you. I expected at least an e-mail or something."

"Sorry," Emily said. "There are no computers where I work."

"Then write a letter," Paige said. "They do have mail somewhere in Zambia, don't they?"

"Yeah. Of course." Emily gazed at her plate for a moment. "I could write you letters."

"I would hope so," Paige teased her. "It's not fair to just vanish from my life like that, not after all the things we've been through together. All this time I've had nobody to share my secret obsession with Twizzlers."

Emily laughed.

"Twizzlers? The candy?" Phoebe asked.

"The best candy in the whole world," Paige replied.

"I didn't know you were obsessed with Twizzlers." Piper wrinkled her nose.

"That's because it's a *secret* obsession," Paige said.

"If you look under her bed, I bet you'll find a stash of emergency Twizzlers," Emily put in, grinning. "In a Tupperware container with a big 'T' on the top."

Paige blushed as her sisters laughed at her. "I got rid of that Tupperware," she said. "And besides, now I keep the emergency stash in my bedside table." She nudged Emily. "See? You disappear for five years, you miss things."

"You're right, I can't believe I wasn't there for the big switch to the bedside table," Emily teased.

A buzzer went off in the kitchen. "Pasta's done," Piper said, getting up. "I hope you like it, Emily. I made it with mushrooms from our garden."

"I'm sure it will be delicious." Emily stood too. "I'm just going to run to the little girls' room before the main course. Where do I go?"

"Upstairs to the right," Phoebe told her.

Emily headed off toward the stairs. Paige watched her go, amazed at how good her friend looked. "They must have some big beauty secret in Zambia," she said, shaking her head. "Emily looks incredible."

"Probably because she's happy," Phoebe said. "She's doing what she loves, so she's got nothing to stress about."

"I think life in the Peace Corps has got to be pretty stressful," Piper disagreed, heading back in from the kitchen. She set out the serving bowl of pasta and began scooping ravioli onto everyone's plates. "Maybe she's just one of those lucky people who always looks young."

"I guess," Paige said. She lowered her voice. "Hey, where did Leo go? Is everything okay?"

Piper nodded. "He had an Innocent in danger, so he had to take off. But I don't think it's anything for us to worry about. I just hope Emily didn't see the light from his orbing."

"I doubt it," Phoebe said, making a funny face at Wyatt. "I didn't notice it. Why would she?"

"I don't know. She probably didn't." Piper frowned. "Have I ever met her before, Paige? She looks so familiar."

"Yeah, she looks familiar to me, too," Phoebe agreed.

"I haven't even seen her since college," Paige said. "She's been in Africa, remember? So unless you two went on safari without telling me, there's no way you'd have seen her before."

The food looked absolutely delicious, but no one ate. Paige

knew they didn't want to be rude—they'd all wait for Emily before they dug in. She glanced at the staircase. No Emily.

Phoebe bounced Wyatt up and down on her lap. Piper stifled a yawn.

Paige checked the stairs again. Still no sign of her friend. "Maybe I should go see if she's okay," Paige suggested. "She's been gone for a while."

She jogged up the steps to the second floor and glanced at the bathroom door. It was open, and the room was dark. So where was Emily?

"Em?" she called, walking down the hallway to her bedroom. "Where are you?" She pushed open her door, but Emily wasn't inside. She wasn't in Piper and Leo's room, either. And she wasn't in Phoebe's. Which left only one place she could possibly be.

Paige took the second flight of steps two at a time. The attic door was open. When she reached the top, she stopped short.

Emily stood inside, behind the podium that held the Book of Shadows. She was reading from it, her lips moving slightly.

"What are you doing up here?" Paige demanded.

Emily started and looked up at her. Then she slammed the Book of Shadows closed. And disappeared.

Piper had just decided to grab one ravioli when there was a shriek from upstairs. Across the dining-room table, Phoebe jumped. "What was that?"

"That was Paige yelling," Piper said with a sigh. "I was afraid that would happen."

Phoebe was already headed for the stairs, carrying Wyatt. Piper followed her. They found Paige in the attic, staring at . . . nothing.

"What happened?" Piper asked. "Where's Emily?"

"She's gone," Paige sputtered. "I came up here, she was reading from the book, and then she vanished."

"Uh-oh," Phoebe said. "That's never good."

"Do you think she did a spell?" Piper asked.

"I don't know," Paige cried. "How could she? She's not a witch. How did she even know the Book of Shadows was up here?" She began pacing around the attic. "Maybe it's not really Emily. Maybe it's a . . . a shape-shifter."

Wyatt began to cry. He never liked it when anyone in the family was upset. Piper took him from Phoebe and bounced him in her arms. "A shape-shifter that you just happened to run into in the grocery store?" she said skeptically.

"It could be," Paige insisted. "It could have gone there to run into me on purpose. To set a trap for me."

"Paige, sweetie, you do the grocery shopping, like, once every six months," Phoebe said. "I doubt that even a shape-shifting demon would think to set a trap for you at the supermarket."

"And didn't you say you were in the Haight?" Piper put in. "That's nowhere near here. There's no reason for an evil *anything* to be looking for you there."

"Besides, the Book of Shadows doesn't tolerate evil near it," Phoebe pointed out. "So whoever she was—or whatever she was—she can't have been evil."

"Then how did she just disappear?" Paige demanded.

Piper eased herself down onto the old couch, settling Wyatt on her lap. "She did a spell. It's the only explanation." She glanced at the Book of Shadows. It was closed. "Didn't you say she was reading from the book?"

"Yeah."

"Then why isn't it open to the page she was reading?"

"Oh." Paige ran a hand through her hair, frustrated. "She slammed it closed. I guess she didn't want us to see what she'd been doing."

"This doesn't add up," Phoebe said. "Did you ever sense anything, you know, *magical* about her during college?"

"No," Paige said. "Nothing. Do you think maybe she got lost looking for the bathroom, and she stumbled across the book? It is pretty cool-looking. Maybe she did her disappearing act accidentally."

Piper frowned. Phoebe and Paige started talking about how to figure out where Emily had disappeared to, but she wasn't concerned with that. Something had been nagging at her ever since Emily had walked into the Manor with Paige. "I know her," she said suddenly. "I swear I recognize Emily."

She jumped up, shoving Wyatt into Paige's arms. "There's a picture of her." She stalked over to the old bookshelf in the corner and scanned the spines of the photo albums. Their mother had kept all the family photos in neatly organized albums, with labels for each and every picture. Finally Piper found the one she'd been looking for—the burgundy leather album with two gold stripes on the spine and one formerly gold stripe that had been colored in with black pen by Phoebe when she was two.

She pulled the book off the shelf and brought it over to the couch. Her sisters crowded around her as she flipped through. There were a lot of pictures of their oldest sister, Prue, who had been killed by a demon a few years back. Piper felt her eyes tear up as she looked at baby Prue playing with a toy phone. Prue riding on a tricycle. Prue holding infant Piper on her lap.

Piper swallowed hard. Now wasn't the time to get all sad about Prue. They had a possibly innocent woman lost out there somewhere, and they had to find her. She flipped to the end of the book. Then back a page or two. And finally she found it.

Little Prue and Piper on the couch in the living room with their favorite babysitter. She heard Paige gasp as she caught sight of the teenage girl. "That's Emily!"

"Yup," Piper said. "I *knew* she looked familiar. This girl was the coolest babysitter ever. After Mom and Dad left for the evening, she'd always give us Oreos and ice cream and all the junk food we wanted. And she let us stay up late." She hesitated, imagining Wyatt with a babysitter like that. "Okay, she totally sucked as a babysitter. But we liked her."

"Wait a minute," Paige said. "This picture is from the 1970s."

Piper nodded. "And her name wasn't Emily. It was Anna, or maybe Emma. I don't really remember her clearly. Prue was older. She would have remembered better."

Phoebe slipped her arm around Piper's shoulders in silent sympathy.

"I mostly just recognized her because of this picture," Piper added. "I've seen it a million times."

"Still, this can't be Emily," Phoebe said. "This babysitter girl has to be almost fifty by now."

"She looks *exactly* like Emily," Paige pointed out. "Maybe it's Emily's mother or aunt. If she lived nearby, there might still be relatives around. Do you think we could find your old babysitter, Piper?"

"Noooo," Piper said slowly. "Something happened to her. I remember Mom and Dad talking about it. I didn't know what they were saying, but Prue told me the babysitter was gone. I think she just took off one day with no warning. Mom was upset about it, but Dad didn't want her to interfere."

"Interfere magically, you mean?" Phoebe asked. "Did Mom suspect that a demon had grabbed her?"

"I have no idea," Piper said, frustrated. "For all I know, Prue was just making up stories to scare me. We were so young, I can't remember any of it clearly."

She stared at the picture for a moment, willing herself to recall anything more about the girl, but nothing came.

"This isn't what I was thinking of," Phoebe said suddenly.

"Huh?" Piper asked.

"Emily looked really familiar to me, too. But it's not from this picture. I don't remember the babysitter."

"You were just a baby," Piper said.

"Yeah. But I thought I recognized Emily from the Book of Shadows," Phoebe said. "I think there's a picture I've seen in there that reminded me of her."

In an instant Paige was on her feet. She grabbed the book and brought it back to where they were sitting. Phoebe began flipping through, but Paige still paced up and down in front of the couch.

"Don't worry. We'll find your friend," Piper told her.

"But *is* she my friend?" Paige cried. "I'm so confused by all of this!"

"Well, we know she didn't pose a threat to us," Piper replied. "Wyatt was near her, and he didn't put up his protective shield."

Paige smiled at the baby. "That's true."

"So chances are that Emily is exactly who you think she is," Piper said.

"Uh, I'm not so sure about that." Phoebe spread the Book of Shadows out on her lap for them to see. There, in Grams's writing, was a page entitled "Amelia Grifton." And in the corner was a sketch of a girl who looked like Emily. *Exactly* like Emily.

Paige's brow furrowed in confusion. "Is that the babysitter?"

"No," Phoebe replied. "It says here that this Amelia person was a neighbor. She lived next door to Grams for five years . . . in the 1950s."

"But she still looks the same age," Piper said. "What else does it say?"

"'It isn't necessarily magical,'" Phoebe read, "'but the circumstances of Amelia's disappearance are definitely odd. One day she was here, the next she was gone. But she left no forwarding address, she didn't take any of her furniture or clothing, and she never said good-bye although we have been friends for years.'"

"I guess that is odd," Piper commented. "But it doesn't really seem worthy of being a note in the Book of Shadows."

"'The reason I am suspicious is this,'" Phoebe continued reading. "'Amelia disappeared the day after meeting Mother, and Mother is positive that she has seen Amelia before. She's getting old now and her memory isn't what it was. But I trust her when she says she recognized Amelia.'"

"Wait a minute," Paige interrupted. "Now we think Grams's *mother* knew Emily, too?"

"It gets weirder," Phoebe said. "There's a note at the bottom of the page that Grams added later. 'When I looked for Amelia, there were no government records on her. And when I scryed for Amelia, I found not a trace of her. It was as if she had never existed.'"

"Maybe Emily's like us," Piper said. "Her family has been in San Francisco for a few generations. Grams knew her grandmother, Mom knew her mother, and Paige knows Emily."

"I don't think so." Paige pointed to the sketch in the book. "This Amelia person had a birthmark on her left cheek, see?"

Piper studied the sketch. Then she pulled the photo album back onto her lap. The babysitter in the picture had a birthmark in the exact same place. "Let me guess," she said. "Emily has a birthmark on her left cheek too?"

"Yeah. She was always talking about getting it removed," Paige said.

Piper sighed. This situation was getting stranger and stranger. "Birthmarks aren't hereditary," she said. "They're completely individual—even twins can have different birthmarks."

"So there's no way that three generations of women could have the same birthmark," Phoebe said.

"Then there's no way that all these Emily-Emma-Amelias are different people," Paige finished. "This is the same person, who's been the same age since Grams knew her . . . and maybe since Grams's mother knew her."

"Yup," Piper said. "And whoever she is, she's been friends with our family for at least fifty years."

"Leo!" Piper called for the fourth time.

Her husband appeared in a swirl of white light, looking frazzled. "Sorry, honey," he said quickly. "I'm kinda in the middle of something."

"Yeah, well, we're in the middle of something, too," she told him. "I need you to watch Wyatt."

"Why?"

"Um, because we have to track down Paige's friend who is also Mom's friend and Grams's friend and who probably did a spell from the Book of Shadows and made herself disappear," Phoebe said.

Leo's eyebrows drew together in confusion. "That girl you were making dinner for?"

"That's the one," Piper said. "Can you take Wyatt?"

"Not really," he replied. "It's a little dangerous, and I really have to get back. Can't one of you stay with him?"

Phoebe let out a dramatic sigh. "I'll watch him," she said. "If I *have* to."

Piper smiled. Phoebe loved Wyatt more than anything on earth. She loved babysitting him. "Okay, go back to your charge," she told her husband. "And say thank you to Phoebe."

"Thanks, Phoebes." Leo gave her a quick wink and orbed away again.

"Think you two can handle it without me?" Phoebe asked, picking Wyatt up and swinging him around.

"Sure," Paige said. "But you're not off the hook yet. We need to figure out what spell Emily did."

"Ooh, I know how to do that," Phoebe said. She grabbed a pen and began scribbling down an incantation as Wyatt played with her necklace. "We need the Book to show us the last spell used." She handed the paper to Paige. Piper came to stand next to them and they all read together:

Halliwell Book,
We need another look;
Reveal your latest secret.

The old leather cover creaked as the book flew open with a loud *thwump!*

"That should be the page Emily was looking at," Phoebe said.

Piper leaned over the book and read aloud. " 'To Return to the Beginning.' "

"What do you think that means?" Paige asked. "Is it time travel?"

Piper scanned the words of the spell. "Sort of. It's to return to the moments before an incantation was said."

"I wonder why Emily would want to do that," Phoebe said.

"There's only one way to find out," Piper replied. "You be good for Aunt Phoebe." She kissed Wyatt's fat little cheek, then turned to Paige. "Ready?"

"You bet." Paige took her hand and they read the incantation from the book:

Powers enacted, magic has gone.
The spell was said,
And done.
Return me there to see it again.

A cold wind blew through the attic, whipping Piper's long hair across her face. She brushed it away—and found everything changed. Well, not *everything*. She stood in the attic, in the exact same place. Paige stood next to her, holding her hand. But Phoebe and Wyatt were gone. The old couch was gone, with two elaborate brocade-covered chairs in its place. The threadbare oriental rug on the floor was a vibrant red color that looked brand-new. The bookshelves in the corner had only a few leather-bound books on them. The rest of the space was taken up by china knickknacks. Underneath the stained-glass window was an old phonograph.

The Book of Shadows sat on its pedestal, closed.

"Okay . . . we're still in the Manor," Paige whispered.

"I think we can speak normally," Piper pointed out. "There's no one here to hear us."

"Yeah, including Emily," Paige said. "Why are we here if she's not here? And why is everything so different?"

"We went back to the beginning, remember?" Piper said. "Now we just have to figure out when that was . . . is . . . whatever."

"Okay, so"—Paige glanced around—"everything is newer. A lot newer. How far back do you think we are?"

"I don't know, but there's no dust on that phonograph," Piper said. "I think that's the current version of an iPod."

Paige's eyebrows shot up. "Doesn't that put us in the 1800s?"

Piper laughed. "The house was only built in 1906, so no. But we're definitely pre–rock and roll."

Paige went over to the door and eased it open. Immediately sound filled the room. Tinkling piano music. The roar of voices talking and laughing. "Uh-oh," Paige murmured. "I think we just crashed a party."

"Well, if we did, then Emily did too," Piper said. "And the sooner we find her, the better. Let's go down."

Paige led the way down the stairs, automatically stepping

lightly on the second step from the bottom—the one that always squeaked. Piper studied it for a second, then put all her weight right in the middle of the step. "No squeak," she announced.

"Wow," Paige said. "We *are* far back!"

"I know—that step has squeaked all my life." On the second floor, Piper hesitated. A girl and a guy were walking down the hallway toward the stairs. The girl had short red hair with a giant peacock eye-feather pinned on one side. Her silky dress hit at her knees, and she wore about five long ropes of pearls around her neck. The guy had slicked-back hair, shiny two-toned shoes, and a dark suit with wide lapels.

Piper took Paige's arm and drew her back up onto the attic stairs. They watched silently as the couple passed them, whispering to each other and giggling on their way downstairs to the living room.

"I know when we are," Piper whispered.

"Their clothes looked like the Roaring Twenties," Paige said.

"Yeah. But this is no party," Piper told her. "In the twenties our ancestors ran a little business out of the house."

A peal of laughter drifted up from downstairs, accompanied by a crescendo in the piano music.

"You think that's a business meeting?" Paige asked skeptically.

"Nope. It's a speakeasy," Piper told her. "Three cousins lived in the house—Grams's mother was one of them. And they ran a secret bar during Prohibition. Grams always said it was how her mother managed to keep the Manor during the Great Depression. She and her cousins made so much money from the speakeasy that they paid off their mortgage before the Depression hit."

Paige looked impressed. "Those were some good businesswomen! It must run in the family, Ms. Nightclub Owner. You take after Great-Grams."

"You know, I never thought of that," Piper said. She'd been

running her own bar for years now and she hadn't even realized how similar her job was to her great-grandmother's. "I guess we inherited more than magical powers, huh?"

The song ended, and a burst of applause floated up the staircase.

"We better get going," Paige said. "Who knows what Emily expected that spell to do? I bet she didn't think she'd end up back in the twenties. We have to find her before she gets into trouble."

"Or before she runs into Great-Grams's evil cousin," Piper agreed. "There are two good witches running this club. And one very, very bad witch."

"Good to know," Paige said. "So let's go find Emily."

Piper glanced down at herself. She wore jeans and a tank top. Her sneakers were made of material that probably hadn't been invented yet. If any of these 1920s people spotted her, they'd stop and stare. Paige wasn't much better, but at least her shoes were basic leather pumps. Her skirt was flirty and cute, but about a foot shorter than a flapper's would've been.

"I think you'll do a little better than I will among the locals," Piper said. "Why don't you check out the action downstairs, and I'll search for Emily up here."

"Sounds good," Paige replied. She buttoned up the top button on her cardigan and yanked her mini down as far as it would go. "Yell if you need me."

Don't make eye contact and no one will notice you, Paige told herself as she stepped off the staircase and joined the throng of people in the living room. It didn't look anything like the living room she was used to. There were no chairs or sofas, just some big overstuffed pillows tossed into the corners. The dining room was taken up by a baby grand piano and an elaborate wooden bar. But the strangest thing was the foyer. There was a wall across the length of the entryway, completely blocking the front door. A tall, thin man with a mustache sat on a stool next to a tiny slit in the wall, looking through it every so often.

Paige glanced around. Obviously that guy was the one who decided whether to let people in or not. But where did they enter?

"'Scuse me, doll," a voice said behind her.

Paige jumped in surprise as a young man and an older woman stepped out of an opening in the wall beneath the stairs. They made their way around her and headed into the crowd.

"Huh. I'm gonna have to see if there's still a secret door there," Paige murmured. "I could pull some nice practical jokes with that one."

She pushed her way farther into the room. The piano music was fast and some of the people were dancing, not caring if they accidentally bumped into each other as they moved. People blew on noisemakers, and over the bar a banner was strung: HAPPY NEW YEAR 1924!! Women sat in groups on the big pillows, heads close together as they gossiped. Everywhere Paige looked, men in suits flirted with girls in flapper dresses.

Change the clothes and you're at a New Year's party in 2005, she thought. But where in all this craziness was Emily?

Paige had checked every inch of the dining room. She made her way into the living room, avoiding eye contact. She'd found that if you didn't look straight at a person, they tended not to look at you, either. But the tall guy watching the front door through the slit in the wall—he looked at everyone. As Paige eased her way through a group of girls in front of him, she felt his eyes following her the whole way. She didn't have much time. He would definitely raise the alarm.

A familiar laugh caught her attention. Paige ducked under the arm of a heavyset man dancing by himself, and made her way across the living room to one of the groups of seated women. There, right in the middle, was Emily.

She wore a dark blue dress with a deep V-neck, and around her forehead was a matching blue ribbon. Her blond hair was chin length, as usual, but now it was curled into an old-fashioned bob, and her lips were painted a deep cherry red.

"Emily!" Paige cried. "What is going on?"

Emily stared up at her, her mouth hanging open. All the other girls glanced up too—and gasped as they looked Paige up and down.

"She has no stockings," one of them whispered, scandalized.

"I've never seen a skirt so short," another added.

Great, Paige thought. *Even in the Roaring Twenties, I'm too radical.*

"Emmeline Graydon, do you know this . . . lady?" the first girl asked, turning to Emily.

"Not yet," Emily said, eyes shining. "But I will soon!" She extended her hand up to Paige. Instinctively Paige grabbed it and pulled her up.

"You're positively courageous!" Emily cried, linking her arm through Paige's. "I'd never have the nerve to show up without stockings!"

Paige had never been so aware of her bare legs as she was right now. "Yeah, I . . . uh . . . didn't have any clean ones."

Emily laughed her throaty laugh and began pulling Paige through the crowd. "It's shocking. You'll see . . . soon it will be all the rage."

"That's what you used to call me," Paige told her. "Paige the Rage."

"I'm sorry?" Emily asked, blinking at her in confusion.

"Em, it's me. Paige. Tell me what's going on," Paige insisted.

Emily looked baffled for a moment, then she giggled. "Oh, did we meet before? I am positively awful with remembering folks. But I'll remember you this time, Paige the Rage." Her grip on Paige's arm tightened. "There she is!" Emily nodded toward the stairs.

A petite woman with a short, black bob was leaning over the banister of the staircase as she spoke to a dapper-looking man near the hidden doorway. Her dress was made of a pale pink gauzy material that clung to her thin frame in a sexy way. She carried a single giant ostrich feather dyed to match the dress, and as Paige watched, she slowly ran the feather up the man's neck. With a lazy smile she turned away and went upstairs. The man stared after her like a hungry puppy.

"Who is that?" Paige asked. "Is that guy her boyfriend?"

"Him?" Emily laughed. "No, she's just playing with him. Let's go."

She maneuvered them over to the staircase, and now she began climbing. "Hold on," Paige said, stopping. "Where are we going?"

"Up to the attic. Shh!" Emily said. "We're really not supposed to, but I simply have to introduce you to my friend up there. She owns the joint."

She owns the joint? Paige frowned. That sexy black-haired girl was her great-grandmother? It didn't seem right somehow. Maybe she was one of the other cousins.

"Come on!" Emily was halfway up the stairs already. "She'll be so excited to meet you. She's very forward herself, as you saw. Still, even she doesn't go out in a dress that short! You two are kindred spirits."

Paige followed her. "Em, what are you doing here?" she asked once they'd left the noise of the party behind. "Why did you come back here?"

Emily looked at her curiously. "Why wouldn't I come back here? This is the keenest speakeasy in town. I come every weekend. I wouldn't want to miss their New Year's party!"

Something didn't make sense. This girl was acting as if she belonged here, not as if she'd just magically sent herself back from eighty years in the future.

"Where'd you get those clothes?" she asked Emily.

"Oh, aren't they spiffy?" Emily replied, running her hands down her dress. "My mama wants me to pinch my pennies, but I'm the one who earns them. I dropped a whole week's salary from the telephone company on these threads." She did a little pirouette to show off. "I go to a sweet little man down in Chinatown who makes them for me."

Paige stared at her. "The telephone company?"

Emily rolled her eyes. "I'd rather get hitched, tell you the truth. But a girl has to have spending money. So I'm working at the switchboard until Mr. Right comes along. What's your story, Paige the Rage?"

Paige didn't know what to think. This girl wasn't acting. She wasn't lying. Paige knew Emily well enough to know that this girl was being completely open and honest with her. But what was going on? Had the spell Emily said not only sent her back here, but erased her memory? But then why did she seem to think she had a whole life here, with a job and a mother and a tailor in Chinatown?

"What did that girl downstairs call you?" Paige asked. "Emmeline?"

"Sure, angel. That's my name. But you can just call me Graydon. All the gals are doing that now."

"You're not Emily Griffin?"

"No." She frowned. "Emmeline Graydon. I thought you said we'd met."

"Yeah. I'm, uh . . . not good with names," Paige lied. "Do you live around here, Emmeline? I mean, Graydon?"

"With Mama, one block away," Emmeline said. "That's why they let me in here for free. I grew up with these girls! My friend Russell up there used to watch me when I was a baby and Mama had to run to the market."

She grew up with Great-Grams and her cousins, Paige thought. She pictured all the different Emilys they'd seen—her college friend, Prue and Piper's babysitter, Grams's neighbor. This girl must be the first one, the original version of Emily.

So we did come back to the beginning, Paige thought, following Emmeline up the stairs to the attic. *But the beginning of* what?

Piper pushed open her bedroom door, hoping to find Emily but half expecting to see her own bed with Leo's rumpled bathrobe flung over one of the wooden posts. But the room was completely different. The walls were painted a pale rose color, half the room was taken up by an elaborate carved armoire, and the bed was just a small twin bed. But on the bedside table was a framed sepia-tone photograph of a middle-aged couple. Piper smiled. This exact framed picture had been on Grams's bedside table when Piper was little. The couple were Grams's grandparents. This had to be Great-Grams's room, and she kept the picture of her parents next to her bed.

"Emily?" Piper called quietly.

There was no answer. The only sounds came from the ticking of the old-fashioned alarm clock on the table and the muted piano music from downstairs. Piper turned to go . . . and found Emily standing in the doorway. She looked astonished to see Piper.

"What are you doing here?" she demanded.

"It's my house," Piper pointed out. "The question is, what are *you* doing here? How did you get here?"

"I read your book," Emily said, coming into the room. "I did a spell. Did you think they only worked for witches?"

"Um . . . yeah," Piper replied. "But why did you want to come here? What did you hope the spell would do?"

Emily opened her mouth to answer, but before she could say anything, a white light filled the room. Wyatt orbed into Piper's arms.

"Wyatt!" she cried. "What are you doing here?"

"Even your baby is a witch?" Emily said.

"Technically he's only half witch," Piper told her. "But that's more than enough."

"Well, why don't you take him back where he belongs?" Emily said harshly. "You shouldn't be here. This is none of your business."

"*What* is none of my business? Emily, what's going on? Paige is frantic, she's so worried about you."

"I didn't mean to drag Paige into it," Emily said. "But when I found out she lived in Halliwell Manor, I couldn't let the opportunity pass me by."

"The opportunity to get upstairs and read the Book of Shadows?" Piper guessed.

Footsteps clomped down the hall, and Phoebe burst into the room. "Oh, thank God." She sighed when she saw Wyatt. "I was hoping he'd be here."

"What happened?" Piper asked.

"He fell and whacked his elbow on the side of his toy firehouse," Phoebe explained. "He was crying for you and he wouldn't let me comfort him. Then he just orbed away."

"How did you get here?" Piper asked.

"I did the back-to-the-beginning spell and just hoped it would take me to you," Phoebe said. She glanced around the room, and then at Emily. "So what's this all about?"

Emily crossed her arms and frowned at them. "It's not about you two at all, or about Paige."

Wyatt squirmed around in Piper's arms, wanting to get down. She bent and placed him on his feet so he could explore the room.

"Why have we been finding pictures of someone who looks just like you during our mother's lifetime, and our grand-mother's?" Phoebe asked Emily. "Are you a witch?"

"No!" Emily spat. "I'm the victim of a witch."

"What?" Piper cried. "What kind of victim?"

"What kind of *witch*?" Phoebe added.

"What are you people doing in my bedroom?" A pretty woman with thick hair who bore an uncanny resemblance to Piper stood in the doorway. She eyed them suspiciously. "Who are you?"

Piper caught her breath. This must be Great-Grams!

"Speak up!" Great-Grams ordered, raising her hands as if she might use her power on them. "Who are you?"

Piper shot Phoebe a questioning glance. How were they sup-posed to explain their sudden appearance to their own ancestor? "Um, we're . . ."

"They're my insurance!" Emily cried suddenly. She bent quickly and snatched Wyatt off the floor. "And so is he."

Piper gasped. Instinctively she lifted her arms to freeze Emily so she could take Wyatt back, but Phoebe grabbed her hand. She shook her head slightly. "He's okay," she murmured.

It was true. Wyatt's eyes were a tiny bit alarmed, but he hadn't put up his protective shield. Since his powers seemed definitely to be working, it was clear he didn't feel endangered by Emily.

Great-Grams was staring at Emily now. "You're that little friend of my cousin's," she said. "Emmeline. Why are you dressed like that?"

"I'm not the Emmeline you know," Emily snapped. "I'm not as naive as she was."

"Excuse me. What?" Phoebe interrupted. "There are two of you?"

"No," Emily said. "I mean, there are right now. I think. Hopefully. But not really." Her voice shook as she spoke, and Piper found herself feeling sorry for the girl. She was clearly freaking out about something. But that was no excuse for grabbing Wyatt.

"Emily, give me my son," she said firmly. "And then we'll help figure out what's happening here."

"No!" Emily backed away, clinging to Wyatt. "I'm not going to be fooled by a bunch of witches."

Great-Grams gasped, her face paling.

"That's right!" Emily cried. "I figured out your secret. You're a witch!" Her gaze swept wildly over Phoebe and Piper. "You're all witches. And so were your mother and grandmother."

Great-Grams turned to Piper. "Who *are* you?" she asked again.

"Um, we're your great-granddaughters," she said quickly. "Nice to meet you."

Great-Grams looked even paler than before, but she managed a small smile. "You too. I think." She turned back to Emily. "Okay, Emmeline. How do you know we're witches?"

"My name's not Emmeline anymore," she said, anger filling her voice. "I've been at least ten other people since Emmeline. I have to change my name every five or six years. I have to move and make new friends and lie to everyone I know. Do you think I *wanted* to run into Paige?" she added to Piper. "I'm just lucky it hasn't been that long since we were friends or she would've realized the truth."

"What truth?" Piper asked.

"That I'm the same age I was when I knew her years ago. I'm nineteen. I've been nineteen for eighty years!"

• • •

"Shhh," Emmeline hissed at the top of the stairs. "I think she went into the attic, so we have to be quiet as mice. She doesn't want people coming up here."

"Who doesn't?" Paige whispered.

"Russell. She says it's off-limits."

Paige frowned at the tightly closed attic door. "Why?"

Emmeline shrugged. "I asked her that, and she just said 'Graydon, there are some things a girl like you simply shouldn't see.'" She giggled. "Isn't it positively intriguing? I can barely contain my curiosity!"

"And you have no idea what her secret is?" Paige asked. She had a feeling she knew all too well what the secret was.

"No, but I know it must be exciting," Emmeline said. "Russell's a gypsy, so who knows what sort of things she might have hidden away in a creepy old attic."

"Wait, she's a gypsy?" Paige asked, confused.

"Not really," Emmeline said. "But she likes to say she is. She tells fortunes and reads palms and everything. The customers at the speakeasy really go for it." She leaned her weight against the attic door. "Ready?"

"No," Paige said quickly. She didn't want Emmeline walking in there to find the Book of Shadows. It was bad enough that one version of Emily had discovered that. "If she doesn't want us going in there, we should probably listen to her."

Emmeline pouted. "Don't be a squawker, Paige the Rage," she teased. "I've been meaning to uncover her big secret for weeks now. Tonight's the night! Then afterward you can meet her."

"Em—uh, Graydon," Paige whispered urgently. "She'll be mad at you!"

"Don't be silly. I'm her best friend," Emmeline said. She shoved open the door and disappeared inside.

Paige followed.

Emmeline immediately ducked behind one of the big brocade chairs, putting a finger to her lips. She gestured with her head to where the black-haired girl, Russell, stood. Paige inched forward and hid behind a brass-bound trunk. She wanted to be close enough to get a good look at her great-great-aunt. Russell stood in the center of the room. On the floor around her feet was a circle of bloodred candles, and she was lighting them one by one from a long wooden match.

Emmeline waved from her hiding spot, grinning like this was all a big game. But Paige couldn't bring herself to smile back. That girl—Russell—was getting ready to do a spell. Emmeline shouldn't see that! She obviously didn't know her friend was a witch, and it wasn't something people could be allowed to find out.

The candles were all lit. Russell took a long, deep breath and languidly raised her arms over her head as she began to speak:

Powers of the earth and the land below,
Witness my beauty, behold my youth.
Though others here continue to grow,
Let age pass me by, keep me young in truth.

She began blowing out the candles in reverse order of how she'd lit them. Paige ran through the spell in her mind, trying to figure out what it would do. She knew as soon as the last candle went out, the spell would take effect.

"Let age pass me by, keep me young in truth," she whispered, staring at Emmeline, who was practically hopping up and down in her excitement as she watched. "Keep me young . . ."

Paige drew in a sharp breath. It was a youth spell, one that would keep the young person that same age forever. But Russell thought she was up here alone. She didn't know Emmeline was hiding nearby. Emmeline . . . Emma . . . Emily.

She was younger than Russell. The spell was going to work on *her*.

"I know you're upset, Emily," Phoebe said. "But what good does holding Wyatt hostage do? You're not mad at *him*."

Emily's blue eyes were wild. "I don't care!" she cried. "I'll hurt him—I will!"

Phoebe shot a glance at Piper, who was remarkably calm. True, Wyatt could protect himself. And if he really wanted to, he could orb to somewhere else. But it was still nervewracking to see this hysterical girl holding on to him so tightly.

"You don't have to hurt Wyatt," Piper said. "Just tell us what it is you want."

"I don't know," Emily said, desperate. "It's not like I had a plan. I just knew I had to get back here if there was any chance of stopping it."

"Stopping . . . what?" Great-Grams asked. She looked as confused as Phoebe felt.

"You!" Emily yelled. "I need to stop you! So you just . . . just sit down and stay where I can see you. Or else I'll hurt this baby. And he's your great-great-grandson." Her voice wavered as she looked down at Wyatt, who was sucking on his hand as if nothing were wrong.

Great-Grams eased herself down on a tall, straight-backed chair next to the door. "All right," she said. "Why do you want to stop me? What do you think I'm going to do?"

"You put this spell on me, witch!" Emily cried. "I remember everything about it. You found me coming down from the attic and you yelled at me for sneaking around. You're so mean. I always knew you were jealous of me."

Great-Grams blinked at her. "Jealous of what?"

"You knew your cousin liked me more than she liked you,"

Emily said. "You got mad at me for being up here, and you didn't like me anyway. So you cursed me."

One big tear rolled down Emily's cheek. Phoebe couldn't decide if the poor girl was more sad or angry. But one thing was certain: Emily was wrong. Their great-grandmother was a good witch. She would never have put a spell on Emily.

Piper seemed to be thinking the same thing.

"Emily, that's not what happened," she said calmly. "This is our great-grandmother. She was a good person, and a good witch. Good witches don't curse people."

"I don't care what you say," Emily replied. "I know I left here that night . . . *tonight* . . . and I felt funny. And I never aged another day. My nails didn't grow. My hair didn't grow. I stopped getting older. Do you have any idea how awful that is?"

Phoebe bit her lip. Never getting old sounded pretty good to her. But she'd never thought through the ramifications of it before.

"Piper, I used to babysit for you," Emily said. "And now you're older than me. That's just not natural. I could never get married or have my own children because they would figure out what a freak I am. My whole life was ruined."

"And you're sure that's going to happen tonight?" Great-Grams asked.

"Yes." Emily narrowed her eyes. "Because you found me upstairs. You banned me from the speakeasy. No one ever let me back in. And Russell dropped me as a friend because I couldn't come by anymore. Then she died a couple months later." She gave a short, bitter laugh. "At first, when I realized what was happening, I thought it was fun. I didn't question it. But after a while I had to leave Mama so she wouldn't figure it out. That was the first time I was forced to change my name—to change my whole life."

"But you didn't really leave," Phoebe said. "You were in San Francisco while Grams was alive, and Mom, and Paige."

"It's the only constant thing in my whole life," Emily said. "I figured this was a big enough city that I could hide from people who knew me. And I also started wondering about who did this to me. I hung around this house, and your family. I finally realized you were all witches. That's how I know it was a curse. And tonight is the night it started."

She suddenly lunged toward the door and slammed it shut. "So no one is leaving this room tonight. Not until my old self—Emmeline—leaves. Unenchanted."

"If that's what you want, that's what we'll do," Piper said. "But it won't fix anything."

"Why not?" Emily glared at them.

"Because I'm not the one who cursed you," Great-Grams said. "My cousin is."

Great-great-aunt Russell blew out another candle. Only two still flickered in the circle. Paige had to do something—*now.*

"Hey!" she cried, leaping out of her hiding spot. "Hi!"

Russell spun around, her brown eyes widening. She looked Paige up and down and frowned. "Who are you?" she demanded. "Get out of here! This is private. The speakeasy's downstairs."

"Um . . . I know," Paige said. "But listen, I just heard you doing a spell to keep yourself eternally young."

Russell's mouth dropped open.

"And that's kinda for personal gain, isn't it?" Paige asked. "I mean, it is."

"Yes. It is." Russell smoothed her sleek hair, recovering from her surprise.

"Well, then you shouldn't be doing it," Paige told her. "Use of powers for personal gain is a big no-no. Don't you think?"

"Hmmm." Russell pursed her lips and pretended to think about it for a moment. "No," she said. "I think it's a dandy idea." She turned around and blew out the second-to-last candle.

"No!" Paige yelled. "It won't work."

"You're getting to be a problem," Russell said coldly.

"Look, the spell won't work, not on you," Paige explained. "I know. I'm from . . . I'm your descendant. I know how it turns out, and you didn't stay young forever."

Russell studied Paige again, paying more attention to her clothes this time. "You're from the future?" she asked. "Are you a witch?"

"Yes," Paige said. "So I know how it will go. Your spell works, but not on you. There's someone else here, and she's younger than you. The spell makes *her* young forever."

Russell's eyes flashed angrily. "Who?"

"Emmeline Graydon," Paige said. She shot an apologetic look at Emmeline, who was cowering behind the chair. "Emmeline, come on out, it's okay," she said. "If you go downstairs, the spell won't work on you."

"Did you say you're a witch?" Emmeline's voice shook as she stood up.

"Yes, you dumb Dora, we're both witches," Russell snapped. "Didn't you hear me doing a spell?"

"No," Emmeline whispered. "I just saw you lighting candles. I couldn't hear over the music. I . . . I don't believe in witches."

"Well, look." Russell flicked her finger and sent a small stream of fire shooting across the room. "Do you believe now?"

Emmeline's eyes rolled back in her head and she fainted.

"What did you do that for?" Paige cried. "Now we can't get her out of here."

"She's annoying," Russell said. "She's always following me around like a little shadow. Now if you'll excuse me, I'm going to finish my spell." She turned toward the last candle.

"But Emmeline's still here," Paige pointed out. "The enchantment will land on her even if she's unconscious."

Russell heaved an impatient sigh. "Fine. I'll get rid of her then." She raised her hand and hurled another fire stream toward Emmeline's unconscious form.

"No!" Paige cried as the fire arched across the room.

Then it slowed. Fingers of flame moved lavalike through the air, inching slowly at Emmeline.

"Paige! Get her!" Piper yelled from the doorway. Next to her stood a woman with chestnut hair, holding her hands up and concentrating on Russell. *She's making the flame move in slo-mo*, Paige realized. Immediately she dove toward Emmeline, grabbed her arm, and rolled her out of harm's way.

The fire stream returned to normal speed as Paige stood up behind Piper. For the first time she noticed Emily—normal Emily, from 2005—standing next to her sister. And holding Wyatt. Paige froze in horror. What was Wyatt doing here?

"Russell!" Emily cried. "What's going on?"

Russell stared at Emily for a split second, confused, then hurled a fire stream at her. This time the flame sped along furiously . . . and bounced harmlessly off the protective shield of white light surrounding Emily. The girl cringed, expecting flame. Then opened her eyes and looked at Wyatt in her arms.

He stared back solemnly, keeping his protective bubble up as the fire dissipated.

"What have you done?" the brown-haired woman demanded, stalking over to Russell. "You just threw fire at an innocent child!"

"Great-Grams, I presume?" Paige whispered, leaning in to talk to Piper. Piper nodded.

"I didn't mean to," Russell said. "I got confused. I thought that Emmeline was a demon. Look, there are two of her!"

Great-Grams frowned at her cousin. "You were doing a spell, weren't you? Not one from the Book of Shadows."

Paige noticed Russell's eyes flick toward the one candle that still burned. If Russell blew it out, the youth spell would take effect.

Paige made a quick move toward it while Russell was being distracted by Great-Grams, and pinched out the flame between her thumb and forefinger.

Russell's eyes betrayed a flicker of anger, but she hid it right away. "I was playing around with something," she told Great-Grams. "Nothing bad."

"An eternal youth spell," Great-Grams said, "that backfired and enchanted Emmeline."

"I can't believe it was you," Emily said. "I thought you were my friend. All these years, I always thought you were good." She glanced at Great-Grams. "I'm sorry I misjudged you."

Russell gave a tinkling little laugh. "I *am* good, Graydon. I wasn't trying to hurt you! I'd never hurt anyone."

"You were doing magic for personal gain," Great-Grams pointed out.

"I know." Russell put on a pout. "It was silly of me. I found a wrinkle on my skin this morning, and I think I went into a tizzy. I only wanted to stay young." She looked at each of them in turn, managing to seem contrite. "Thank heavens you stopped me. I was about to make a huge mistake."

Paige didn't know what to say. This woman was an evil witch . . . but did Great-Grams know that yet? If not, could they really be the ones to tell her?

"Yes, you were," Great-Grams said. "Don't do it again."

"Of *course* I won't," Russell assured her. "I think I'd better toddle back down to the bar now. I could use a pick-me-up after this close call." With her head held high, she walked right through the Charmed Ones and down the attic stairs.

Paige bit her lip. Piper and Phoebe were exchanging worried looks. "Um, listen, Great-Grams," Phoebe said. "I know a little bit about what's going on with your cousin. And—"

"She's become evil," Great-Grams interrupted. She smiled sadly. "Is that what you want to tell me?"

"Well . . . yeah." Phoebe raised an eyebrow. "Did you know that before tonight?"

"We've been suspicious lately," Great-Grams said. "My other cousin and I. But this episode confirms it."

"So what are you going to do?" Piper asked.

"I don't know yet," Great-Grams said with a sigh. "I don't want to hurt her, but maybe we'll have to."

"Paige? Take the baby." Emily suddenly gasped. She shoved Wyatt into Paige's arms, and stumbled backward. Phoebe grabbed her just before she fell to the floor.

"What's wrong?" Paige asked. "Em?"

Emily smiled at her, then gestured to the still-unconscious Emmeline. "Think she'll remember any of this?" she asked.

"No," Paige said. "She didn't really understand what was going on."

Emily nodded. "Good." She leaned forward with Phoebe's help, unsteady on her feet, and kissed Wyatt's cheek. "Thanks for saving me, little guy," she murmured. "You saw right through me the whole time. I could never have hurt you. You're just as sweet a baby as your mom was."

"Aw, I'm blushing," Piper joked.

Emily looked up at Paige. "It was good to see you again," she said with a wink. "Good-bye, Paige the Rage."

Paige opened her mouth to answer, but her friend was gone.

"How come I can remember her, then?" Paige asked for the fifth time.

Piper led the way up the stairs to the attic, carrying her sleeping son. "It's magic," she told Paige.

"So she's just gone. Like *gone* gone?" Paige asked. "That stinks."

"She never got enchanted this time," Piper replied. "The Emily you knew never existed."

"But then why do I remember everything about her?"

Piper shook her head. Sometimes leading a magical life was hard to wrap your mind around. "You know what, Paige the Rage? I'm not sure. Maybe you'll forget after a little while."

"Huh," Paige said. "I don't think I want to forget."

"You know, I bet she never even went to Africa with the Peace Corps," Phoebe put in, shutting the attic door behind them. "I bet that was just a story to keep Paige from realizing that she'd been living in San Francisco with a different name."

"It must've been lonely, having to change her whole life so often," Piper said. She settled Wyatt on the couch and began flipping through the Book of Shadows. "I guess eternal youth isn't all it's cracked up to be."

"This time, maybe she got married and had kids and lived to a ripe old age," Paige said.

"So, how did you like meeting your ancestors? It was kinda weird, don't you think?" Phoebe said.

Paige nodded. "But I'm glad we were around to right the wrong Russell did," she said. "And to see what the Manor was like back then. This was some jazzy joint!"

Piper raised her eyebrows. "Looks like you've picked up the lingo there, Matthews."

Paige stuck out her tongue as Phoebe laughed.

"Here it is," Piper said, smoothing out the page. There was still a sketch of Emily there, but this time the handwriting belonged to Great-Grams, and it contained a message to them. There were only three words: *She grew old.*

The Crucible

Micol Ostow

"You are never going to believe this one!"

Phoebe Halliwell burst through the front door of Halliwell Manor brimming with cheer and energy. She practically spun into the front hall, unloading her jacket, keys, and wallet in one well-executed pirouette of glee.

"There's a ring of fish-demon running an underground racket through the local coffeehouse?" Paige Matthews guessed, bounding down the stairs and into the hallway to join her half sister.

"What? No. Huh?" Phoebe asked, running her hand through her short, dark hair in confusion. "There is?"

"It's just a hunch," Paige admitted. "A theory I came up with after being charged four fifty for a small skim latte. I mean, really, what is that? There's got to be something evil behind those prices."

"Um, okay," Phoebe agreed, her good mood not to be diminished. "Is Piper home?"

Paige nodded. "Yeah, she's in the kitchen, trying to feed Wyatt before starting on dinner for the rest of us."

The girls' other sister, Piper, had been a chef once, though now she worked full time managing her club, P3. She still preferred to handle most of the domestic aspects of their life together at the Manor, claiming that preparing meals was actually her hobby now that it was no longer a profession.

"Great," Phoebe said. "I can give both of you my news at the same time." She made her way toward the kitchen, motioning for Paige to follow.

"Hey, Phoebes, what's going on?" Piper asked as Phoebe and Paige came into the kitchen and collapsed at the table. "I could hear you come in. Good day?"

"Great day," Phoebe enthused, reaching out and taking a slice of banana from the plate in front of Piper.

Piper slapped at her hand. "That's your nephew's dinner, missy."

"Ooops," Phoebe said, looking sheepish. She leaned forward to where Wyatt sat gurgling in his high chair. "Sorry, Wyatt," she cooed, smiling at him. She turned back to her sisters. "You guys, you're going to love this. It's so cool."

"Tell, tell," Paige said, waving her along impatiently.

"Right, okay," Phoebe said, sitting straight up in her chair. "Okay, so you know how the column's been doing so well lately, right?"

"Of course," Piper said. "You've had amazing publicity! Your face has been all over town." She was referring, of course, to Phoebe's advice column, "Ask Phoebe," which ran in the *Bay Mirror*. Phoebe had a huge fan base and was constantly being interviewed for television and radio. She'd become a total local celebrity almost immediately since she'd started writing.

"Well, it turns out that even high-school kids are reading 'Ask Phoebe.' And they really like it! A school approached Elise about coordinating a high-school internship program and she agreed! I'm going to have an intern! Can you believe it?" She clapped her hands together with glee. "Me, a mentor!"

"That's awesome!" Paige exclaimed. "You're going to be such a great boss!"

"I agree," Piper said. "I can definitely believe it. I'm sure you'll be fantastic. *And* you'll finally have the help you've been wanting down at the paper."

"I know," Phoebe said. "We get so many letters, it's really getting to the point where it's hard to read all of them. It'll be good to have someone to sort through them with me."

"The burden of fame, huh?" Piper teased. "All those people clamoring for your attention. *Begging* for your advice—"

"All right," Phoebe said, mock pouting and slapping her sister playfully. "You're just jealous."

"You're right," Piper agreed. "I am."

Wyatt let out a particularly noisy gurgle and flung a slice of banana directly at Piper's forehead. It smacked her squarely between the eyes and slid to the floor. Wyatt laughed maniacally from his perch in his high chair.

Piper sighed. "Do you think mommies can get interns too?"

"Probably not," Paige said, rising from her chair to help clean up the banana fallout. "But they have sisters who are willing to lend a hand when the baby starts going bananas."

Piper groaned at the pun. But she smiled. "Thanks, Paige," she said. "And congratulations, Phoebe."

A week later Phoebe sat slumped over her desk, pushing resumes back and forth. It was late and most of her co-workers had gone home hours ago. Her eyes were blurry with exhaustion. The students from a tenth-grade English class had come in for a tour of the office and they had all sat through a Q&A period with "Ask Phoebe" herself. The problem—if it could be called a problem—was, each of the students from the class was bright, eager, and utterly capable. How was she supposed to choose only one?

They'd each submitted a resume to her, but the truth was, that after twenty minutes of comparing one to the next, she'd realized that they were all solid. *More* than solid. She couldn't think of one particular reason to hire one student over another. Each one had straight As and lots of extracurriculars. Each one was interested in going into journalism. They had all asked interesting, engaging questions. Was this what they meant by an embarrassment of riches? It was giving her a headache.

With a grunt she collapsed facedown onto the heap of papers. "Forget it," she mumbled into her arm. "There's no way to choose."

As she said it, though, she felt a breeze pass through the room. Which was odd, she realized, given that the windows were closed. She sat up, rubbing her hands over her elbows, puzzled. "Hello?" she called out. "Is anyone still here?"

As if by response, a single sheet of paper fluttered from the top of the stack to the floor and landed, facedown. Without rising from her seat, Phoebe rolled her chair over to where it lay and fished it up off the ground. She flipped it over, scanning it. "Marissa Hargrave," she read aloud. "A-plus student, debate team, honor roll." She frowned. "Weird, she dropped out of debate after ninth grade, even though she won all sorts of awards."

"Phoebe? Are you talking to yourself?"

Phoebe looked up to see her boss, Elise, standing in her doorway, looking puzzled. She was so startled she nearly jumped out of her seat. "Elise! I didn't even know you were still here."

"I wasn't, actually," Elise said, making a face. "I thought I had made a clean getaway, but I was halfway home when I realized I'd left some copy here that I wanted to edit. The question is, what are *you* still doing here?"

Phoebe sighed. "I still haven't picked an intern. They're all really qualified." She paused, and waved the resume she was holding in her hand by way of demonstration. "What do you remember about this girl? Marissa Hargrave?"

Elise looked surprised. "Nothing, to be perfectly honest. Nothing at all." After a moment, she nodded with recognition. "No, wait. Wasn't she—I think she was the quiet one, who didn't really ask any questions. But I think she was dressed . . . well, she was dressed kind of oddly. All in black, with big boots. I remember lots of eye makeup."

In a flash Marissa's face appeared to Phoebe. "Yes! She had black hair. But dyed black, not natural. She was wearing a black denim skirt and a black tank top. With fishnets and black boots!" Off Elise's look, she asked, "What? I notice things like that." She paused, considering. "She was quiet, yeah, but I think I heard her crack a few jokes when she thought no one was listening. But it must have been hard for her. I mean, she was definitely the only one of her classmates dressed . . . well, you know . . . dressed that way. It seems like it's preppyville over at that school. Maybe she was just quiet because she didn't have too many friends."

"Maybe," Elise agreed. "So, does that make her a better or worse candidate for the position?"

Phoebe shook her head. "I have no idea. But it sets her apart. That's something, isn't it?" She bit her lip. "Is it bad practice to hire someone for wearing butt-kicking footwear?"

"Hey, I trust you, Phoebe. It's your call. Just double-check her writing samples—they should be around here somewhere—and as long as they're okay, it's fine."

"Writing samples!" Phoebe said, smacking her forehead with her palm. "Why didn't I think of that?"

"Because it's after eight o'clock and you really should have gone home two hours ago," Elise said gently. "Which is what I am going to do, finally. I completely trust your judgment. Just let me know in the morning who it is you decided to pick."

"I will," Phoebe said, rubbing at her temples. "I'll look through the clips, like you suggest. I can't let this drag out any longer."

Elise said her final good-byes and left the office. Phoebe was alone again, for real, this time. She dove right back into her pile of paperwork, this time pulling Marissa's writing samples from the mix. A quick read through told her that the girl would be perfectly fine to keep up with the paper's workload. She immediately called the number on the resume to give Marissa a phone interview.

Phoebe was so eager to find a qualified candidate, it never occurred to her to wonder how, exactly, Marissa's resume had drifted to the top of what had been, in all reality, a very hefty pile.

Any concerns Phoebe may have had over selecting the right student for the internship dissipated within the first hour of Marissa's first day on the job. She showed up fifteen minutes early for her after-school shift, butt-kicking footwear firmly in place. Phoebe gave her an abridged tour of the office, since luckily Marissa remembered most of it from her class visit. Marissa was friendly and much more outgoing than Phoebe remembered. She was starting to think that her antiprep theory might actually hold water. Maybe the girl just needed to be taken out of her environment in order to better come out of her shell.

"So what do you think you might like to work on?" Phoebe asked, suddenly nervous. She'd never had an intern before and she really wanted to make a good impression. "I was thinking maybe you could read through the letters I've been getting. There's been . . . well, there's been sort of a backlog lately," she said, feeling sheepish. "So maybe if you could pick out some top choices for next week's column?"

"Definitely," Marissa said, a smile playing lightly on her black-red lips. She scooped up the bundle that Phoebe had set aside for her and parked herself at the available cubicle that Phoebe had set up just outside her office.

Marissa and Phoebe worked in tandem quietly for an hour or so, Phoebe every so often glancing out her door to check on the girl. She could see, based on the piles that Marissa had created on her desk, that she had plowed her way through at least half of the mail that Phoebe had set aside for her. Phoebe was impressed. Usually it took her a week to get through a stack that size.

Phoebe found that Marissa's rather extreme fashion sense—the black-on-black look—was actually kind of appealing. She was really taking a liking to the girl. After all, Phoebe had been sort of a rebel herself in high school. And after high school. And, well . . . kind of until she'd come back to San Francisco and semiaccidentally activated the Power of Three. Down deep she believed that it had been fate working on her all along, that inner sense that she was, somehow, different from everyone else. Who knew? If she had chosen a more conventional lifestyle, maybe she wouldn't have been so open to accepting her powers as a Charmed One. And then where would she and her sisters be?

Deep thoughts for a school night, she decided, rubbing the back of her neck. She checked the small clock she kept on her desk and was stunned to discover that it was seven. She stood up, stretched, and walked out to the main office where Marissa was sitting. "I'm going to be arrested for violating child-labor laws if I don't send you home soon," she joked, pulling up a chair next to the girl's cubicle. "Why didn't you tell me it had gotten so late?"

Marissa shrugged. "I was enjoying reading the letters. What

else do I have to do? And besides, I'm not a child."

"Of course you aren't," Phoebe said, "but the last thing I want is for you to think I'm some kind of slave driver. You'll never come back again. And based on how much of the mail you've gotten through there, I know that I need you to come back."

Marissa snorted. "Are you kidding? Please. I'd come back here every day if I could. This totally beats school. I wish I could swap."

"So I take it you're not a huge fan of high school?" Phoebe asked softly, taking this opportunity to figure out what the boots, the black, and the big-time frown she'd seen the other day were all about.

"Understatement of the year," Marissa said, looking down.

Phoebe could tell she'd struck a nerve. "Yeah, me neither," Phoebe said.

"But you turned out okay. Better than okay!" Marissa said, obviously impressed.

Phoebe sighed. "Well, it took a while for me to get to 'better than okay.' In fact, it took me a while to take school seriously at all—but once I did, it was worth it." She looked at Marissa. "Even after I graduated from college, it was rough. It was hard for me to find the right job. You should see my resume. You would have thought I was going through some sort of multiple-personality disorder. You name it, I tried it. But nothing felt right until I met Elise and stumbled into my column. It took a long time to find my place." She tilted her head and looked at Marissa, considering. "But now I'm being all preachy grown-up instead of hip, cool mentor. And anyway, I'm thinking it's not the classes that are the issue?"

Marissa nodded her head slowly. She shrugged again. "What can I say? I don't wear polo shirts and jeans that cost more than twenty dollars. I'm not a 'joiner.' I don't . . . I don't fit in." She took a deep breath before continuing. "My grandmother just died, and we were really close. It kind of hit me hard. But maybe that's weird? Being so close to my grandmother? I don't know. I don't know what other kids my age would think. I don't . . . I really don't talk about this stuff with them."

Phoebe thought about her own grams. Ironically it was Grams's death that had brought her back to the Manor and into her powers as a witch. Even though she had fought with Grams more often than memory would admit, and she was glad that she had returned to become a Charmed One, Phoebe would have given anything to have her grams with her, alive. Though she did get to communicate with her grandmother in spirit form, it wasn't the same. Nothing was the same as having your loved ones alive, surrounding you every day. "I don't think that's weird," she said. "I was very close to my grandmother too."

"Too bad other people just don't get it," Marissa said wistfully.

"You know, I think everyone feels like that in high school, at least for a little while," Phoebe said. "I think it's some kind of horrible rite of passage, or something."

Marissa bristled, sitting up tall in her seat. "It's different for me," she said abruptly.

Phoebe could see instantly that she had offended the girl. "No, I'm sure it is," she agreed hastily. "I didn't mean . . . I didn't mean to suggest that what you were feeling wasn't real, or wasn't unique."

"Whatever," Marissa said, clearly insulted and regretful of having opened up. "Look, I finished half the letters. But I'll be back on Thursday to finish the rest of them. Or whatever else you want me to do."

"No, Marissa, wait—," Phoebe started, feeling terrible. "You know I wasn't trying to be condescending. I just meant that I underst—"

"Sure," Marissa said, shouldering her bag and heading down the hallway toward the office exit. "No problem."

And then she was gone.

"Marissa!" Phoebe called after her, frustrated. She contemplated getting up and going after the girl, but she decided that maybe Marissa just needed time to cool off. Besides, who was she to presume that Marissa needed her support? The girl obviously didn't want it.

Phoebe sighed and lifted out of her seat, figuring she was just about ready to pack up and go home herself. She stopped, though, when she noticed a book sitting on Marissa's desk. It was *The Crucible,* the play about the Salem witch trials. Was Marissa reading that for school? She supposed it didn't matter. She'd return it the next time Marissa came into the office. She reached down and picked up the book.

The premonition hit her like a tidal wave, washing over her body with a force that nearly sent her backward in her tracks. *Marissa, in a back alley. It's broad daylight, but she's being chased by a pack of . . . teenagers? Down the streets of San Francisco? This is no pep squad meeting, this is an angry mob, minus only the torches and the chanting.*

Breathing hard, Phoebe dropped the book.

So the girl had been right about her high-school woes; they were different than the norm. Way different.

What had Marissa gotten herself into?

"Leo," Phoebe called, stalking into the Manor full of purpose. "I need you!"

She slammed the front door behind her and strode into the living room to find, to her surprise, her sisters and her brother-in-law/Whitelighter already assembled.

"You are so lucky that Wyatt just woke up," Piper said.

"Haven't we talked about reckless door slamming in this house?"

"I'm sorry, Piper," Phoebe said, collapsing on the couch and exhaling deeply. "It's just, we've got an Innocent to protect." She suddenly stopped and looked up at Leo, as if noticing him for the first time. "Wait. Why are you here?" She groaned. "Don't tell me we have two Innocents to protect. I'm burned out as it is."

Leo shook his head ruefully. "Sorry to be the bearer of bad news," he said, patience etched across his smooth, handsome features. "But the Elders just sent me some information."

"High-school girl. Wild child," Paige said, rubbing her hands together and shimmying in her seat. "I'm sort of excited about it, actually. I mean, hello? I can completely relate." Much like Phoebe, Paige had gone through her own rebellious period when she was a teenager living with her adoptive parents, though, also like Phoebe, she had completely reformed and was now totally devoted to her role as one-third of the Power of Three.

"High-school girl?" Phoebe asked. "That's weird, because—wait," she said, suspicion dawning. "Who's your charge, Leo?"

"Her name is Marissa," Leo said. "The Elders think she's a rebel with a cause. And she's gotten herself into some trouble. I'm going to need to track her down at school, which is where you girls come in."

"Leo has this ridiculous idea that I can still pass for a high-school student," Piper said, flipping her long, dark hair over her shoulder. "Which I love you for," she added, grinning at her husband. "And you should know, Leo, that your charge is just about the *only* thing that could get me to go back to high school again." Piper had been very shy in high school, and her class reunion a few years back had sent her into a tailspin. Magic had worked its way into the evening, bringing out Piper's more flamboyant alter ego. She shuddered, recalling the memory of "Coyote Piper."

"Don't worry, Piper. If it's just a basic recon mission, I can go with Leo," Phoebe said. "I need to get in touch with Marissa, anyway."

"Oh, okay," Piper said agreeably. She paused. "You do? Why?"

"Because I need to give her this," Phoebe said, pulling *The Crucible* from her bag and dropping it onto the coffee table.

"So what do you think Miller is saying about the nature of mass hysteria?"

Marissa looked up to see her teacher, Miss Peterson, pacing back and forth in front of the classroom, looking thoughtful. She glanced around at her fellow students. Next to her, Warren James was tracing his hand onto a piece of looseleaf paper. Margaret White was stealthily text messaging from her lap. Absolutely no one had volunteered an answer to the question. In fact, most people looked as though they hadn't even heard it being asked. Too bad. Miss Peterson was nice, but she was too young, and she just couldn't seem to get the class interested in her lessons. Which was a shame. She was really cool. Take, for instance, the internship at the *Bay Mirror*. That had been all Miss Peterson's idea. Marissa was really grateful to her for that, too— even if Phoebe had gotten a little too close for comfort the other night.

"Marissa? Did you have any thoughts about this?"

"Huh?" Marissa asked, startled out of her reverie by the question. She could hear a few of her classmates tittering. "Um, mass hysteria . . ." She considered the question. "I guess, just that it's . . . quick to catch on? You know, that people need a scapegoat?" *Way to state the obvious, Marissa,* she thought to herself.

Fortunately Miss Peterson seemed satisfied with the response. She opened her mouth to reply, but at that moment the bell rang. Students immediately gathered their bags and books and made a beeline for the door. Marissa moved a bit more slowly, in no rush.

"Nice answer, freak. Did it take you all night to think that up?"

Marissa turned to see who had hissed the derisive words at her. *Oh. Of course.*

It was Natalie Kent. Natalie was essentially everything that Marissa wasn't: tall, blond, popular. She was even a cheerleader, for pete's sake. It was such a cliché. Not that Marissa was jealous of Natalie at all, but she did have to wonder what it'd be like to spend a day at school with the entire student body practically falling at your feet in adoration. The entire student body other than Marissa, of course.

Marissa wasn't interested in having a battle of wills with Natalie—not that it would have been much of a battle, anyway— so she just ignored her.

"Excuse me, but are you deaf? Loser, can't you hear that I'm talking to you?" Natalie stepped in front of Marissa, blocking her way threateningly. When Marissa still didn't reply, she mumbled, "Whatever. Nice outfit. No wonder you know so much about *The Crucible,* little Miss Black Magic. You probably would have fit in back then, huh?"

"Give her a break, Nat."

It was Matt Eding. He was to the football team what Natalie was to the cheerleaders. That is to say, he was their leader, their MVP, their demigod. Their captain. He was also Natalie's boyfriend.

"You *would* defend her," Natalie screeched, just a shade closer to hysteria herself than Marissa would have liked. "Maybe you'd rather be with her than with me?" She put her hands on her hips, challenging him.

"Hey, relax," Matt said, holding up his hands in a gesture of truce. "All I'm saying is that maybe you're overreacting. She didn't do anything to you. Live and let live."

"I can't believe I'm hearing this," Natalie shrieked.

"Nat, forget about him. If he wants to get with the freaky chick, let him," said one of Natalie's cronies, a short, stocky brunette with an unfortunate pug nose. Her name was Chloe. Chloe's big issue was that she hadn't been deemed "talented" enough to join the cheerleading squad, which she, of course, had read as not being attractive enough. She mainly contented herself by playing second fiddle to Natalie, happy to bask in B-level popularity-by-association.

Marissa took advantage of Natalie's temporary distraction to shove her way past the cheer nazis. As she approached the door, however, she tripped, sprawling flat on her face. From her vantage point on the floor she could see Chloe's outstretched size-seven Skechers extended just so.

"Ooops," Chloe said, giggling nastily. "Did I do that?"

Still silent, Marissa pushed herself up off the ground and fled, willing herself not to cry.

She made it out all the way down the hall and through the front door without being accosted or otherwise approached. Once outside, she leaned against a large tree in the front of the schoolyard, trying to catch her breath. *They're not worth it,* she told herself, calming her heart back to its regular pace. *They're totally not worth it.*

"Marissa!"

Marissa froze. *What now?*

"It's me, Phoebe Halliwell."

Feeling slightly less panicked, Marissa turned to see that indeed, "Ask Phoebe" had somehow tracked her down and now stood before her, brandishing a book. *The Crucible.* Oh. So *that's* where she had lost it! It had been majorly humiliating in class when she'd been bookless, with no one in her immediate vicinity willing to share.

"What are you doing here?" Marissa asked, confused.

"Well, you left this at the office," Phoebe replied. "And I was afraid you might need it before you came in again. But, well . . . it's more than that."

"Who's he?" Marissa asked, suddenly noticing Leo standing just behind Phoebe, looking concerned.

"That's my brother-in-law. And this is going to sound completely weird. But hopefully you'll just trust me."

"Trust you with what?" Marissa asked, baffled.

"We need to talk to you," Phoebe said.

"Okay, so I get that you're worried about me," Marissa said, taking a long swig from the glass of soda that Piper had poured for her. "But I don't think you hijacked me from classes just because I'm not a Gap girl. What gives?"

"This is going to sound really weird, but we . . . well, we sort of help people," Phoebe explained tentatively. "My sisters and I. And now we want to help you."

Phoebe and Leo had managed to convince Marissa to come back to the Manor with them, where Piper and Paige were waiting. Now, the five of them sat, gathered around the kitchen table, nursing soft drinks and trying to get to the bottom of the magical issue surrounding Marissa. It was hard to do without being able to actually tell her that they were witches, but of course, they needed to keep their identities as the Charmed Ones on the down low. Phoebe assumed that Marissa would never believe the truth even if they'd been willing to share it.

"Just as long as you're not going to, like, try to give me a makeover or something," Marissa teased, gesturing at Paige's tight, stretchy jeans and clingy sweater. "That's really not my . . . thing," she finished tactfully.

"We wouldn't touch a hair on your head," Paige said. "I've

gotta tell you, I think that look you're rocking is pretty cool. I always wanted a nose ring, myself."

"Yeah?" Marissa asked, looking slightly more hopeful than Phoebe had ever seen her. She was glad Paige was there, as she and Marissa seemed to have more than a few things in common.

"Why don't you tell us what's going on with you at school?" Piper prodded gently. "'Cause we're thinking that maybe the kids you go to school with don't have the same attitude about your appearance as we do."

"What do I care what they think?" Marissa scoffed, huffily folding her arms across her chest.

"Well, it'd be great if you didn't care at all," Paige said. "But something tells me that's not the case. Trust me," she continued, her voice earnest. "I've been there. I know what it's like to pretend you're not interested in being part of the 'in crowd.' Or at least, to pretend you don't care about being on the outside."

Marissa paused, as if considering how much to share. Finally she began to speak. "Here's the thing. I was never, you know, supersocial. I have my friends, and we mainly keep to ourselves, but I never set out to be a total outcast. The piercings were pretty recent. Anyway, it was last semester, in science class. I was paired up with this guy, Matt Eding. Total jock. All-American, tall, cute . . . And he . . . well, he seemed really into me. Which was weird because I am *so* not his type."

"What, he doesn't like pretty, smart, funny girls?" Phoebe teased.

Marissa blushed, clearly uncomfortable with the compliment. "Anyway. He was always sort of pressuring me to go out with him, and I kept saying no. I don't know why. Maybe I was nervous. But either way, eventually he started dating this girl, Natalie. You know—the queen bee of the social scene. It was a perfect match. So I figured, he'd moved on, and he was going to leave me alone."

"But not so much?" Paige guessed.

Marissa nodded. "Exactly. And it started making me really uncomfortable. I mean, he had a girlfriend! He was sending me notes, and calling me all the time, and hanging around my locker. One day I came home and he was waiting at my door for me. I decided that was totally creepy. So even though I didn't want to—at all—I told our guidance counselor." She looked down, feeling guilty.

"And what happened then?" Phoebe asked.

"They talked to Matt. Gave him a big afterschool special talk about stalking. Which wouldn't necessarily have been so bad, but then they benched him for, like, a week. And our team kept losing. It was really embarrassing for him, especially because he didn't want anyone to know why he'd been penalized. Anyway, Natalie found out, and went ballistic. Now she hates me. Not Matt. Me."

"Displaced anger," Leo commented. "It's much easier to use you as a scapegoat."

"Right," Marissa said, thinking back to her English-class lesson. "Which is what she and her friends have been doing. Of course, she stayed with Matt, though she goes nuts if he even so much as looks at me. *He* doesn't have any hard feelings. But lately she and her friends seem to be going a little bit over the top. *More* than a little," she said. "Insults, I can handle. But they've been getting physical. Tripping me, stealing things from my locker. Gym class has become, like, the *Lord of the Flies*. They think I'm a goth chick, all into voodoo and whatever."

"Well, you do dress sort of goth," Paige hedged. "Not that anyone has the right to judge you on superficial appearances, but it's possible that on some level, that's the image you're trying to project."

"But what you're telling us—minus the stalking—is really basic high school BS," Piper interjected impatiently. "It's crappy, but we've all been there. There must be something more to this story."

Marissa squirmed impatiently in her seat. "There may be a little bit more," she admitted.

"I knew it!" Piper said triumphantly.

"So, Natalie was being such a jerk that my best friend, Laurie, and I decided to play a little joke. See, she had this spell book that someone had given her for her birthday, so we decided to put a hex on Natalie. We met in the chem lab one day after school. We didn't know that Natalie was going to come by for some extracurricular assignment. She saw us, and flipped." Marissa sighed. "It doesn't even matter how I dress now. She is completely convinced that I am all into the black arts. Which is so crazy. I mean, magic is just make-believe, right?"

She looked up to find the three sisters leaning halfway across the table, their faces tight with anxiety. The room was swathed in a nervous silence. Marissa swallowed, the sound echoing in her ears.

Leo cleared his throat, breaking the silence abruptly. "So," he said. "A spell. Could you, ah, show it to us?"

The next afternoon Marissa came by the Manor with Laurie's spell book in hand. Piper opened the door to find the girl looking disheveled, her signature fishnets torn and her hair mussed. "What happened?" she asked.

"Natalie," Marissa said simply, pushing past Piper and into the house. She didn't elaborate.

"Wait, is she getting violent with you?" Piper asked, worried.

"It's fine," Marissa said dismissively. "I can take care of myself." She strode into the living room and pulled her book out of her bag, opening it to the page of the spell she had used. "Here," she said, pushing the book underneath Piper's nose. "But we had to make a substitution. We had no idea what 'wolfbane' was." She chuckled, obviously amused at the absurdity of the situation—and the gravity with which Piper was reacting.

Piper quickly scanned the spell. She didn't like the sound of the word "substitution." "What did you use?" she asked.

"Some dried, powdered mushrooms that we found at the health-food store," Marissa said. "Please. I don't get why you're spazzing. Magic isn't real!"

Piper sighed. She had no idea what wild mushrooms would add to the mix she saw listed. And she was going to have to ask someone who would. Unfortunately that would involve a little witchcraft, for which she couldn't have Marissa around. "Magic may not be real, Marissa, but there's something going on here," she said. "Maybe it's just fate, or a self-fulfilling prophecy. But we need to get to the bottom of this."

"What does that mean?" Marissa asked.

"Well, for now, it means that you go home and get some rest while my sisters and I do some research," Piper said. "We'll give you a call later."

Marissa furrowed her brow at Piper in disbelief. "Fine, okay, if that's what you want," she conceded. "Though I have absolutely no idea what you think you're going to research." She turned and left.

Once she was gone, Piper headed into the kitchen to gather some magical ingredients of her own. Her sisters would be home in an hour or so, and they were going to need to do a summoning spell. They might not have understood what dried mushrooms would do to Marissa's spell, but they knew someone who would. And they were going to have to talk to her.

But in order to do that, they'd have to summon her first.

"Here it is. *Hete*. From the Old English, 'hate.'"

Grams raised her hand and flipped the Book of Shadows open to its appropriate entry, gesturing for the girls to gather around to read along with her. They had summoned her, knowing that she was more educated on the subject of spells than the three of them combined. Now they were in the attic of the Manor, devising a strategy to combat the problem. "Hete is a demon who foments hatred among humans. It looks like Marissa was trying to draw him forth against Natalie. But because of the substitution she made in the spell ingredients, she accidentally turned him on herself."

"What does that mean?" Paige asked, nervously chewing a thumbnail.

"Well, unfortunately, it means that before too long, she is going to become the focus of a whole lot of anger. Hete's job, basically, is to sow discord. Not surprisingly, he's the one behind most incidents of mob violence throughout history."

"So that's why Natalie was getting more and more irrational in her attacks against Marissa," Piper said, thinking aloud. She stopped, realizing. "Oh, God. Marissa said that the attacks were getting really physical. Is she in actual danger?"

Grams nodded grimly. "I'm sorry to say," she replied.

"Okay," Phoebe said, rising from her perch at the attic window. "Here's what we need to do. We need to summon Hete, first of all, from out of Marissa. That should protect her. I can work on a spell this afternoon."

"And it says here"—Paige jerked her index finger back toward the book—"that he can be bound with a potion. I can work on that."

"I'll get Marissa's address from my Palm Pilot. Hopefully we can orb in tonight, while she's asleep. With any luck we can draw Hete out without her ever knowing the difference," Piper said.

The sisters squared off like drill sergeants, each marching out of the attic with purpose. Grams stood at the Book of Shadows, looking lost. "I'll just wait here, then," she offered, to nobody in particular. Wearily she closed the book.

"Ow!"

"Shh!"

"I'm sorry, but you're standing on my foot!"

"Will you two *please* keep it down?" Piper turned to glare at her sisters reproachfully, stage-whispering. "We don't want Marissa to wake up."

"Well, excuse me if someone needs to work on her orbing skills." Phoebe sulked. "She kicked me when we orbed in."

"It was an accident!" Paige hissed. "*You* try orbing three people at once. I'm not an airlift! Where's Leo, anyway?" she asked.

"Babysitting," Piper reminded them. "We can handle this ourselves. That is, if you two can put a lid on it. Phoebe, where's the spell?"

Phoebe fished a wrinkled sheet of paper from her pocket. "We just have to recite this together," she said. "But keep it down."

The sisters clasped hands and tiptoed to the foot of Marissa's bed. Thankfully the girl was clearly a very heavy sleeper, her head buried under several layers of pillows.

Mark of hatred, hear our plea,
Bring the demon forth, to be fully seen.

The girls stepped backward, bracing themselves for an impact. After a beat they looked around the room uncertainly. "Was that it?" Paige asked quietly.

Suddenly a dark shadow rose from the bed.

"No, actually, I think *that* might be it," Phoebe replied nervously.

The shadow gathered and began to take shape. A deep, black

cloud morphed to solid being, arms, legs, and a rocky exterior carved of cast iron. Red-rimmed eyes bore down upon them.

"So that's what hatred looks like?" Piper mused. "Ugly little guy."

In a flash the demon sprang overhead and out the window.

"Piper, the potion!" Paige whispered.

"Freeze him!" Phoebe put in.

Piper flung her fingers out the window desperately. She ran to see what, if any effect she'd had. "I hope Marissa's parents weren't especially attached to that white oak," she said sadly.

Phoebe sighed, hands on hips. "So what you're saying, basically, is that the demon got away."

"Yup," Piper said. "Although, on the bright side? Marissa slept through the whole freakin' thing. Teenagers."

"Well," Paige said, pulling her hair up and out of her face, "we've got a big, slobbering demon of hate on the loose out there somewhere." She looked hard at her sisters. "That can't be a good thing."

"It's not working!" Phoebe tossed her scrying crystal back onto her map of San Francisco with a cry of frustration. "The stone is just going completely out of control. What does that mean?"

"Exactly what you think it means," Leo explained, his eyes wide with concern. "Hete's influence has spread. The entire town is contaminated."

Phoebe's eyebrows flew up her forehead in dismay. "Yikes."

"How did you let the demon get away?" Leo asked.

"Okay, first of all? We didn't *let* him anything. That demon was big, and bad, and ugly. I mean, more intimidating than your average evil. And we know from evil. And second of all?" Phoebe continued. "We didn't *let* him anything." She folded up her map and placed her scrying crystal back in its drawer. "Look, Piper, Grams, and Paige are almost done making more of that potion, and I've got the new spell that should draw him to us. This time, we'll be on our turf. And we'll be prepared."

Leo stopped, staring off into space.

"Hello?" Phoebe asked. "Earth to Leo."

"It's Marissa," he said. "I can sense her. She's in trouble."

"What is it?" Phoebe asked.

Leo shook his head. "I'm not sure. But we're about to find out."

"Huh?" Phoebe asked. "How?"

Just then the doorbell rang.

Leo glanced at Phoebe knowingly. "Because she's here."

This time, when Piper answered the door, she full-on panicked. "What the heck happened?" she asked, peering beyond where Marissa stood and shuttling the girl inside hastily.

"Lunch period," Marissa said, picking a leaf out of her hair. "I was reading, with Laurie, like we always do, when Natalie came by and started with me. First she was just talking, but then she started shoving. Finally she and her friends pinned me down."

"You're *bleeding*," Piper said, grabbing Marissa by the hand and ushering her into the kitchen, where the rest of the group was gathered. "Here." She handed the girl a wet washcloth to staunch the flow of blood that was trickling down from her nose. "How did you get away?"

"I just pushed until the pileup had dispersed," she said. "And then I ran. I didn't look back once. I hope it's okay that I came here," she said, suddenly shy. "It's just . . . you guys seemed to take all this pretty seriously and I . . . I didn't really have anywhere else to go."

"Of course, dear," Grams said.

Marissa looked up, and froze in place.

She's remembering her grandmother, Phoebe realized, her heart breaking for the poor girl. "This is our grams," Phoebe said. "She's just, um, visiting with us."

"Hi," Marissa said, looking dazed.

"Leo," Piper said quietly, jerking her head at her husband and indicating that she wanted to talk privately. The two discreetly made their way out into the hall.

"Obviously Hete's influence is getting stronger," she said. "What if it affects us?"

Leo shook his head. "Not possible," he said. "Phoebe already thought of that—she put a protection spell on the Manor so that no evil will be allowed in."

Piper sighed with relief, collapsing against Leo's warm chest. He kissed her on her forehead.

The moment was broken, though, by an enormous crash from the kitchen, followed by a shriek. Piper and Leo exchanged worried looks, separated, and took off in the direction of the noise.

They got to the kitchen to find the French doors smashed and a group of teenagers standing in the room, their eyes dark with murderous intent. At the center of the mob was a tall, statuesque blonde.

"I'm guessing you're Natalie," Paige said.

Leo glanced at Piper. "Hete's pull must have drawn them here," he said.

"And obviously, the protection spell doesn't hold if you've already been spooked," Piper said.

Leo looked at her and nodded. "I'll take Marissa upstairs." He instantly descended on Marissa and swooped her up protectively, rushing out of the kitchen and upstairs to the attic, with Grams following closely behind.

Natalie and her crew were storming through the kitchen like a tsunami, pulling things off shelves and counters and smashing them against the floor, yelling and screaming the whole while. "Where's Wyatt?" Phoebe shouted nervously.

"He's in his nursery," Piper said. "Don't worry, his force field will protect him."

"Wish we had one of those," Paige mumbled, thinking fast and grabbing at the vials of potion they'd just mixed.

Suddenly the room was rocked by a sonic boom. What remained of the French doors was blown inward, glass flying through the air. The sisters dropped to the ground, wrapping their arms protectively around their heads.

"What the hell was that?" Phoebe yelled.

Cautiously Piper peeled one eye open. "Oh, my," she murmured.

"I'm thinking Hete," Paige said.

"He must have been drawn to the dark energy here," Phoebe said.

"Ya think?" Piper shouted, struggling to be heard over the sounds of riotous destruction.

She looked up. Hete towered behind the mob, massive, thunderous, and slobbering. Fortunately they were too involved in their fevered frenzy to notice. She reached out and froze the room, leaving Hete in all his black fury.

Hete roared, shaking the Manor to its foundation. Piper reached her hands out again to explode him, but was thrown back by the contact for her troubles. She slammed against the far wall of the kitchen. "The potion!" she cried. "Where is it?"

"I've got it!" Paige said. She pulled it from her pocket and waved it triumphantly.

Hete's fist crashed into the wall next to her, leaving a deep crater at the place of impact. Paige orbed silently out of harm's way, onto the floor next to Piper. She noticed a nasty tear in Piper's jeans. "You're bleeding!" she said.

"I'm fine," Piper said, waving her away. "Phoebe, behind you!" she called.

Phoebe whirled in time to see Hete's monstrous fist coming at her full force. She levitated overhead just in time to miss the crunch of steel against flesh. She maneuvered herself in-air to the corner where her sisters huddled. "Do you have the potion?" she asked.

"Right here," Paige said, brandishing it. "Do you have the new spell?"

"No!" Phoebe said. "The new spell was to draw Hete to us. And, I hate to state the obvious, but it looks like we've taken care of that just fine. Oh, God," she said, wracking her brain for a new, more appropriate rhyme. "All right," she said, after a moment. "Give me your hands. I think I've got it."

The sisters clasped hands and awaited the new spell. Phoebe squeezed her eyes shut in concentration.

Demon of hatred,
be gone from this place,
remove your evil influence from our deeds.

"Paige, now!" she commanded.

Paige leaned forward and flung the vial of potion at Hete with all of her might. The vial shattered against him, and his torso began to smoke. Deep fissures began to appear in the beast, cracks that deepened and drew apart. Finally he began to crumble from the outside in, until nothing more was left but a pile of dust. Then, all at once, the dust gathered and swirled out the window in a hurricane vortex.

Then the room was still.

Piper looked up cautiously. "Is that it?"

• • • •

"What happened?"

After the sisters were sure that Hete was gone, Piper unfroze the angry mob. Phoebe walked into the living room to find that the mob had essentially dissipated into . . . well, into a crowd of very-confused-looking high-school girls. "Hi, uh, guys!" she said brightly, straightening out her clothing and pasting a huge smile onto her face. "Did everyone have fun?"

"Are you . . . are you 'Ask Phoebe'?" Natalie asked, wonderment etched across her lovely features.

"Yes, she is."

Phoebe turned to see Marissa, Leo, and Grams coming down the stairs of the Manor, Marissa walking with a grace and poise she previously hadn't seen. Reaching the foot of the stairs, Marissa quickly crossed to where Phoebe stood in the living room. "Thanks so much for agreeing to have us all over to talk more about your job," Marissa said, ad-libbing rather convincingly. "That was really cool of you."

"Oh, anytime!" Phoebe chirped, relief washing over her. "It's great to know that you guys are so into my column!"

One by one, the students came forward to shake Phoebe's hand and shyly ask questions. Phoebe patiently answered them all while hustling everyone to the door. Fortunately no one asked about the state of the house, or specifically, why half the living room was smashed to pieces.

Twenty minutes later Phoebe stood at the front door, waving beatifically. "I love to meet the fans!" she shouted. Then she went back inside and closed the door.

"Well, that was . . . an interesting afternoon," Paige said, collapsing into a chair at the kitchen table and sinking forward, chin in hand.

"What will be *really* interesting is the cost of the repairs to our kitchen and living room," Piper quipped wryly. "Just once,

I'd like to battle evil from somewhere other than our home."

"Well, I for one am just relieved that Hete is gone," Phoebe said. "That was spooky."

"Actually," Leo interjected, "Hete's technically *not* gone. He's just bound again."

"Do you mean to tell us that someone could release him again if they wanted to?" Phoebe asked sharply.

"Of course," Grams said. "Hete is a demon, but it's impossible to vanquish him." She settled herself at the table with the girls. "After all, he's really just the manifestation of our own evil impulses. So he never truly goes away."

"Marissa was reading *The Crucible* at school," Phoebe said, remembering. "Hete was behind the Salem witch trials, wasn't he?"

Grams nodded. "Of course. And World War Two, and the Crucifixion . . . Any point in history that you can recall that was driven by hate and anger."

Paige sighed, absorbing this depressing news. "So basically we're the ones who keep him going. People."

"Yes," Grams said. "And it never ends."

"But hey," Phoebe said, determined to look on the bright side, "at least we stopped him for now. That's something, right?"

"Yes," Leo said, clapping her on the shoulder supportively. "It definitely is."

Three days later Phoebe found herself working late again. It never ceased to amaze her how she could go from fighting evil and back to her normal life so seamlessly. She always felt that there should be some sort of vacation, a break . . . *something*, but obviously, that was just wishful thinking.

She sighed, and clicked open her latest e-mail. Ever since the

Bay Mirror had agreed to start an internship program, Phoebe had noticed how many of her letters were coming from high-school students. This one rang more than a little bit familiar.

Dear Phoebe:

I'm sure you probably hear this a lot, but I'm having a hard time in high school! I'm a freshman, and I just moved to San Francisco from Seattle, so I don't know anyone here. It's really hard; I miss my friends so much, and I feel like nothing I do here is right. Kids dress, talk, and act different in San Francisco and I get treated like I'm some kind of alien! I don't want to just conform, but it would be nice to be able to actually make a friend, you know?

Anyway, at the risk of sounding pathetic, I would totally love your advice. Is this something you can relate to? Please—I'm begging you!

Thanks,
Frisco Freshman

Phoebe shook her head ruefully. She stood up and walked outside her office where Marissa sat at her cubicle, studiously scanning the e-mail printouts Phoebe had left with her.

Thankfully Grams had distracted Marissa while they were upstairs in the Manor, so Marissa hadn't heard any of the goings-on downstairs. She definitely thought that the whole thing with Natalie was a little weird, but she certainly didn't suspect magic. And spending time with Grams had been good for her in a way. It reminded her of her own grandmother and helped to ease the pain of the loss just a bit. When Marissa had come back to the paper the next day, Phoebe was pleased to hear that things had basically gone back to normal at school. Maybe Marissa and Natalie weren't going to be having sleepover parties or braiding each other's hair, but they could manage basic civility just fine. And that was enough for Marissa.

"Seriously, I need for you to stop working overtime," Phoebe said. "You know I can't afford to pay you."

Marissa smiled. The darkness that had enveloped her on their original encounter had disappeared, leaving in its wake an outgoing, eager apprentice who happened to have a distinct style of dress. "What can I say? I love it here. You're a total inspiration."

"Oh, flattery will get you everywhere," Phoebe said, grinning. "But I've got a new job for you. I could use your advice on how to answer this reader. . . . How'd you like to take a crack at it?"

"Really?" Marissa asked, her eyes lighting up. "Oh, my God—that would be such an honor! Are you sure?"

"I'm sure," Phoebe said, nodding. "I'll look it over before I submit it to Elise, but you might be better at answering the question. It's from a new student who's looking to fit in. I'm thinking you might have some insight."

Marissa beamed with pride. "Hmm, 'Ask Marissa' . . . ," she said, smiling impishly. "I kind of like the sound of that."

Patty's Awakening

Greg Elliot

Patty Halliwell walked through the thick, gray, San Francisco dawn, her arms wrapped tightly around her. When walking through the fog, she knew the trick was to move fast enough to build up some body heat, but not so fast as to allow the damp air to penetrate her clothes. The soggy air could be chilling. But Patty wasn't thinking about how fast to walk in order to best stay warm. She wasn't thinking about the long walk from her best friend Mandy's house to the Manor. Instead she was replaying over and over the fight, the harsh words between Mandy and her, the reason she had abruptly left the sleepover at Mandy's at such an early hour. The evening had started out pretty well—How had things gone so wrong?

Mandy had barely blinked when Patty invited herself over. Instead she'd gushed about all the new 45-rpm singles she wanted to play for Patty, and had insisted that Patty tell her about Hugh, the boy she had just begun dating.

"He's *so* dreamy," Mandy had said as soon as they were upstairs in her bedroom and out of her mom's earshot. "What's it like to date someone older?"

"He's not that much older than me. Only one year."

"But he's *seventeen*. Which means next year he'll be *eighteen*! And he's *captain* of our football team."

"Yeah."

Patty had wondered herself what Hugh saw in her. She was slim and not nearly as well developed as Mandy, or many other girls in her tenth-grade class for that matter. But Hugh had acted as if he didn't even notice. He'd smiled at her in trig. Then walked right up and talked to her in the hall between classes. Now, they'd become a couple.

"Tell me everything," Mandy insisted as she put another 45 on her turntable. "Is he a good kisser?"

"I guess."

"You *guess*?"

"He's been kind of shy about it. We haven't done that much kissing."

"Hugh Stenstrom? Shy? That's not what I've heard."

Patty had heard the stories too. Hugh Stenstrom, party animal. Hugh Stenstrom, masher. Jock. Stud. She didn't want to believe that he would be that way with her.

She stuck up for him. "Maybe he's changed. I told him I wanted to take things slow, and he's really respected that."

"Wow," said Mandy. "We all thought he was being a jock so he could try to live up to his dad."

"He does talk a lot about his dad," said Patty. "He wants to be like him. Hugh plans to join the ROTC when he goes off to college. He says he even wants to be a fighter pilot, like his dad, and go to Vietnam. But I hope," she added, "that the war is over by then."

"Me too," added Mandy. "The war is so wrong."

That had been the first sign of trouble. Mandy told Patty all about the teach-in she'd attended with her older brother, Frank, who was a student at USF. When Patty asked, Mandy explained that at the teach-in several professors talked to the students, telling them, as she put it, "things that the government won't tell you about this war." Mandy and Patty had got a little loud while hashing this out, and Mandy's mom had come in and insisted that they stop playing records and go to bed. Under the covers the conversation continued at a volume intended to stay under Mandy's mom's radar, and Patty had changed the subject to how weird her own mom was.

Of course, Patty couldn't tell anyone, even Mandy, that her mom was a witch. That might mean, among other things, explaining how being a witch was passed from mother to daughter, and how she, herself, was a witch, and was well on her way to developing her own powers, powers she wasn't sure she wanted. So, instead, Patty had complained to Mandy in detail about her mom's latest attacks of weirdness, altering the parts about witchcraft.

It had worked. Well into the night, Patty was able to talk about the things that bothered her about being a Halliwell. Then the conversation had drifted back to boys, and Hugh, and Vietnam, and Mandy had said that she couldn't see how *anyone* could date someone who was for the war—this being 1966, and all; we knew better now—and Patty had risen, donned her sweatshirt and her sneakers, pulled on her backpack with her toothbrush and change of clothes, and stalked out.

Now she was sorry. Not because of the long walk, not because of the cold, damp air, but because she had to return to the Manor. This was the night of the Beltane Ball, an event she dreaded, and the real reason she had invited herself over to Mandy's. During Beltane, the Wiccan spring festival of fertility and renewal, her mother would gather other witches and invite the fairies to join them in a celebration of Mother Earth. It lasted from sundown to sundown, ushering in the month of May, and wouldn't even be half over at this hour.

Patty stopped in front of the Manor and stared, sullen. Even from here, she could hear the faint sounds of merriment. Nothing loud enough to disturb the neighbors—Penny Halliwell would have taken care of that with some spell or other—but loud enough for Patty to know what she was walking into.

The fog surrounded her, chilling her, practically forcing her inside. Patty sighed, walked up the front steps, and opened the door.

A shriek of laughter undiluted by any spell greeted her. Gossamer-winged fairies, wisps who could defy gravity more gracefully than any dancer, darted by, chasing one another or the witches who filled the house. They didn't acknowledge Patty's entrance, further darkening her sulk.

"You'd think they'd notice when someone walks in on them," she muttered to herself.

"But you're not just someone, dear." Penny had appeared suddenly at Patty's side. "You're a witch, and a very important one."

"Well, you'd think they'd notice *that.*" Patty was in no mood to be coddled by her mom. She glared at the witches and fairies, all of whom seemed to be having a wonderful time. "Why can't we ever have a normal party, with normal people? It's always witches, or fairies, or even worse things."

Penny smiled. "Would you like to have a normal party? We could try it."

"No, because right in the middle of a *normal* party, some demon would show up, try to kill us, and you'd have to destroy it, and then you'd erase everyone's memory, and what's the point of my having a party that no one will remember?"

Penny studied her daughter a moment. "I take it the sleepover didn't go well?"

Patty turned, walked straight through the gaggle of swooping,

gravity-defying fairies, and started up the stairs. She turned back
to her mom. "I'm going to get some sleep, so please tell everyone
not to try and drag me down here for all this *fun.*" Without waiting for an answer, she stomped up the stairs and into her room.

Lying on her bed, she became aware of how tired she was. She
was sorry she had fought with Mandy, but Mandy had been so
wrong. She listened to the laughter, rising like waves breaking on
her door, and she wished she'd learned the muffling spell her
mom used on the outside of the house.

She'd just drifted off when the scream of a fairy or a witch
passing right by her door startled her awake. The scream came
again, breaking this time into laughter. Patty caught her breath.
No demon was wreaking havoc, bent on destroying them all; it
was only more of the merriment she'd been trying to sleep
through. She looked at her alarm clock, which read 7:02. She
knew from experience that things would not get any quieter, not
for hours. She spotted her backpack, still crammed with a
change of clothes and her toothbrush. She put on a heavier
sweater and slipped the backpack over her shoulder, huffing her
way out her door and down the stairs.

"Can't sleep, dear?"

Penny had appeared by her side again, and Patty was sure
her mom had been standing watch for just this opportunity.
"What do you think? It's louder in here than any concert I've
ever been to."

Penny glanced from the backpack over to Patty's face. "Don't
leave just yet. It's still cold outside. At least have some breakfast."

"Breakfast?" Patty looked at the array of feast food laid out on
the dining-room table. "You call this breakfast? Mom, I want
some sleep. Then I want to wake up in a normal house and have
a normal breakfast on a normal Saturday morning."

"But where can you go so early? If you and Mandy are fighting—"

"Anywhere but here, Mom," she said. She swept her hand behind her for emphasis. "*Anywhere* but—" She stopped, aware of the sudden silence. She turned slowly, taking in the room, the house.

Every fairy was frozen, pinned in time like a 3-D picture. Mouths were still open; eyes still flashed in merriment. The witches, too, stilled; not frozen, but bewildered at this spell in their midst. Halfway up the stairs one witch, a look of chagrin on her face, reached for a wine goblet that had been knocked askew by a passing fairy. The goblet had tipped beyond all hope of recovery, its contents now free of the glass and headed, in frozen droplets, on a trajectory beyond the banister and toward the floor several feet below. "Sorry," she said to Penny.

"Catch what you can," said Penny. She turned to Patty, admiring the total motionlessness of the tableau. "That's really well done. I think that's the best freeze you've ever accomplished."

"Oh, *mother*. Don't you get it? I don't want this." She gestured at the fairies frozen above them. "I don't want to know how I did that. I don't want to be *able* to do that. I want to be normal. I want to be *anything* but a witch."

With that, she stalked to the door, threw it open, and slammed it on her way out. She was aware of the dim resumption of gaiety as she walked down the steps, and felt an odd mixture of anger and sadness that her departure had set the party in motion again.

Patty sat on the bus bench, shaking her head no at the bus driver, as she had at the three previous drivers who pulled up to this stop. The bus drove away and she glanced up at the sky, wishing the feeble sun would break through the morning gauze and warm her up. She closed her eyes, sure that it was only the cold that kept her awake as she sat there. She felt miserable, and, for the first time in her life, alone.

Her mom had been right about Mandy. To go back now would only put her once again into the same argument, the same tension. Besides, she'd have to wake Mandy's mom to get back in, then explain where she'd been. She looked at her watch. Eight ten. She wondered what time Hugh's family arose on a Saturday morning. She wondered what his mother would think if she met the girl Hugh was dating under these circumstances. Then Patty remembered Hugh saying something about being an early riser. She decided she was too miserable to worry about the first impression she might make on Hugh's mom and walked to the pay phone behind the bus stop.

She fed the coin slot, dialed Hugh's number, and hoped he would answer.

"Hello, Mrs. Stenstrom? Hi, this is Patty. Patty Halliwell. I'm sorry to call so early, but I was wondering if I could speak to Hugh."

She waited for Hugh to come to the phone, relieved that his mom had seemed so pleasant, so unconcerned as to why a girl was calling her son at this hour. When she heard Hugh's voice, she only said that she was fighting with her mom and wanted to talk. She was greatly relieved when he invited her over. In the background she heard his mom say, "Be sure she knows she's welcome for breakfast."

Patty hung up. For the first time in what seemed like ages, she felt the tension drain out of her. She didn't even mind the cold anymore.

When Hugh answered his door, Patty wanted nothing more than to fall into his arms, heave a great sigh, and wait for his embrace to make everything better. Instead, she shifted her weight, gave him an awkward smile, and said, "Hi."

"Come on in. You can meet my mom."

Patty stepped inside and stopped, looking around.

It was like she'd just crossed the border into another country. The Stenstrom house wasn't any bigger than the Manor, perhaps it was even smaller, but it could not have been more different. The Stenstrom house was subdued, quiet, like entering a library. Dark wood paneled the walls, muted shag carpet covered the floors. Every object seemed to know its place, and to be there. The Manor, on the other hand, was bright, casual, its already ancient hardwood floors and old-fashioned wooden banisters home to dozens of objects scattered about for practical, utilitarian reasons. It seemed sloppy in comparison to the tidy orderliness of this home.

"I like your house," she said to Hugh.

"Thank you," came a woman's voice from behind them.

Patty turned to see Mrs. Stenstrom standing in the entry to the kitchen. She wore dark slacks and a crisp, white blouse that set off her short, neat haircut. Patty couldn't help comparing their two moms, just as she had their two houses. Mrs. Stenstrom looked tastefully put together; her mom often spent the day in some tie-dyed muumuu. Mrs. Stenstrom's makeup and hair looked perfect; Patty's mother sometimes went all day without makeup, her hair piled in a bun on her head, while she worked on some potion or other.

Hugh's mother broke Patty's musings, walking toward her with her arms raised in a greeting. "It's nice to finally meet the young woman whom Hugh talks about so much. Welcome. Please, come into the kitchen and have some breakfast."

Mrs. Stenstrom laid out platters of pancakes and scrambled eggs. Patty dug in, suddenly aware that she was starving. She worked to slow her eating, lest she appear to be some ill-mannered cretin raised in a barn—or raised in the Manor.

Even Mrs. Stenstrom's breakfast small talk was reserved, careful. Patty was reminded that her mother seemed to blurt out whatever was on her mind, then sort it afterward, almost as if she were thinking out loud, assembling her thoughts in the open.

Finally Patty was full and stopped eating. She was also very, very tired.

Mrs. Stenstrom turned to her son. "Hugh, would you be a dear and go down to the corner market for some things? The list is on the fridge." She smiled at Patty. "While Hugh's dad is overseas, it's just him and me, so he's needed to take on some more responsibilities." She moved to the refrigerator, handed Hugh the list, and discreetly gave him money for the groceries.

"Back soon," Hugh said as he walked out.

Mrs. Stenstrom poured herself another cup of coffee and moved back to the table, sitting across from Patty. "I love Saturday mornings, don't you?"

"Yes, ma'am—Mrs. Stenstrom." Patty flushed, sure she'd just sounded like a complete idiot.

"Please, call me Stella."

Patty smiled, feeling a bit better. "Okay."

Stella glanced to the corner, where Patty's backpack was neatly stored. She sipped her coffee. "Patty, I don't mean to pry, but it looks as if you've left your house with more than just a sweater. Are you planning on being gone for longer than breakfast?"

"I guess."

"Would you tell me what happened?"

"I was at a sleepover at my best friend Mandy's, and we had a fight about the war."

"Ah," said Stella. "Mandy's against it, is she?"

Patty nodded. "But I know Hugh's dad is fighting over there. And I don't think it's right to say terrible things about it while people are risking their lives."

"Good for you."

"Anyway, I came home this morning, and told my mom, and

she's against the war too, and then *we* had a fight." Patty didn't dare tell Stella that her mom was in the middle of a twenty-four-hour party or that they'd fought over witchcraft. She suddenly felt tears stinging her eyes. "Anyway, I didn't mean to run away, but my backpack was already packed, and I had to get out and think, and I'd been up all night—"

"Oh, dear. You've been up all night?"

Patty nodded.

"Well, no wonder you're so out of sorts. No wonder you can't think." She leaned over, putting a comforting hand on Patty's shoulder. "Here's what let's do. First, please call your mother. Let her know that you're here with me and that you're all right. I'm sure she's worried." Stella crossed to the counter, picked up a Princess phone, unrolled its long cord, and carried it back to the kitchen table. "Here. Give her a call while I draw you a bath. We'll get you put right again in no time." She gave Patty a reassuring smile and left the room.

Patty was grateful that Stella was out of earshot when she called. The party was still in full swing. Patty could barely hear her mother over the din. "I'm fine," Patty said. "I'm with Hugh's mom. She made me breakfast."

There was a loud crash on the other end of the phone, and Penny said she had to go.

The bathroom was steamy and smelled of lavender when Patty walked in. The tub was nearly overflowing with huge mounds of sweet-smelling bubbles piled on top. Patty shed her clothes and stepped in, sliding down among the scented bubbles. She felt her whole body relax, as if she were suddenly turning to liquid. She closed her eyes, thinking it felt like heaven.

She awoke, aware that the bubbles were gone. The bath was cooler now, and not nearly as pleasant. She got out, dried off, and donned the thick terry robe Stella had laid out for her. She realized she'd left her pack of clean clothes in the other room, and peeked out cautiously.

"There you are," said Stella pleasantly. "I was afraid I was going to have to come in and rescue you."

"I need my clothes," Patty mumbled, looking around.

"Don't worry, Hugh's still out. It's just us girls." Stella walked over, leading Patty down the hall. "Before you dress, why not lay down in the spare room, take a little nap? I'll bring your clothes in to you."

Patty lay under the soft warm comforter in the quiet, quiet room of the quiet, quiet house, feeling at peace. This was what normal felt like. This was what she wanted. She fell asleep smiling.

Patty awoke, feeling refreshed, alive. Her clothes were out of her backpack now, neatly laid out on top of the dresser. She looked at her watch: It was nearly five thirty. She jumped up, dressing quickly.

"Hey, lazy bones," Hugh said as she emerged from the bedroom. "I thought you were never going to wake up."

"Hugh." Stella's voice carried a gentle reprimand. "Our guest needed some sleep. You quit your teasing."

"I'm sorry," said Patty. "I can't believe I slept all day."

"Nonsense," said Stella, crossing to her. "Don't you mind Hugh. You needed a day to sort yourself out. Are you hungry?"

"Yes," Patty replied without thinking. Then: "But you've been too nice already. I'll get something at home."

She cringed as soon as she'd said it. It wasn't yet sundown; the ball would still be in progress, the fairies and witches wringing the last of the merriment from the celebration while they could.

Stella watched her face a moment. "Don't feel like you have to rush off. You just woke up." She stepped closer, lowering her voice, almost closing Hugh out of what she said next. "You still need a little time to think about how best to patch things up with your mom. Why not stay for dinner?"

"Thanks, I'd like that."

At Stella's insistence Patty called home once more to check in. This time Stella stayed in the same room, and Patty was sure she would be able to hear the laughter coming through the phone. "I'll be home soon," she told her mom, and hung up quickly.

Dinner was wonderfully simple. No conversations about spells, no one getting up suddenly in midmeal to rush over to the kettle and turn it down/add some frog's eyes/keep it from blowing up the kitchen. Instead they talked about school, about Hugh's plans to get an after-school job to begin saving for college.

"This is so nice," Patty said, "just sitting and talking, like normal people."

Hugh looked up, surprised. "What do you and your mom talk about at dinner?"

Uh-oh. Patty had been so relaxed, she'd gotten careless. She glanced up into Hugh's waiting face. "We don't talk," she managed, "we fight." She felt bad about making her mom sound like some ogre, but she'd needed an excuse. Maybe, she told herself, if she and her mom had more dinner conversations like the talk she was engaged in now, she wouldn't have to make up such lies.

Stella began to clear the table.

"Let me help," said Patty.

"No. You're company." She turned to Hugh. "Why don't you two go and watch some TV," she said. "I'll join you in a few minutes."

Patty reveled in the simple luxury of watching TV. She even allowed herself to snuggle a bit with Hugh, wishing this day didn't have to end.

Stella came in and switched to the nightly news. They watched coverage of the war.

It was a grim business. Flame throwers. Distraught, homeless villagers. Death. Patty thought of the deaths recently of two witches her mother knew who had been slain by demons. "The world," she said out loud, "can really be an ugly place."

"Yes," Mrs. Stenstrom agreed, and turned the TV off.

"I'm sorry," Patty said to Hugh. "I know your dad's fighting over there. I didn't mean—"

"I'm sure you didn't," Stella interrupted. She glanced at her watch. "Well, it's getting late. We'd better get you home." She looked at Patty. "Do you think you're ready?"

"Yes." The ball would be over now, making it safe to go home. "Thank you, Mrs. Stenstrom."

"Stella."

Patty smiled. "Stella. Thank you. Thank you for everything."

"Anytime. I'm glad we could help." Stella turned to get her car keys, then stopped, as if struck by a new thought. "Would you like to come back?"

"Oh, yes." Patty felt embarrassment flush across her face. Not only was her response corny, it also made her sound desperate. But Stella only smiled.

"You're welcome here anytime. In fact, why not stop over after school on Monday? Hugh tells me you get wonderful grades, perhaps some of your good study habits will rub off on him."

"Really? I'd love that."

"Good. Check with your mom. Assuming it's all right with her, then it's settled."

The inside of the Manor looked like a trailer park in the aftermath of a tornado. Penny sat in the kitchen, drinking tea and looking haggard. She smiled when Patty walked in. "Hello, dear. You missed a splendid ball."

"Really?" Patty glanced around. "It looks more like this place was ransacked by a demon."

Penny sipped her tea.

Patty looked from the house to her mom. "Oh, no. Mom. Demons? *Again?*"

"We did have a party crasher that we had to . . . dispatch."

Patty felt her sulk returning. "Why even bother with the party? Why not just put a permanent sign on the roof that says 'Demons, attack here'?"

"We have a lifestyle," her mother said calmly, "and I'm not about to stop celebrating it because I'm afraid of what might happen."

"But . . . don't you get tired of creepy things trying to kill you?"

Her mother regarded her for a moment. "Do you ever wish you were male, because men have it easier?"

"No," Patty said immediately. "Of course not. I like who I . . ." Her mother's point hit home. "I like who I am."

"So do I." Penny reached over, patted her daughter's arm. "But right now, I'm very tired. I'm going to get some sleep."

The two of them spent all day Sunday putting the Manor right again. And since Penny couldn't use magic for help without suffering the consequences, it was old-fashioned work. Scrubbing. Washing. Sweeping up. They didn't finish until sundown.

"I can't wait for tomorrow, for school," Patty said out loud. She remembered Stella's offer. "Mom?"

"Yes, honey."

"Is it okay if I go over to Hugh's to study after school? His mom will be there."

Penny stopped her work. "You had a good time there yesterday, did you?"

Patty nodded.

"Sounds all right. I'll call Mrs. Stenstrom to make sure."

"Thanks, Mom."

"Here are my rules. You and Hugh are never alone in a room with the door closed. And you're never on any piece of furniture together when you don't have at least one foot on the floor."

Patty rolled her eyes. "Mom, it's for homework. It's not a make-out party."

"Fine. But I don't know Mrs. Stenstrom, so we'll do it my way." She held out her hand, as if to shake hands with Patty, then bent her wrist so her hand angled to the side. Patty did the same, touching palms with Penny.

"I promise, Mom."

They held this witches' promise a moment, then Penny moved closer, stroking her daughter's hair. "I know it's tough on you right now because you're fighting with Mandy. And Hugh *is* a handsome young man."

"It's more than that, Mom. I mean, I really like him, but I like his mom, too. They're so . . . normal. It makes me wish I was normal. Makes me wonder if I want to be a witch at all."

Penny nodded, the slightest look of pain crossing her face. "I had that same wish sometimes, when I was your age. Don't worry, you'll grow out of it."

Patty felt her irritation return. "But what if I don't want to grow out of it? What if I never want to be a witch as much as you do?" She took a breath, saying out loud what she'd been thinking for some time now. "What if I wanted to . . . give up my powers?"

"Give them up?" Her mother looked bewildered, then concerned. "That would leave you defenseless. *Then* how would you stop the creepy things that come for you?"

Patty hadn't thought of this. Her mood darkened. Of *course.* She wouldn't have any powers, but she would still be aware of all things witchy. She would still be a target. She was trapped.

"You're right," she said, "as always." She turned and clumped up the stairs to her room, angry at herself for getting her hopes up that she could ever be like everyone else.

Monday, after school, Patty walked home with Hugh. The walk was longer than she usually liked, but this time she had no complaints. They were together, alone, walking and talking trig and California history and why the new gym teacher was so weird. When they walked into the Stenstrom house, it smelled of baking chocolate. As they began studying at the kitchen table (Stella's ideas about how best to study seemed remarkably like Penny's), Stella put out milk and chocolate-chip cookies. The cookies were still warm, the milk ice-cold, and Patty couldn't imagine anything she would have liked better at that moment.

For the rest of the week the routine was the same. Twice the studying went long, and Patty was invited to stay for dinner. For Patty, it was a happy, peaceful week. Almost perfect. There was only one real problem.

Hugh had left on another errand and Patty was sitting at the kitchen table, putting away her books before she headed for the bus stop. Stella entered the doorway to the kitchen and saw her sitting, staring out the window at nothing in particular.

"Patty?"

She turned, startled, and gave Stella an awkward smile. "Sorry. Just . . . thinking."

"Don't apologize. Is everything all right?"

Patty sighed. "I miss Mandy."

Stella crossed to the chair next to Patty and sat down. "You're still not speaking?"

"She barely even looks at me. No apology, no nothing. And there's so much I want to tell her."

Patty blushed, realizing that what she wanted most to share was how happy she was at Stella's house and what a dream it was to be able to spend so much time with Hugh, even if most of it was doing homework.

"It's hard to lose a friend." Stella thought for a moment. "Have you considered apologizing to *her*?"

"What?" Patty looked up, surprised. "But, she thinks we shouldn't be over there. She thinks everything we're doing is wrong. She thinks soldiers, like Hugh's dad—"

"She's your best friend. You don't have to agree with her about everything to be friends, do you?"

"It's more than that. It's the *way* she talked to me. Like I was the enemy or something. Like she didn't really know me. And, I guess, that's the way I feel about her."

"But now you're lonely."

"Yeah."

Stella smiled, wan. "I know how that feels. I miss Rodger, Hugh's dad, very much."

"I guess I didn't think about that."

"Sometimes, when it's important, we all have to make sacrifices. When we stand up for what we believe in, we have to accept that there are going to be some costs."

Patty thought about the sacrifices Stella had made, that every soldier's family makes. She thought about her own family and about making sacrifices to stand up for what she wanted.

That's when the idea hit her.

"Thanks, Mrs. Stenstrom."

"Stella."

Patty smiled. "Thanks, Stella. Thanks a lot. You've been a big help."

Patty left for the bus, excited. Giddy, almost. She had an idea.

She had a plan. It would be a sacrifice, but it just might bring her what she wanted most.

"I want to give up my powers. Forever."

Patty sat across the kitchen table from her mom, biting her lip, wondering how she'd found the courage to say those words out loud.

Penny sat, looking alternately at Patty then back into her teacup. "Patty . . . ," she began carefully.

"Mom, I want to be normal. I want that more than I've ever wanted anything. I think this is how I can do it."

"What about the dangers to you if you're a witch with no powers?"

Patty smiled, leaning forward, her eyes sparkling. "See, that's just it. That's the part I've figured out." She took a breath, choosing her words more carefully. "I know you're right about that, Mom. I know there are demons out there. But I've seen what you can do with the Book of Shadows. I know you can find something for just about any situation, or brew up some combination of spells to fit what you need. So, I was thinking . . ." Here her nerve began to fail her. _Don't stop now,_ she told herself. _You can't back down._ She looked straight at her mom. "Brew me a potion that erases all my knowledge of anything witchy. Cast a spell so I never again understand what witches can do. Then no demon would ever have a reason to come after me."

From the look on Penny's face, Patty knew that such a thing was possible. She watched her mom struggle with this idea.

"That could still be very dangerous," Penny said at last. "Besides, even without demons chasing you, what would you think of all the things that happen around here?"

"I'd think I have a weird mom, like everybody else does. If it gets really bad, you can erase my memory again. You do it for the normal people who see things they shouldn't."

The look on Penny's face turned to anguish. "Patty, you are talking about breaking a tradition that goes back hundreds of years. You are talking about changing the very essence of who you are, of who we are. Please take some time and think very carefully about this."

"I already have thought about this, Mom. A lot. I'm sure this is what I want to do."

Patty rose and left the room, a feeling of power coursing through her. She had, at last, hope that she might soon be as normal as the other kids she knew.

The next day was warm for San Francisco, almost balmy. Hugh, having an after-school errand, had headed off in another direction, and Patty walked alone toward the Manor, happier than she'd been in a long, long time.

It started as something she saw out of the corner of her eye, but it quickly overtook her, like a dream that swallowed her waking self whole: *She lies in a hospital room, in pain, exhausted. She can feel her damp hair plastered to her head. She hears a baby's cry. Someone in scrubs hands her a tiny new life. "It's a girl, Patty." Others are in the room, but her attention zeroes in on this baby. Her baby. Everything else falls away. Exhaustion is pushed aside by the elation of motherhood. She feels a joy she hadn't known was possible.*

Patty wobbled on the street, weak, staggering to a nearby bus bench. She sat, breathing quickly, feeling her dry hair. It had been so real. She had *been* there, had been in that delivery room. She had felt the pain, the joy. . . .

Patty realized she must have had a premonition. She didn't know how, or why, but she didn't care. She rose off the bench, elated, beaming. This must have been a sign. This *had* to be the right decision for her. She would give up her powers, marry Hugh, have his child, and all would be right with the world.

"Mom," she called, coming in the door.

Penny moved out of the kitchen. From the look on her face, she'd already guessed what Patty was about to say. She stood in the doorway, leaning on the doorjamb as if for support.

"I've made up my mind," Patty said, her smile refusing to stay hidden. "I want to go through with it."

Not even the doorjamb seemed enough support now. Penny reached for a chair, as if she were afraid to walk the two steps unsupported, and sat. "I've been thinking about this too," she said. Her voice was soft. Weak, almost. Patty had never heard her like this. "If you give up your powers, there are so many things that you and I will never be able to share. . . ."

Patty sat as well. "Mom," she said, reaching for Penny's hand, "we'll still do stuff. You'll still be my mom."

Penny shook her head sadly, started to say something more, then changed her mind. "I've been thinking about your safety, as well. I'm still not sure you'd be as secure as you believe."

"But why would any demon want to come after me if I have no powers? What would make me any more of a target than the next girl on the street?"

Penny looked down. "Please take some more time, before you—"

"No. Mom, I *have* thought about this. Being normal. For a long time now. No matter how long you make me wait, this will still be what I want."

Penny moved her mouth, but at first no sound came out. "Very well," she said at last. "I'll prepare the ceremony."

Patty nearly leaped out of her chair. "Mom, you're the greatest! Thanks!" She left, not daring to look back at her mom's face.

Patty headed for the Stenstrom house. Hugh would be back from his errand by now. The homework didn't matter, though. She wanted to be there. With him. This premonition thing was so cool. Now she knew what her future held. She could hardly wait to get there.

She reached the bus stop and was about to sit when it came again, overwhelming her. Like stepping into another version of herself.

A different hospital room. She smells the antiseptic. She looks down at the baby girl in her arms. The door opens. A toddler stands there, with a man. "Piper. Come here. Come see your sister." She smiles as the girl moves over shyly. She looks up to the man. "Where's my other girl? Where's—" Something is wrong. She can't see his face. She looks harder, but it's as if he's being sucked into the hallway, which is turning black. All around her the blackness swirls, swallowing up the man, then the toddler. "Piper, no! Stay with Mommy!" The girl disappears. The baby is wrenched from her arms. She screams, trying to go after them into the blackness. Her family is gone.

Patty landed hard on the ground next to the bus stop. She winced at the pain in her elbow, her hip. She struggled up, sitting on the bench. What had just happened? She shook involuntarily. The images from the premonition flooded by again. Her family. Her three girls. There had been three, she knew. But who was the man? And what was that horrible, evil blackness that swept them all up? This was too much for her to sort out on her own. She forgot about the Stenstrom house, and headed back to the Manor.

"Patty?" Concern radiated from Penny's frame. She rushed to her daughter's side.

"I'm okay, Mom. . . ." Patty shrugged her mom off, then slumped down at the kitchen table. "I'm okay . . . ," she repeated, as if trying to convince herself.

"What happened?"

Patty stared, wondering how it could be so obvious that she'd experienced something terrible. "I'm not sure. Maybe nothing. Maybe just . . ." She didn't know how to explain it.

"Patty, you are about to undergo a process that is life-changing, that is irreversible. If something has threatened you . . ."

"That's just it, Mom. Something did happen, but I can't tell if it's a good thing or a bad thing."

"Tell me what it was, exactly."

"I saw my future."

Penny sat back. "That shouldn't be." She looked at Patty. "Honey, your gift is freezing, not precognition."

"But, Mom, it was so real. Like I was there."

"Tell me everything you saw, everything you felt."

Patty began to tell her mom of the vision. Penny prompted for details, and Patty filled them in, as if she were relating a dream. By the time she got to the end of the second premonition, her mother's face was pale and etched with worry.

"What does it mean?" Patty's voice was a whisper.

"One of your premonitions was almost certainly a transmitted vision."

"What's that?"

"A vision given to you, which shows you what you want to see. It's flattering, but it tries to lead you in a false direction."

"Hey, that's not fair." Patty turned this idea over. "You mean, a witch with this power, this ability to see the future, might be given wrong information?"

"Yes. By something evil."

"How can any witch with this power ever be sure she's

seeing the real truth, and not a transmitted one?"

"That comes with time. But it looks like someone is watching out for you. I believe that your other premonition came from a different source. A good source."

"But, how do I know? How do I tell which vision was the good one, and which was the bad one?"

"I think you know already."

Patty fought to hold back her tears. "No, Mom. I loved that first vision. I had a family. I was happy."

"You had a family in both visions, dear. So that much looks to be a part of your real future. Now you must be on your guard to protect that future."

"How? By giving up my powers? By keeping my powers?"

"I can't answer that for you. But please take more time to think this over."

Patty nodded, shaken. She didn't want to have to do this. She didn't want to be forced to guess which action—keeping her powers or relinquishing them—would best protect her future family.

Exhausted, she dragged herself to her room, looking to sleep, looking to push all decisions away, at least for the moment. Sleep, though, would not come. She closed her eyes only to see, over and over, her family being sucked into blackness.

After school the next day, Patty saw Hugh waiting for her outside. She walked up to him, let herself sink into his embrace. This was the man she was to marry, whose children she was going to have. But as a witch or a regular mortal?

Patty snuggled under his arm as they walked away from the school, but the sense of evil lurking somewhere, watching her, refused to stay away. Something terrible was waiting to happen.

She stopped.

"Patty? Something wrong?"

"It's just that there's this thing . . . with my mom. . . ." She sighed. "Would it be okay if we didn't study together this afternoon? I really need to talk to her."

"Sure. No big deal."

She smiled, kissed him, and turned back for the Manor.

Patty found herself once again across the kitchen table from her mother. "Mom, tell me about being a witch and having a man."

Mother and daughter talked for a long time, about how to know when love is right, about Penny's love for Patty's father.

"So, how do I know what's right for me?"

"You trust your judgment, your instincts. You listen to your heart . . . carefully."

"But Mom, I've seen my future. I've seen—"

It came this time in midsentence, that feeling of being overwhelmed, of being suddenly underwater, only instead of water it was a whole other reality.

Two hallways, each with a man, with children. Both look happy. The blackness returns, swirling, sucking both families into a vortex. There, behind each family, stands a woman, strong in the blackness. One fights against the dark swirl. One becomes it.

Patty blinked, feeling the kitchen table under her elbows. Her mom reached out, grasping both her hands. "What did you see this time?"

Patty described every detail she could remember, down to the bookshelf in the hallway. She tried to put faces on the men, tried to see Hugh in one of them, but she couldn't be sure.

"Tell me about the women," Penny said.

"They were both in shadow. The one on the left didn't do anything, but I could tell she was holding back the darkness. The one on the right . . ."

"Go on."

"She didn't do anything either, but I could tell . . . I could feel . . . that she *was* the darkness."

"What does she look like?"

"I didn't get a good look."

"Go back," Penny said, "and look again."

"But how—"

"Close your eyes." Her mom's voice was gentle, soothing. "You're in that hall again."

"She's too dark, too far away."

"Step closer. Slowly. Don't worry, she can't hurt you."

"She's all dark. Not clothes, really, just darkness in the shape of a body."

"What about her face?"

"I can't see it."

"Yes, you can. Step closer. Relax. Tell me what you see."

Patty mentally took a tentative step, then another, toward the dark woman. She leaned closer, closer.

"I see her now. She's . . ." Patty stopped, opening her eyes. She gripped her mom's hands tighter. "It's Stella."

Penny leaned back. "I was afraid of that."

"What . . ." Patty felt her lower lip tremble. "Mom, what does it mean?"

"She's a demon," Penny said gently. "And she'll come after your daughters. *You* may give up your powers, but they'll still be born with theirs. And when you're defenseless, she'll take your girls from you."

Patty instinctively wrapped her arms around herself. "Are you sure? She's been so nice to me. I mean, what if you're wrong about her?"

"Sit quietly for a moment. Relax. Put away your fear."

"Yeah, like that's going to happen."

"You can do this, Patty. You must. For the sake of your family."

Patty stilled, closed her eyes, tried to shed the fear that gripped her.

"Nothing can hurt you here," Penny said. "You're safe. Your future is not yet here. You have time."

Patty listened to her mother's words and felt a strange calm slowly push away the fear.

"Good," Penny said, watching her. "Now, from here, from this place of peace, of power, tell me what you know."

"Stella isn't who she appears to be," said Patty. "And Hugh isn't the man for me." As soon as she said it, her hands flew to cover her mouth. She felt the tears, hot in her eyes. "Mom, I wanted that so much."

"I'm truly sorry," Penny said. "But it's better to know. Now we must do what we have to to keep your family safe."

For the first time, Patty opened the Book of Shadows as a practitioner, not simply an observer. "This is your spell," her mother said, "your future. I'm here to help you, but this invocation must be yours."

"So, how do I begin?"

"The book will guide you. Ask."

Patty addressed the book. "How do I protect my future family?"

The pages of the book fluttered, stopped, fluttered again, pausing on several spells.

"I think," her mother said gently, "that you need to be more specific."

Patty tried again. "How do I protect my family from a demon who's acting like a mortal?"

The book's pages turned slowly, thoughtfully, as if it were thinking this over, finally resting on a page. Patty read the passage:

When demons come in human form
To threaten those you love with harm,
Wait until the moon's full pow'r,
And cast your spell at the witching hour.

Patty reread the words softly, out loud. "When demons come in human form . . ."

"This is advice, dear," said her mom, "not a spell. You don't have to memorize this part."

"Right." Patty brushed her hair back, embarrassed. "I knew that."

"It's understandable if you're nervous. This is an important milestone for you. For many reasons."

Patty was aware that all her thoughts of becoming normal had vanished. This surprised her until she realized they'd been replaced by the desire to protect her family, her future charges. "Mom, I'm really sorry about the . . . you know, the giving-up-my-powers thing."

"Don't be. You're finding your own way, what's best for you. I'm here to help you do that, whatever it is."

Yeah, but I bet you're glad I've decided to stay a witch. Patty thought this, but she didn't say it out loud. Right now she was grateful for her mom's help. She needed her guidance. This vanquishing-demons stuff was pretty scary, and she didn't even know yet what it was she would have to do.

"The spell," her mother said, as if reading her mind. "Ask about the spell."

"Right." Patty addressed the book again. "I need a spell to vanquish the demon who dwells in the form of Stella Stenstrom."

The book opened to a blank page. Calligraphy began to form, the ink drying slowly as an unseen hand etched these words:

Take four objects, wrapped in care,
One for each child you will bear.
With this bundle, and your spell,
Cast this demon back to hell.

"Four? Mom, I only saw three girls in my vision."

"Apparently, there's going to be another. And we wouldn't want to leave her out."

Patty smiled. "That's so cool. To know that—" She stopped herself. "Wait. It says 'and your spell.' What spell?"

"The book isn't going to give you the incantation. You seem to be on your own for that."

"What? Mom, I can't do that."

"Yes, you can. I'll help. We'll do it together."

For the rest of the afternoon they pored over the book, mother and daughter, looking for a spell that Patty could modify.

"Here's one," Penny said. "Listen to this. 'Demon in the form of man—'"

"She's not a man, Mom, she's a woman."

Penny gave her a slight smile. "Many of these spells were written hundreds of years ago. There wasn't much thought given to the feminist movement."

"I don't care about that. I just want a spell that works." Patty heard the irritation in her voice. It surprised her. "Sorry, Mom. I just—I just want to get back to"—she laughed—"to our *normal* life."

"We already know you're going to have to come up with your own spell. Why not listen to the rest of this one and see what you can do with it?"

Patty sighed. "Okay. Go ahead."

Penny read again.

> *Demon in the form of man,*
> *Leave this quest, this life, this land.*
> *Return unto your natural form.*
> *No longer do my loved ones harm.*

"Wow." Patty leaned closer, reading over her mother's shoulder. "Mom, that's perfect. Except for the 'man' part."

"That's probably why you have to write your own," Penny said. "The book knew you wouldn't go for that."

"Okay," said Patty, "let me try: Demon who is known as Stella . . ."

"I'm not sure you should be so specific. After all, you're going to enter this into the book. It will need to be something those who come after you can use."

"I'm going to—" The idea stunned Patty. "I'm going to write? In the Book of Shadows?"

"Of course, dear, that's how it works." Her mother regarded her. "You are coming into your own now. You're taking your place as a Halliwell witch."

Patty mulled this over a moment, accepting the idea. She tried her own spell.

> *Demon in this kindly form,*
> *Quit your quest to do me harm.*

"That's good," Penny said. "Nicely alliterative. Those lines will protect you. Now you need lines that will send her back to where she came from, so she can't harm others."

Patty thought again.

> *Stay no more in this earthly world.*
> *Back to the darkness you are hurled.*

She looked at her mom. "Is that too . . . corny?"

"How does it make you feel?"

"Powerful," Patty said. "Like I can take care of myself, my family."

"Good. Then that's all that matters." Penny checked her lunar calendar. "The moon is full on the fifteenth, this coming Saturday."

Saturday. Patty's heart pounded so hard in her chest she could feel it. "So . . . what's the plan? How do we . . . you know."

"Vanquish her? First you create the bundle the book mentions. Then we lure Stella somewhere, and you cast your spell."

"And what if it doesn't work? What if she doesn't come, or I do it wrong, or—"

Penny placed her hands on her daughter's shoulders. "I know how scary this is. But you can do it. I'll help you. Now, you need to make that bundle."

Penny left her alone until dinnertime. Patty toured the house, ransacked her belongings, scoured her scrapbooks, looking for four mementos, each of which would somehow protect one of her unborn daughters. She chose carefully.

At dinnertime she laid out the items she'd chosen on the kitchen table.

Penny picked up the rag doll. "I made this when you were three," she said.

"And I always thought I'd pass it on to my firstborn."

Penny smiled. She held up another item, a muffler. "I knitted this. . . ."

"Mom, they're all things you've given me. Things I'll pass on. That seems only right."

Penny nodded.

"So, I just . . . take these things with me?"

"Remember the incantation," Penny said. "'Take four items

wrapped in care.' Not 'wrapped *with* care'. The book is very specific, but it can also be very subtle. You must pay close attention."

"Wrapped in care," Patty mumbled. "Wrapped in . . . what?" She looked up at her mother. Both of them smiled at the same time.

Penny left the room and came back with Patty's baby blanket. "I crocheted this—"

"I know, Mom. It's perfect."

Patty feared her knees would give her away. She was so scared they were shaking. She held on to Hugh as they walked into the Stenstrom house. *She'll know,* Patty thought. *She's a demon. She'll take one look at me, and she'll know. She'll fry me on the spot.* But this part was up to her. She was about to lure this demon to her demise. Or, at least, she was about to try.

She and her mother had gone over and over this part. "Whenever possible," her mother had said, "tell the truth. Just don't tell too much of it."

They stepped inside. Stella greeted them, her welcoming smile freezing in place. "Patty? Is something wrong?"

"No. Everything's fine." A wave of fear swept over her.

"Are you sure? You look terrified of something."

Patty looked down. She and her mom had planned even for this. "It's this thing . . . with my mom . . . I'm not supposed to talk about it." *Stick with the truth, and you can't go wrong. Just stick very carefully.*

Stella stepped closer. "I don't want you to break a confidence with your mother, but something is clearly bothering you. Can you tell me a little? Give me a hint?"

Patty shook her head.

Stella led her to the couch, sitting down with her. "Hugh—"

"I know," he said, sighing, "the grocery list is on the fridge."

After Hugh was gone, Stella leaned closer. "It looks almost as if you've made some decision you're not happy about."

Patty looked up, then down again. "Remember when you and I talked about sacrifice?"

Stella nodded.

"Well, I went home that day and had a long talk with my mom. We went over some stuff we've never talked about before. And afterward, I realized that I *do* have to make a sacrifice, but not the one that I thought."

"I'm afraid I'm not following you."

Boy, do I hope that's the truth. "I thought I was going to go my own way, to sacrifice . . . some of the things my mom and I do together, so I could be who I wanted to be." She broke off. "I'm sorry I can't be more clear, but I made a promise . . ."

"It's all right," Stella cooed. "Just tell me as much as you can."

"Anyway, my mom and I came to a decision. I'm going to stay . . . who I am. And my mom is going to help me."

Stella looked bewildered. "But, I thought you were going to change in order to be happy."

"I did too." Patty allowed her regrets to show. "But I think my mom is right. This is for the best. It's just a different kind of sacrifice."

"This sounds serious."

"It is. To tell you the truth, I'm scared. But we're going through with it."

"With what?"

She took the bait. "With this . . . ceremony thing. Tomorrow night. Late."

Stella looked concerned. "Are you sure this is what you want?"

"I'm not sure of anything, Mrs. Stenstrom. Stella. But my mom and I have agreed. So tomorrow, out by the lake—"

"What lake?"

"I shouldn't tell you any more." *Please ask Hugh which lake.*
Please *ask Hugh which lake.* "In fact, I should go." Patty got up
and walked to the door, trying to control her still-shaking knees.
"Thanks. For all your help." *Yeah. Thanks for showing me that not
all demons look like demons.*

For the first time, Stella had no parting remarks. Patty closed
the door behind her.

Patty and her mom stood at the side of the lake, watching the
moon and the clock.

"She may come for you in the form that you know," Penny
said, "or she may look like her older, truer self."

"You mean hideous."

"Yes. But don't let that get to you. The spell is simple. We're
here, under the moon, it's almost midnight. . . ."

"And I have my bundle." Patty held the items, wrapped in her
baby blanket, as if the bundle were one of her children. In fact,
she told herself, it was more: It was the future of all four of them.
"Mom?" Her voice wobbled. She took in a ragged breath.

Penny pulled Patty into an embrace, held her close, then
stepped back. "You'll be fine," she said. "I'll be here. In the shadows. I'll help you if you need me."

"But, how will I know if I need you?"

"Don't worry. I will."

Penny backed away, and Patty stood inside the circle they had
drawn.

She heard something approaching. *Demon in this kindly form,*
Patty repeated to herself for the forty-seventh time. Then she had a
horrible thought: *What if she isn't in a kindly form tonight? What if
she looks like her demon self?* Panic swept through her like ice water.

Something stepped out of the shadows by the lake. Not
human. Tall. Hairy. Walking stiffly on two legs that looked more

like wolf's haunches. Its eyes glittered in the moonlight, focusing on Patty. A low growl emanated from its snout.

Her mother's voice, almost a whisper, came from behind her. "Now, Patty."

D-demon . . . in this kindly form . . .

The demon stepped forward, twitching. The twitching turned to shudders, and before Patty's eyes, it turned back into Stella. Stella looked up, confused, then smiled. Eyeing the bundle, she advanced once again on Patty.

Without warning Stella sprang, as if she were still wolflike. Her arms arched, fingers curving into claws. Fangs protruded from her mouth as she opened it with a snarl.

Patty screamed, clutching the bundle to her with one hand and holding up the other arm for protection.

Stella froze, half demon, half woman, hanging in midair only a few feet from Patty.

Penny rushed forward. "The spell. Now!"

Demon in this kindly form,
Quit your quest to do me harm.

A sound, like ice floes breaking, boomed from the demon's body. Stella's head slowly became mobile again, her eyes fixing on Patty, her fangs curling into a smile.

"She's too powerful to freeze for long," Penny said. "Finish the spell quickly."

Something akin to rage replaced the ice water flowing in Patty's veins. She leaned closer to the demon hanging in front of her. "You won't touch my daughters," she said. She began again, almost shouting the words.

Demon in this kindly form,
Quit your quest to do me harm.
Stay no more in this earthly world.
Back to the darkness you are hurled!

Surprise crossed the demon's face as she was flung backward, body dissolving into the dark, swirling mass that was her truer self. A void, like the mouth of a black hole, opened, and the demon's darkness disappeared into it.

The void closed. The lake was quiet again, tranquil in the moonlight.

"It's over," Penny said. She wrapped her arms around Patty, who began to shake uncontrollably.

"Mom, did I just kill Hugh's mom?"

"No," Penny said quickly. "You just vanquished a demon. Stella was never Hugh's mom. She was his stepmom. If you can call a demon a stepmom."

Using her magic, Penny moved Stella's car into the lake, where it could still be found. Then she removed all traces that she and Patty had ever been there. "This was one of those accidents," she said, "where the body will never be recovered. That's the kindest thing for Hugh and his father to hear."

At the funeral Hugh introduced Patty to his dad, then explained they would be relocating to the East Coast, to be closer to his dad's family. Hugh's body language was stiff, formal, and Patty realized his attraction to her had been manipulated by Stella, along with everything else the demon had presented to Patty as normal.

Back home at the Manor, Patty sank into the couch, allowing her mother to wrap her in her arms, as she had when Patty was little.

"Her life was so perfect," Patty said, "and it was all such a lie."

Penny smoothed her daughter's hair and said nothing.

"But I guess," Patty went on, "that it makes me appreciate what I have here. I mean, our life *is* a little weird, but it's ours, you know?"

"Yes," said Penny, "I do know."

"This whole good-and-evil thing, it's so complicated."

"Not really." Penny smiled. "You strive to be good, and you watch out for evil."

"But I mean, the *power,* in the world, to do harm . . ."

"Or to do good," her mother added.

"Yeah." Patty snuggled farther into her mother's embrace. "Mom?"

"Yes, dear."

"I'm really glad I have you to go through all this with me."

"We have each other. We're a family. And we will be, for a long time to come."

"Yeah." Patty smiled. "A family of witches." Patty felt warm, safe. She knew she'd made the right decision.

Penny reached into her pocket and pulled out an old, worn, leather pouch. "This is for you."

Patty opened the pouch. A pendant in the shape of a pentagram slipped into her hand.

"It was your ancestor Melinda's," her mother said.

Patty gasped. "Mom. It's for me?"

"It is now. I wore it when I was your age. My mother wore it before me, and her mother before her."

Patty fingered the pendant carefully. "This is so . . ."

"Yes. This is a big deal." Penny took the pendant back. "You'll get it officially at your initiation. Now that you've made your decision, it's time."

"So, I'm a full-fledged witch now?"

"You've cast your first spell, written in the Book of Shadows, vanquished a demon, protected your family. Yes, I'd say you're a full-fledged witch now. And I couldn't be prouder of you."

Patty looked into her mother's eyes. For what might have been the first time, she felt that words were completely unnecessary.

Something Old, Something New

Paul Ruditis

"I swear that thing is getting bigger," Piper said as she made a wide curve around the attic to get to the Book of Shadows.

"Nope. It's still exactly seven feet in diameter," Phoebe replied. "I measured it five minutes ago."

"You've been measuring it every fifteen minutes."

"Well, it's not like we've come up with any other ideas on what to do with it," Phoebe said. "You keep looking in the Book of Shadows, even though we've been through every page at least three times."

"On the bright side, the light from the thing is nice to read by," Piper admitted as she went for her fourth read of the book.

"Well, that's something at least."

Piper looked up at the swirling mass of blue-and-silver light. The vortex had appeared, without ceremony, in the middle of the attic about twenty-six hours earlier. They wouldn't have even known it was in the Manor if Paige hadn't gone up to the attic to check a spell and stumbled across the thing.

In the twenty-six hours since the discovery, they were no closer to finding out the origin of the vortex. Piper certainly had her suspicions. Swirling circles of color weren't entirely unusual around the Charmed Ones, but this one had a familiar air to it. That, more than anything, was cause for concern.

"Still nothing?" Paige asked as she joined her sisters.

"Nope," Phoebe replied. "And what's with the outfit?" Paige was dressed in a long-sleeve peasant blouse with a floor-length green skirt. It was definitely out of the norm for the always trendy youngest Charmed One.

"You said you think this is a time portal, right?" Paige said as she stepped up to the churning mass of light. "Like the one that took you guys back to Melinda Warren's birth."

"We said it *looks* like a time portal," Piper corrected. "But that one sucked us in as soon as it appeared."

They had cautiously stepped up to the vortex several times over the past day and felt no gravitational pull beyond that which kept them glued to the floor. On a whim Phoebe had even thrown a tennis ball into the vortex, but as far as any of them could tell, nothing happened.

"It's been here for a whole day," Phoebe noted. "And the only thing we know for sure is it doesn't suck."

"Besides, the last one was sent by the Elders," Piper added. "And Leo's already confirmed that they had nothing to do with this."

"Yeah, cause they always tell the truth," Paige muttered.

Piper felt no need to comment. Paige was only speaking the truth herself.

The frustrating thing about it was the waiting. If they were expected to use the portal to take them somewhere, it would have been helpful if there had been some kind of sign telling them what to do. And if something was going to come through it and try to kill them, well, Piper wished it would just get it over with.

"Which brings us back to your outfit," Phoebe said.

"It's something I learned in high-school chem class," Paige said.

"When all other areas of observation fail, it's time to experiment."

Without further comment Paige walked into the vortex and disappeared.

"Paige!" Piper yelled as she came around the vortex. "Why would she do that? Why would she do that?!"

"So we'd do this," Phoebe said as she followed.

Piper looked at the swirling mass. It had not grown. It had not changed. It just stood in the middle of the attic as it had been doing since it got there.

"Leo!" Piper yelled downstairs. "Keep an eye on Wyatt! We'll be back!" Then she added to herself, "I hope."

She followed her sisters through the portal. The trip was less jarring than the last time she, Phoebe, and Prue had been through one of those portals. She just stepped in from the attic and stepped out in the forest. Her sisters and one lone tennis ball were waiting for her.

"Paige, you can't just go walking through portals like that," Piper admonished. "You never know where they're going to lead you. We could be in some alternate reality . . . some demon dimension."

"The shoe department at Nordstrom's," Phoebe added.

Piper shot her a look that said, *You're not helping.*

"Well, unless we were planning to redecorate the attic around the glowing disk of light, I figured this was the best way to get things moving," Paige responded. "Besides, I think it was a time portal. Check this out." Paige raised her hand. "Tennis ball."

The ball remained where it was on the ground.

"My power's out," Paige said. "So that's usually a sign we're in the past."

"Yeah, in the middle of a forest," Phoebe said. "Big help."

"No. Listen." Piper heard noises that weren't native to any forest she had ever been in. "I don't think we're in the *middle* of the forest."

Piper led her sisters around a clump of bushes. She could distinctly hear voices calling out and horses clomping in the distance. As it turned out, they were only a few feet from the edge of the forest and on the border of a fairly large colonial town. It was much larger than the village they had visited in Virginia a few years earlier.

"Looks about sixteen or seventeen hundreds," Piper said, giving Paige's outfit another look. "How'd you guess?"

"Played the odds," Paige said. "Besides, you can get away with a long-sleeve top and floor-length skirt in almost any time."

Piper looked out at the townspeople. The women were dressed even more conservatively than Paige, if that was possible. Wherever they were and whenever it was, Piper would definitely stand out dressed in pants. Phoebe, on the other hand, who was wearing a miniskirt and a halter top, would cause nothing short of a scandal if she were seen.

"You two wait here," Paige said. "I'll find out where we are and try to pick up some clothes."

"How are you going to do that?" Piper asked.

"The less you know," Paige said, "the better for you." She turned and hurried off toward town before either sister had a chance to say anything.

"Impulsive, isn't she?" Phoebe asked as she sat on a large stone.

"That's one word for it," Piper replied as she paced the forest greenery. Once again they were lost in time with no clue how they really got there, what they were expected to do, and how the heck they could get back.

"Why don't you sit down?" Phoebe asked.

"Why don't you pace with me?" Piper shot back. "We've got to figure out why we're here."

"No, we don't," Phoebe said. "We can just sit here and wait for the answer to come to us. It usually does."

Piper tried to argue with the logic, but she knew it was sound, in a mixed-up–Charmed-Ones way. Someone obviously wanted them to do something in this time. Odds are they'd find out what it was soon enough. Piper joined her sister on the ground and waited, though her mind was still going a mile a minute.

After several minutes and numerous miles of thought, Piper heard someone shuffling through the forest.

"There we go," Phoebe said softly, hopping to her feet. "You know, I didn't really expect it to be that easy."

"Somehow I doubt it will be," Piper said as she joined her sister.

They followed the sound through the trees to a clearing, where they found a young woman hunched over the ground. The girl had long brown hair and appeared to be a few years younger than Paige. She was digging through a patch of leafy green plants that looked like mayapples. Piper couldn't really tell from her vantage point.

"If she's doing what I think she's doing," Phoebe whispered, "she's not doing it right."

Piper agreed. If the girl was digging up the plants for a spell, she was obviously not well versed in her craft, because she was doing it all wrong. As part of the mandrake family, the mayapple plant had to be tended to carefully, or else it would be useless. Piper was always careful when she found a new herbalist shop, because an improperly pulled mayapple could lead to an ineffective potion that might endanger their lives.

The girl stopped halfway through her work. At first Piper wasn't sure why. But when she noticed the girl's shoulders shaking—even at that distance—it was clear to see that she was crying.

"Hey, what's the—"

"Shhh!" Piper said as she spun to find Paige standing with her arms draped with clothing. Piper led Paige and Phoebe back through the bushes so they would not disturb the girl.

"What did you find?" Paige asked in a whisper.

"Odds are, our Innocent," Phoebe replied. "What about you?"

"Here you go." Paige handed over the outfits. "I was able to find out that we're in Boston at some point in the early seventeen hundreds."

"Couldn't you narrow it down a bit more than that?" Phoebe asked as she slid the long skirt over her leather mini. The smaller skirt was so thin that it barely made a line in the fabric covering it.

"Sorry," Paige said. "It's not like there's a conveniently placed newspaper stand with the date emblazoned across the headlines."

"I don't think we really need specifics," Piper said. The general date gave her a suspicion as to why they were there. "Let's go make a friend." She led her sisters out to the clearing. The girl was still on her knees, but the crying had apparently stopped. She was back to work carelessly ripping out the mayapples.

"Pardon us," Piper said softly as they entered the clearing.

The girl looked up at them but didn't speak.

Piper stepped forward. She figured it was time to take a move from Paige's playbook and just go the direct route. "I was wondering if you could help us," Piper said. "We have traveled quite far to find our cousin . . . Prudence Warren."

The girl's face lit up with an excited, confused look. "Why . . . that would be me!"

Phoebe tried to cover her own surprise. She didn't know why she hadn't figured it out on her own. The timeframe worked out. Even the location made sense. But that once again raised the question of who wanted them to meet Prudence and what they were expected to do.

"Cousins?" Prudence continued at a near manic pace. "I did not know of any relatives. I was always told that I was alone in the world. How did you hear of me? Was it the wedding?"

"Yes," Phoebe said, playing along. "We came for the wedding."

"We lost track of you," Piper said. "Following . . ."

"The death of my mother?" Prudence said solemnly.

The sisters nodded.

"I'm Piper," the eldest Charmed One started the introductions. "And these are my sisters, Phoebe and Paige."

"Prudence, Piper, Phoebe, and Paige?" Prudence echoed their names. "I had no idea I came from a family with such an infatuation with the letter 'P.'"

"Yeah, it's kind of a thing," Phoebe said, thinking fondly of her own sister Prue.

"Did we interrupt some wedding preparations?" Paige asked, pointing to Prudence's half-filled bucket of mayapples.

"Just collecting some plants," Prudence said evasively. "I fear it was more taxing work than I had imagined."

"We can help," Phoebe said as she grabbed the bucket and Paige. They dropped to their knees among the plants.

"So . . . ," Piper said, directing Prudence's attention away from her sisters. "When exactly is the wedding?"

"Tomorrow," Prudence said with a smile. "On what is certain to be the most beautiful day of the year."

Phoebe made sure that Prudence was not looking in their direction. She spilled the poorly collected mayapples out of the bucket and set to work pulling more plants the correct way with Paige. She hoped that Prudence was planning to use the plant in a spell, because if she was merely pulling some wedding decorations, they didn't really have to take the care they were in getting the plants. She half listened as Prudence detailed the wedding plans.

"But you must tell me how you came to find me after all these years," Prudence insisted once she had exhausted the wedding details.

"It's a long story," Piper said.

Phoebe took that as her cue. "Here we are," she said as she stood with the refilled basket of mayapples. "Is there someplace we can go to clean up?"

"Certainly," Prudence said. "You must stay with me and Elizabeth."

"Elizabeth?" Piper asked.

"She moved us from Salem and raised me following my mother's death," Prudence said. "Elizabeth is the closest thing to a mother I know. Come. This way."

Phoebe and her sisters followed Prudence through the forest and into Boston. Phoebe's head was twisting in all directions, taking in the history surrounding them. It was beautiful. The buildings had character as opposed to the cold architectural designs of the future. There was an exciting energy to the town. The people moved differently than they did in the future, which may have had something to do with the fact they didn't all have cell phones attached to their ears.

In their crazy magical lives it was often easy to forget to enjoy the opportunities it afforded them. How many people from their time got to witness eighteenth-century life firsthand?

The journey to Prudence's home was interesting but uneventful. Unfortunately the arrival was not as welcoming as they had been led to believe.

"Melinda had no sister," Elizabeth Hasting said upon introduction.

"We're distant cousins," Piper added quickly.

"Our mother died when we were very young," Paige added, not exactly lying. "We've always been a little unclear how the family lines diverged."

Elizabeth seemed skeptical. Phoebe didn't blame her. She'd be suspicious too if long-lost relatives showed up at their door.

"Why would you arrive at this particular time?" Elizabeth asked.

"We received word of the wedding," Phoebe replied. But there was a nagging feeling that Elizabeth was referring to something else that was about to happen.

"Where?" Elizabeth asked.

"Where what?" Paige asked.

"Where were you that you heard of the wedding?" Elizabeth asked. "Where have you been all of Prudence's life?"

Phoebe was tempted to say New York, but it seemed unlikely that news of the wedding would have traveled that far. Salem would have been the wrong choice, considering Elizabeth may have kept in touch with people in that town. Phoebe chose the only town in the area that she knew was established in this time.

"Charlestown," she said. "We're from Charlestown. It's amazing that we lived so nearby all this time without knowing about our cousin."

"It is interesting," Elizabeth said.

"Oh, Elizabeth, can you never be happy?" Prudence asked. "After all these years, I have finally found that I have family."

"I am only looking out for your best interests," Elizabeth said.

"We are too," Phoebe said. "We didn't mean to intrude on your wedding. If you'd like us to leave, we will go."

"Please stay," Prudence said to the Charmed Ones, but she was looking at Elizabeth. "I would love to have you at my wedding."

"You are welcome to stay," Elizabeth relented, though her expression indicated that she was not happy about it. "Now, if you will excuse me, I am expected at the livery."

"I believe she has a gentleman friend there," Prudence said conspiratorially after Elizabeth left. "She is being so secretive. I do apologize for the way Elizabeth spoke. She is very protective."

"We understand," Piper said. "Especially considering how your mother died."

"You know of that?" Prudence asked. "Of course you would. Certainly that story of her death would have reached your own mother. It was horrible. To be accused of such wretched falsehoods."

"Falsehoods?" Phoebe asked. She wasn't sure if Prudence believed that her mom wasn't a witch or if she was covering for herself. "You believe the rumors of her . . . abilities . . . were lies?"

"But what else could they be?" Prudence asked. Her voice seemed strained, but Phoebe wasn't sure if she was reading too much into it. They were discussing a sensitive subject. "Elizabeth has assured me that my mother was not evil."

Phoebe stepped forward. "Not all witches—"

"Phoebe!" Piper said, laying a hand on her sister. "I think it would be nice to explore the town. I have never been to Boston before."

"Oh, but you must visit the harbor," Prudence said. "My fiancé's ship is in port. I would take you there myself, but I have an appointment to keep."

"That sounds like a wonderful idea," Piper said. "We certainly don't want to get in the way."

"I shall not be too long," Prudence said as she picked up her bucket full of mayapples. She also grabbed a satchel off a shelf in the kitchen area. "We can meet back here before nightfall. Then I can take you to see my fiancé."

"That would be great," Piper said.

Prudence pointed out the direction of the harbor, and turned off to go back to the woods. Piper led her sisters a few feet until Prudence had turned a corner and was out of view.

"Paige, you go follow Prudence," Piper said.

"What are we going to do?" Phoebe asked.

"Look in on Elizabeth," Piper said. "I'm sure we can figure out where the nearest livery is."

The Charmed Ones went their separate ways. Phoebe didn't like splitting from Paige, but she liked Prudence going off on her own even less. There was a reason they were sent back in time, after all.

"I knew you didn't trust Elizabeth," Phoebe said as they walked toward the center of town.

"It's not that exactly," Piper said. "She could just be concerned about Prudence. Elizabeth has taken care of her all these years."

"What better way to get control of the power of the Warren line?" Phoebe asked.

"That's a concern," Piper said. "Or she could really care about the girl."

It didn't take long for Piper and Phoebe to wind their way through the dirt roads to find the livery. Elizabeth was just leaving the stable, but she did not head back toward her home. Instead she went off in the opposite direction.

"Here we go," Phoebe said as they followed.

Elizabeth led them through town and into Boston Common. Phoebe got a chill as she entered the park area. She figured she would get the same chill if they entered the common hundreds of years in the future. This was the place where women found guilty of witchcraft were hanged.

There were only a few people in the common, which made it harder for Phoebe and Piper to remain hidden. They had to keep their distance, because Elizabeth kept looking back as if she were expecting to be followed.

"What's she up to?" Phoebe wondered aloud.

They continued to follow her through the common, to a graveyard on the other side. Phoebe wanted to believe that this was where the poor hanged souls were laid to rest, but she doubted that they were buried in consecrated ground. It was possible that Elizabeth was just visiting a deceased friend or family member, but that didn't explain why she kept looking over her shoulder.

The graveyard was on a small patch of land with only a few rows of headstones. Elizabeth bypassed the graves, heading straight for the lone mausoleum in the center. It was a small building made of concrete. Elizabeth took one last look behind her. Phoebe and Piper dropped to the ground beside a headstone, pretending to be mourners overcome by grief. The ruse seemed to work, as Elizabeth continued into the mausoleum.

"Wait here," Phoebe said as she left her sister.

"Be careful," Piper whispered after her.

Phoebe hurried up to the mausoleum. She wasn't surprised to find that the only windows were small slats up by the roof to let in the light. It wasn't like anyone inside was going to be looking out to admire the view. If she had her powers, she could rise up to them to look inside, but she'd never be able to peek in on her own.

She carefully stepped up to the door. The name "Lancaster" was etched in the metal. She wondered if Elizabeth was related somehow. It seemed unlikely that her family would rate a mausoleum. Her home was nice, but by no means did it indicate that she came from a background that could afford such a stately burial.

Phoebe searched her memory banks, but knew of no ties to any Lancasters in the Warren line.

Even with the door closed, she could hear the sound of stone sliding against stone. She wanted to peek inside the door, but knew that was too risky. As she leaned against the door, she could hear footsteps approaching from the other side.

Phoebe dashed to the corner of the mausoleum and hid around the side. She turned and peeked out to see Elizabeth exit the mausoleum with something bundled in her arms.

As Elizabeth exited the graveyard, Phoebe considered grabbing her sister and continuing to follow, but the mausoleum interested her too much. She went up to the door and pushed it open.

The interior was dark, even with the small slats by the roof providing light. She kept the door open to brighten the room. It looked like an ordinary crypt. There were two stone slabs in the center, presumably with bodies resting inside. Along the wall there were several openings for future bodies, as well as a few sealed ones with more residents.

"Find anything?"

"Jeez!" Phoebe nearly jumped out of her anachronistically high heels. "Don't do that!"

"Sorry," Piper said as she peered into the room. "Any idea what she took out of here?"

"Whatever it was, it's gone now," Phoebe said. "So I doubt looking in the graves is going to do any good."

"I agree," Piper said.

"But I'd say there's a good chance that Elizabeth is the reason we were brought back here," Phoebe said as she let the metal door slam behind them on the way out.

Paige followed Prudence through town and back into the woods. It was more than a little odd for the girl to go back to the very place she had just been. At first Paige figured it had to do with running into her and her sisters, but she realized Prudence must have needed to get the sack that she was carrying. Either way, secret trips into the woods rarely tended to be portents of good times as far as Paige was concerned.

As they went deeper into the forest, Paige found she didn't need to keep too much distance as there were many places to hide. That was especially good since she was concerned about getting lost. She did need to be careful not to make a sound while walking through the brush.

They walked for quite a while. Paige wished she had worn a watch to mark just how long they had been in the forest. When she had prepared for the trip she didn't want any anachronistic things like watches to expose her. Now, she wished she had brought one . . . and some bottled water . . . and better hiking shoes.

After what must have been close to a half hour, they came to a small house in the woods. Prudence knocked three times. Then an additional two times. Then she entered without being invited.

"Well, this is never good," Paige said to herself.

She walked up to the house and moved to an open window. Peering inside, she saw Prudence with an elderly woman who looked as if she had been through a very harsh life. From her vantage point, Paige could hear everything they said.

"I collected the items you requested," Prudence said. "But I do not know if we should do this tonight. I have recently received some unexpected visitors."

"You are the one who set the wedding date for tomorrow," the woman said in a condescending tone. "You are the one who insists we enact the spell before you are wed."

The spell part piqued Paige's interest. This was the first mention of magic she had heard since they arrived.

"For the spell to work," the woman continued, "you need to do this of your own free will. You cannot have doubts."

That part concerned Paige. Anytime something was done "of your own free will," it was usually something that shouldn't be done.

"And what if I am unsure?" Prudence asked.

"We shall have to wait for the next full moon," the woman replied. "And hope that your new husband does not find your secret before that time."

There was a long pause in the conversation. Paige was tempted to peek in the window, but there was no real need. She had enough information to know that this must be the reason the portal appeared in the attic. This old woman was trying to get Prudence to do something that a good witch should not do.

"I shall do my best," Prudence said.

"See that you do," the woman replied. "I will meet you in the clearing tonight. Do not be late."

Paige listened as the door opened. She watched Prudence start back through the forest. Paige considered staying to watch the old woman a bit longer, but she would never find her way back to town on her own. She hurried off after Prudence. It was much easier now that she wasn't bothering to hide her approach.

"Prudence!" Paige called, once she was sure they were clear of the house and out of earshot.

"Who's there?" Prudence asked. There was a noticeable quiver in her voice.

"It's me," Paige said. "Sorry. I didn't mean to scare you."

"Scare me? Is that your only concern? Did you not mean to follow me either?"

"Okay, true . . . that's not the nicest thing to do," Paige said. "But there's a reason, I promise."

"I should certainly hope," Prudence said as she started through the forest again. It was fairly obvious to Paige that the girl was trying to put some distance between them and the house.

"But first, who was that woman?"

"No one important."

"I heard you talking to her," Paige said, knowing they didn't have time to be coy with sunset approaching. "You're working on a spell."

Prudence froze. She had a horrified look on her face. "You

should not speak of such things. My mother died from false accusations like that."

Paige could understand why Prudence would fear being found out, but since the girl thought that Paige was part of the family, she might understand that they shared the trait. The problem was figuring out how to approach the subject without terrorizing Prudence.

"Listen, I know this is hard to—"

"You do not know," Prudence said. "You do not know anything about me. You come into my life on the eve of my wedding and start making accusations—"

"I haven't accused you of anything," Paige replied. "But I can help."

"Stay away!" Prudence threw up her hands. Paige's body flew through the air and slammed—hard—into a tree.

"Well, that wasn't very nice," Paige grumbled as she tried to stand. Her whole body ached. She wished that she wasn't used to this kind of pain, but she had been through much worse in the fight against evil.

Once Paige got back to her feet, she found that she wasn't the only one caught off guard by what had happened. To say that Prudence had a look of horror on her face would be an understatement. She looked terrified at what had just happened. She was staring at her hands.

"Prudence, it's okay," Paige said.

"Stay away from me!" Prudence started running.

Paige ran after the girl. That had not gone at all the way she had hoped. She had to find a way to calm Prudence before she reached town. There was no telling what she would do in that state.

"Prudence, slow down!" Paige called out. The long skirt she was wearing was not made for sprinting, but neither was Prudence's for that matter.

The girl refused to listen. She continued through the forest at a brisk pace for a while. Even in her long skirt, she managed to do well at avoiding rocks and hurdling over downed tree trunks. Eventually her emotions took control and she dropped to the ground, sobbing.

"Yeah, I need much better shoes," Paige said as she caught up and tried to catch her breath.

"What have I done?" Prudence asked, more to the skies than to Paige. "Is it really true?"

This was something Paige had not prepared for. It was one thing to assume that Prudence was hiding the fact that she was a witch. Certainly that would have been the logical thing to do in this time. It would also explain why she would be so secretive about the old woman in the woods and the spell they were working on.

But Prudence was acting like this was all news to her. Then Paige realized that maybe it wasn't an act. Maybe Prudence didn't know about her gifts. It was the only logical explanation, really. Melinda Warren had bound her daughter's powers before she died.

"So the stories are true," Prudence said, near tears. "My mother used magic."

"Very powerful magic," Piper said. "And a very good magic."

"There is no such thing."

"Of course there is," Piper said. "We can use the same magic."

"Just not at the moment," Paige added dryly.

Piper knew that outing herself and her sisters in the seventeen hundreds wasn't the smartest idea, but it was the fastest way to get Prudence to understand they were in this together. The day certainly wasn't shaping up the way she had expected it to when she was feeding Wyatt his breakfast a few hours earlier and a few hundred years later.

Piper and Phoebe had gone back to the house following their trip to the graveyard. By the time they reached the front door, Elizabeth was already heading back out. She no longer had the mysterious bundle in her hands. They exchanged strained pleasantries while Elizabeth let them back inside, then excused herself for more errands. Piper thought it odd that the woman would just leave them unattended, but she had apparently hidden the mysterious object fairly well. A search of the house turned up nothing out of the ordinary.

Then again, considering they didn't know what they were looking for, they could have easily overlooked the item. It wasn't like they didn't give the place a thorough search. They had over a half hour to dig around before Prudence burst in the door with Paige on her heels. Paige was quick with the update, bringing her sisters to speed. Piper decided to take over from there.

"So, you are . . ." Prudence couldn't bring herself to say the word.

"Witches?" Phoebe completed the thought. "Yep."

"Then it runs in the family?" Prudence asked.

"You could say that," Piper replied. "It's nothing to be afraid of."

"But my mother was killed because of it," Prudence cried. "Why should I not fear it?"

"She's got a point," Paige mumbled.

Piper shot her sister a look.

"And why did I not know this before now?" Prudence asked. "How could I throw Paige into the air without even touching her?"

"You didn't have any idea?" Paige asked. "Then why did you go to see that woman about a spell?"

"I did not *know*," Prudence confirmed. "But I had my suspicions. I started seeing odd images in my mind . . . images that came true."

"Premonitions," Phoebe clarified. "You were seeing the future."

"Well, I did not want to see it," Prudence said. "So I went into the forest to find the lady Helena. I had heard tales of her magical ways since I was a child. I sought her out and told her of the images. She said she could remove them. I only hope she can remove all of these powers."

"No," Piper said calmly. At least they had their answer. They were sent back in time to stop Prudence from giving up her powers. On the bright side, there didn't seem to be any big hulking demons around to deal with. "These are gifts. I know they don't seem like it at the moment. But believe us, they can be used for good."

"And how do I explain it to my Michael?" Prudence asked. "We are to be wed tomorrow. He will not want to marry a . . . a . . ."

"Witch," Phoebe said.

Piper shot her sister a look.

"What? It helps to say it out loud," Phoebe said defensively. Then she turned to Prudence. "I know it did for me. Please understand, Prudence, all three of us were once exactly where you are."

"Well . . . maybe not exactly," Paige mumbled, taking in their surroundings.

"We each had to accept the truth about ourselves," Phoebe said. "And then we had to decide how to share it with loved ones."

"If at all," Piper added. She was well aware that the decision was somewhat easier in the twenty-first century. As much as she and her sisters understood what Prudence was feeling, there were parts that they would never fully realize.

"But I was told that it was all a lie," Prudence said.

"That is not exactly true," Elizabeth said as she entered the house. "Whenever the question arose, I diverted your attention from the subject. I never truthfully provided an answer."

"You knew?" Prudence asked.

"Melinda died to protect you," Elizabeth said. She walked through the room toward the far wall. "As her friend, I felt it was my duty to see to it that she did not die in vain. I knew one day we would have this discussion. I am only sorry that I waited so long. It should have come before the eve of your wedding."

Elizabeth bent and pulled up a loose floorboard. From the secret space beneath it she removed the bundle that she had been holding earlier.

"I knew it was here someplace," Phoebe muttered.

"This was your mother's," Elizabeth said. "I had kept it hidden in the only place I knew would be safe. Someplace far from the house."

Prudence reached in the bag and removed the Book of Shadows. It was much thinner in this time since it did not yet have the collected wisdom of the Warren witches.

"This is a sort of family heirloom," Piper said. Technically that wasn't true yet, but she figured it was best to keep the story simple. "It is where we collect all that we have learned about our powers."

"This is . . ." Prudence froze on a page. Piper could not see what it was, but it was obviously not pleasant. "This is too much. I must . . . I need . . ."

Prudence slammed the book closed and dropped it on the table. She looked up at Elizabeth, then her strange, newly found cousins. Without a word she turned and fled the house.

Piper turned to her sisters. "Paige."

"I'm on it." Paige sighed and went after her.

"I should not have waited so long to tell her the truth," Elizabeth insisted once they were gone. "On the eve of her wedding."

"Trust me, she wouldn't have been ready no matter when you told her," Piper said.

"She's been conditioned to think magic is evil," Phoebe said.

"It makes sense, considering the attitudes around here. We just need to prove that her magic is a gift."

"How will you do that?" Elizabeth asked.

"By showing her the good that she can do with it," Piper said. "Phoebe, I need you to come up with some potions to show Prudence how magic can benefit her in everyday life."

"And how am I supposed to do that?" Phoebe asked. "It's not like there's a good herbalist shop around here."

"But there is an apothecary not far," Elizabeth suggested. "On Great Street. They may have the items you need. I have an account there."

"Just be careful," Piper warned. "Don't call too much attention to yourself."

"No problem," Phoebe said and was out the door.

"What shall we do?" Elizabeth asked.

"Do you know anything about this Helena woman?" Piper asked.

"I made a point of seeking out any stories of witches when we came to Boston," Elizabeth explained. "Helena is more of a sorceress. She can be very dangerous even though she only possesses minor powers of her own. Her true strength comes from her ability to tap into nature, the elements, and other beings. I fear she is always looking for more power."

"Which means she isn't in this solely to help Prudence," Piper said. "Helena wants the magic for herself."

Paige hurried after Prudence through the streets of Boston. She was worried that night was about to fall and she could easily lose Prudence in the darkness. The fear soon proved to be unfounded when Prudence stopped suddenly.

Paige ducked behind a building as Prudence turned in her direction.

"Are you following me again, Cousin?" she called out. "It would be best if you revealed yourself instead of playing this game!"

Paige considered her options. There were none, really. Prudence would wait in the middle of the street until Paige revealed herself. She stepped out from behind the building.

"I am without family for twenty years," Prudence said, "and now I find I cannot rid myself of them."

"We were worried you were going to do something rash."

"Why would you fear that?" Prudence asked. Paige could tell she was being sarcastic. It was oddly comforting to know that sarcasm existed hundreds of years before she was born.

"Come back to the house," Paige said. "We can talk some more."

"Oh, we shall talk," Prudence said. "But first I must end my engagement to Michael."

"You can't do that." Paige was careful in choosing her words since they were having this discussion in the middle of a fairly busy street. "You need to know more about what you found out today before making any life-altering decisions."

"But surely he would not want me now," Prudence said. "I must look out for the interests of my love."

"Not without all the facts."

"I know all that I need," Prudence said as she started off again. "I would bid you not to follow me, but I imagine that would be ignored."

"You got that right," Paige said.

They continued to tramp through the streets of Boston as the sun set. It did not take long for them to reach Boston Harbor. The docks were crowded with people. Paige worried that Prudence would try to lose her in the throng, but that did not happen. The crowd thinned as they reached the last ship in the harbor. Paige had seen similar tall ships at a Fourth of July festival when she was younger. It was quite different seeing them as they originally appeared, before they were cleaned up and polished by historical restoration.

"Michael!" Prudence called out to a man disembarking the ship. The handsome sailor's face lit up as he waved.

"Nice catch," Paige said. "Captain?"

"First mate," Prudence explained as she pushed her way through the few stragglers at the end of the dock. "His ship sails to England in one week."

"Some honeymoon," Paige said. "If you don't call off the marriage, that is."

"Prudence, my love," Michael said as he hurried to her and gave a chaste kiss on the cheek. It took him a moment to notice his fiancée was not alone. "And who is this?"

"I am told she is my cousin Paige," Prudence replied. "Though I suspect the story is more interesting."

Paige tried to look innocent. She failed.

"Your cousin?" Michael asked. "Why, that is marvelous! To finally find a family member on the eve of your wedding. Paige, it is wonderful to meet you."

Considering his exuberance, Paige was expecting to be wrapped up in a hug. She braced herself, but only got an enthused bow. She stood for a moment, then realized that she was expected to curtsy in return.

"This is indeed a special wedding gift," Michael said, beaming.

"Yes, Michael," Prudence said. "That is the reason I came to see you."

"I'll be over here," Paige said as she shifted herself out of earshot. As much as she was afraid of losing Prudence, she did not want to participate in this conversation. It was bad enough that she had to watch.

Prudence apparently cut right to the chase because Michael's expressive face went from joy to confusion to misery in mere moments. Paige couldn't hear what was being said, but Michael was not taking the news well. He fought back tears as he fought to keep his fiancée. Prudence handed him something, but Paige could not see what it was.

"We must go," Prudence said as she rejoined Paige. "It is getting late. Helena will be expecting me."

"I assumed you weren't going to go through with that," Paige said. "Now that you broke up with Michael, what's the point?"

"I may never marry," Prudence replied as they moved down the dock. "But—what if I do?" She checked around to make sure no one could hear. "I cannot marry anyone in good faith and give birth to his children. Or to any children—not while I still have these powers. I fear that they too will be cursed."

Paige wasn't worried about that at all. There was no doubt in her mind that if Prudence had her powers removed, the Warren line would cease to exist as witches. Paige and her sisters often wondered what life would be like if they never found out they had powers. On one hand, it wouldn't be such a horrible thing to live a normal life again. The problem was that Paige knew that wasn't an option.

The world would be a different place, certainly. There's no telling what demons could accomplish over the next few centuries without the Warren witches to fight them. She suspected that the powers of good might be able to maintain balance without the Power of Three. Some other force could always rise to take their place.

Piper and Phoebe could very well return to the future never having known that they were once witches. Paige wasn't sure how Michael fit into the family tree, so it was possible the ancestry would not be greatly altered. Piper and Phoebe could return to their time thinking they belonged to a normal family with a normal mother and father. Their own Prudence from the future may even still be alive.

The same wouldn't be true for Paige. If the Warren witches did not exist, there would be no need for Whitelighters to protect them, and Paige's mother would have never met her father. If the magic left their family line, Paige would never be born.

"I'm almost ready," Phoebe said as she stirred a pot over the fire. Elizabeth sat by the kitchen table, nervously glancing out the window to make sure no one else was approaching.

"What's cooking?" Paige asked as she and Prudence came into the house.

"We're going to show Prudence how her powers can be used for good," Piper said, mainly for Prudence's benefit. "We're working on a potion to show you how it can help in daily life."

"At least, we think we are," Phoebe corrected. "I had to substitute a few ingredients. It's surprisingly difficult to find unicorn-horn shavings around these parts."

"Is that really a good idea?" Paige asked. "Couldn't we try a simpler spell?"

"Next time *you* visit the apothecary and try not to come across like a witch," Phoebe said. "It's the best I could come up with, considering the things they had on hand."

"Sorry," Paige said as she showed Prudence to a seat at the table.

A bucket sat at the center of the table. It was filled with dirt and a rather sad-looking sunflower. The flower was a few shades of brown past healthy, missing numerous petals, and drooping to the side.

"We took this from the garden," Phoebe said as she carefully walked over with a spoonful of potion. "It's looking pretty sad, isn't it? Well, watch what happens when we pour a little of this potion into the soil."

Phoebe did as she said. For a moment nothing happened.

Then the rest of the petals started to drop off the flower. The stem turned black. The entire flower disintegrated into the dirt.

"Yeah. Kind of saw that coming, didn't we?" Paige mumbled, shooting a glance at Phoebe.

"Okay, that wasn't our best work," Piper said.

Prudence, however, seemed totally fine with the results. "It does not matter. Everything could have gone perfectly. You will not change my mind. I am going to give up my powers if Helena can take them."

Prudence moved to the door. Piper considered simply knocking the girl down and tying her up until morning, but there was something unsettling about that course of action. Besides, it would only stall Prudence until the next full moon, and Piper didn't feel like waiting it out, stuck in the past. She looked at her sisters for ideas.

There was a knock at the door. Prudence went to answer it.

"Helena?" Prudence seemed surprised to find the old woman when she opened the door. "I thought we were going to meet later in the woods."

"I had the sense that something might be wrong," Helena said as she took in the room. "Some of your wedding guests?"

"They claim they are my family," Prudence said.

Helena eyed them cautiously. Piper suspected that the woman was taking stock of the magic in the room, calculating ways to convince them all to give up their powers.

"I hope you have not changed your mind," Helena said.

"What's in this for you?" Phoebe asked. "Why are you doing this?"

"Women come to me for help," Helena replied as her eyes went over the other women in the room. They rested for a moment on Elizabeth. "Yet the good people of this town fear me too much to allow me to live among them. I simply enjoy the company when they visit." Her lips curled in a grin as she threw a trio of rocks onto the floor. The rocks sparked blue light.

"Get out of my house, you evil creature," Elizabeth said as she stood and crossed to Helena.

"Elizabeth, no!" Piper yelled.

She was too late. As Elizabeth stepped up to the stones she slammed into an invisible barrier that knocked her to the floor, as well as trapped Piper, Phoebe, and Paige behind it. Piper dropped to her knees to check on Elizabeth. She'd merely had the wind knocked out of her.

"Elizabeth!" Prudence yelled. She moved toward her guardian, but Helena put a hand on the girl to stop her.

"She will be fine," Helena said. "Evil creature? Such cruel words. I merely offered to help this child. To remove what she sees as a curse. And for that I am attacked?"

"Help her?" Paige was incredulous. "You're only doing this for yourself. Helping Prudence is the last thing on your mind."

"If you want me to remove your powers we must go now," Helena said. "We have much to prepare before we can enact the spell."

"I thought we were going to cast the spell at midnight," Prudence said.

"As long as the moon has risen, the spell will work," Helena said.

"Prudence, wait," Piper begged. "You can't just give up your powers. The world needs them in ways you will never understand."

"Oh, they are not going very far," Helena said. "I will give her powers a safe home . . . in me."

"We could always bust through the back wall," Paige suggested halfheartedly.

"Let's save that as a last resort," Piper replied.

Phoebe pulled a walnut out of a jar and flung it at the invisible barrier. She watched as it arced through the air, made contact, and was thrown back at her. Phoebe ducked as the walnut breezed past her head, hit the wall, and fell to the floor beside the other walnuts she had thrown over the past hour.

"Still there," she said. She was getting annoyed. Playing dodge-walnut wasn't nearly as fun as one might think. She wished she had that tennis ball with her.

"Maybe we can use the things we have on hand to make a potion that will dissolve the barrier," Piper suggested as she looked through the bottles Phoebe had brought back from the apothecary. "What are these things, anyway?"

"I picked up a few extra items," Phoebe said. "Never know what might come in handy. None of them will help get us out of this particular predicament, however."

"Does that mean we're out of options?" Paige asked.

"It looks like it," Phoebe replied. If they didn't get out of the house soon, Prudence would give up her powers and the Warren witches would cease to exist. Phoebe assumed that the spell hadn't been cast yet. The moment it was cast, she and her sisters would be returned to their own time with no knowledge of any of this. It was tempting, but there was no telling what the altered future would have in store for them.

"Prudence!" a male voice wailed as fists pounded on the door.

"Michael!" Elizabeth yelled as she approached the barrier. "Michael! We need your help!"

The door swung open and Michael barreled into the room. "Where is Prudence?"

"Stop!" Phoebe yelled. Michael froze a foot from the barrier.

"Yes, Michael, come no farther," Elizabeth added.

"What is wrong?" Michael asked. "And who are these people?"

"Hi," Paige said. "Remember me? Paige. These are my sisters, Piper and Phoebe."

Michael bowed politely, but impatiently. "Where is Prudence?" he asked.

"That's kind of a long story," Paige replied. "But right now we need your help. See those stones on the ground?"

"Yes."

"Could you maybe try to kick them away?" Paige asked. "We tried it from our side and got nowhere, but I'm thinking your side might work."

Michael looked confused. Phoebe could understand that. He wasn't aware of the invisible barrier creating an "our side" versus a "your side."

"Certainly," he said uncertainly.

"Wait!" Phoebe cried. "Use that broom. We don't know how the stones are going to react."

Phoebe gave the guy credit. What they were saying made absolutely no sense, but he did as instructed. He was going to make a good husband, if Prudence ever gave him the chance.

Michael grabbed the broom from the corner and brushed away the stones. Blue light crackled as the barrier came down.

"What madness is this?" Michael asked, staring at the air that was glowing mere moments before.

Phoebe picked up another walnut and threw it across the room. Its flight continued unobstructed as it landed by the front door.

"We have to find Prudence," Piper said.

"I have an idea," Phoebe said. She gathered some of the bottles on the table. "I need something that belongs to her."

"Take this," Michael said, handing her a necklace. "It was a gift she returned to me this afternoon."

"Thank you."

"Elizabeth," Michael continued. "Can you please tell me where Prudence has gone? And what her cousins are doing?"

"It is a difficult story," Elizabeth replied. "And one that Prudence will need to tell you when she is ready. For the moment, you should know that she has been led astray by a mischievous woman."

"Is that why she ended our engagement?"

"In part," Elizabeth replied. "But it is far more difficult a reason than that."

Phoebe did not envy Michael's position in all this. Strange things were happening all around him, and he had no idea what was wrong with the woman he loved. She wished she could warn him that things were about to get stranger, but there simply wasn't time to explain it all.

She poured the last of the powders onto the necklace and thought of Prudence. At first she wasn't sure it had worked. But slowly she saw the necklace start to shake. It rose off the table, floating in midair.

"Madness," Michael whispered.

"This is certainly more direct than scrying," Paige said to Phoebe as the necklace started to move through the house. "We should use this more often."

"Darryl might have a problem with that one since one of the powders I got from the apothecary is fairly illegal in our time," Phoebe replied as they followed the floating necklace out the front door.

"Grab it! Grab it!" Piper said as they hit the street. It wasn't exactly busy, but there were a few people out enjoying an evening stroll.

Paige was the closest to the necklace so she did as instructed. She could feel the necklace straining to get out of her hand and return to its owner. Technically Paige suspected the true owner was Michael, but apparently the necklace hadn't gotten news of the breakup yet.

"Scrying tends to draw less attention, too," Paige added as the necklace pulled at her. "This way."

"How is it that we can follow Prudence's necklace?" Michael asked. "Where is it taking us?"

"Hopefully, to Prudence," Phoebe said. "You know, if this is a bit much, you can stay back at the house, and we'll bring Prudence to you so the two of you can talk."

"If my Prudence is in trouble, I want to be by her side," Michael replied.

"Good guy," Paige cheered. She hoped that she would find someone just as faithful—and heedless to danger—someday.

The necklace led them to the forest, as expected. Once they reached the edge of town, Paige let the necklace free to guide them. It floated slowly, but directly, lit by the full moon and lanterns held by Elizabeth and Michael.

"I do so dislike being in the forest at night," Elizabeth said.

"I'm not so crazy about it either," Paige agreed.

The necklace wound the group through the trees for several minutes. Paige wasn't sure of her surroundings, but she could tell that they were not heading in the direction of Helena's cottage. After a while she heard rushing water and saw the necklace start to speed up.

"Grab it!" Phoebe whispered urgently. "Douse the lanterns. We're here."

Paige grabbed the necklace again. This time it was *really* fighting to break free, obviously sensing its owner was nearby. Phoebe hurried over to Paige with a small bottle full of a new powder.

"Hold out your hand," she instructed.

Paige did as she was told. The necklace was straining against her now. Phoebe sprinkled some of the powder over Paige's hand. The struggling ceased, but she could still feel the necklace quivering.

"Open your hand," Phoebe said.

Paige did as she was told. As the necklace started to slowly rise, Phoebe sprinkled some more powder directly on it. The necklace dropped into Paige's hand.

"You killed it," Paige said. She shook the powder off and wished she had a pocket to stash it in. Instead she handed it to Michael. "Here. You can give this back to Prudence later."

"I can only hope," he replied.

"Good thoughts," Piper added encouragingly.

The group walked quietly to the edge of the tree line and peered out. Prudence and Helena were standing by the edge of the river. Helena had set up an altar by a blazing fire. Paige figured that whatever the spell was she was about to use, the elements of fire and water were necessary for it to succeed.

"So what's the plan?" Piper asked.

"Prudence!" Michael yelled as he burst through the trees.

"I say we use the direct approach," Phoebe said.

"Ya think?" Paige said as they followed.

"Michael, stop!" Prudence yelled as her former fiancé approached the fire.

"Listen to her, Michael," Helena warned. "You do not want to be involved in this."

"He's already involved," Piper said. "He loves her."

"And she loves him," Paige insisted.

"And considering some of the things he's seen tonight, something tells me he's going to be okay with your news Prudence," Phoebe added.

"It's too late," Prudence said. She was positioned directly between the fire and the water. From Paige's vantage point she could see that Prudence was standing in a circle of stones.

"No, it's not," Paige insisted. She knew that as long as she still existed, they had time. "Listen to him."

"Ah, but it *is* too late," Helena said, holding what appeared to be a small robin's egg. It was hard to tell with only the light of the fire.

Michael rushed Prudence in the moment that Helena dropped the egg into the fire. The fire exploded, catching Michael's sleeve and setting his woolen jacket ablaze.

"Michael!" Prudence yelled.

"Stop, drop, and roll!" Piper yelled as she rushed to him.

It was unlikely that he was familiar with those instructions, but it didn't really matter. Michael was in a state of panic as the fire quickly spread over his clothes. He was clearly not thinking straight, as he ran toward the trees and away from the river.

"Prudence!" Paige shouted. "The river!"

Prudence looked confused, but she figured out what Paige meant. Stepping out of the circle of stones Prudence waved her hand at the river. A torrent of water shot up and out at Michael, knocking him to the ground and dousing the flames.

"Wow, she is powerful," Phoebe whispered aloud.

The stone circle was glowing as Prudence rushed to the side of her love.

"Are you all right?" Prudence asked Michael.

"I will be fine," he said, though his voice was strained. His hands and the side of his face were burned, but not horribly so.

"Prudence, get back in the circle," Helena said.

"Do not leave me," Michael begged.

"Just for a moment," Prudence replied. "I promise it will make things better."

"For whom?" Piper asked. "If you are doing this for Michael, I can assure you, he's handling this stuff pretty well."

"He does not know what to make of this," Prudence said. "Once he has the time to think it over, he will no longer want me."

"Prudence, you are making a mistake that you're going to regret," Paige said.

"There will be no regrets," Prudence said.

"Yes, there will," Piper said. "Elizabeth, tell her how much she will regret this decision."

"I don't know what you mean," Elizabeth replied.

Paige didn't know what Piper meant at first, but she was beginning to have an idea. "You weren't able to help Melinda," she said.

"She would not let me help," Elizabeth explained. "She did not want Prudence's life to be threatened."

"You knew Melinda bound her daughter's power," Phoebe said.

"And that she'd be safer if she was not raised by a witch," Piper said.

"I had very limited abilities," Elizabeth said. "Nothing compared to Melinda. But I did not want to risk Prudence losing another guardian." She looked directly at Prudence. "I gave Helena my powers soon after we arrived in Boston. I wanted you to be safe."

"Why did you not tell me sooner?" Prudence asked.

"Again, it was because I was afraid," Elizabeth admitted. "The day I gave Helena my powers, I felt as if I had lost a part of myself. I feared if you knew the whole story, you might make the same mistake as I did. Take the easy solution."

"You gave up your powers for me?" Prudence asked.

"Just as you are about to give up your powers for Michael," Elizabeth replied.

"Time is running out, child," Helena said softly.

Prudence looked at the circle. The stones were not glowing as brightly as they once were. She turned to look at her cousins, and then her love, Michael.

"I do not think I will take you up on your offer, Helena," Prudence said. "I may need my powers to look after my husband."

"He'll be fine," Paige said, feeling a tremendous amount of relief. "There's a potion for a healing salve in the Book of Shadows. I flipped through it while we were trapped behind Helena's force field thing."

"What about Helena?" Elizabeth asked.

"Yes, what about me?" Helena asked. She sounded more than a little annoyed.

"Well, all she really did was try to take Prudence's powers," Piper said. "She may have misled her, but nothing she did really calls for our usual punishment."

"We don't go around killing every sorceress we meet," Phoebe added.

"True," Paige said. "Not *every* one."

The time portal reappeared before Paige even finished the sentence. All the colonial residents were understandably shocked. The future visitors were caught a bit off guard too.

"I guess our work here is done," Piper said. "It was a real pleasure meeting you all."

"We had a blast," Phoebe added. "Well, not so much a blast, but not the type of nightmare we usually have in these situations. So that's a plus."

"Remember the salve," Paige instructed. "I think you and Michael have a bright future together."

The Charmed Ones took a step toward the portal.

"Who are you, really?" Prudence insisted before they could get away.

"Family," the trio said in unison as they stepped into the portal.

"Well, that was interesting," Piper said as they exited the portal. "And look, no bruises, bleeding, or broken bones whatsoever."

"Speak for yourselves," Paige said, rubbing her shoulder. "Prudence didn't accidentally fling either of you into a tree."

"I'm still wondering who sent us there in the first place," Phoebe said.

The portal blinked out, replaced by their answer.

"Grams!"

"Hello, girls," Grams, or more specifically, the spectral image of Grams replied.

"You were behind this?" Piper asked.

"You might say that. It was actually the combined power of the Warren witches. We created the portal to send you back. Of course, we didn't expect that it would take more than a full day for you to step inside the darn thing in the first place."

"You were the one who taught us to keep away from dangerous objects like hot stoves, busy streets, and glowing vortexes of light that suddenly appear with no warning," Phoebe reminded her.

"Why didn't that thing just pull us into it?" Piper asked.

"A bunch of dead witches can only summon so much power," Grams replied.

"And you couldn't have sent a note or something?" Paige asked. "Told us what to do?"

"Where's the fun in that?" Grams asked with a smile. "We knew you'd figure it out. The story had been passed down through generations. When Prudence Warren was faced with the decision whether or not the magic ended with her, the Charmed Ones came and helped her see the light. It was preordained, one might say."

This was met with silence.

Finally Paige was the one to ask the question on all of their minds. "Okay, wait a minute. How did the story get passed along for generations before we were even born? How did we go back in time before we existed?"

"I've found it best to leave questions of magic and time travel alone," Grams said. "Even in the afterlife it can give you a headache."

Preconceived

Erica Pass

PROLOGUE

"Oh, honestly, Patty," said Penny Halliwell, sighing. She stared up from her spot at the foot of the stairs at her teenage daughter, who stared defiantly back. "You're being a royal witch . . . pardon the expression."

"Exactly, Mother," said Patty, securing a rubber band around her long brown hair. "I'm being a witch. Or at least I'm trying to be—if you'd only let me."

"How many times do I have to tell you: Spells are not to be used for personal gain," said Penny.

"And I say," countered her daughter, coming down a step, "what good is having the ability to cast spells if you can't use them to help your friends?" She jumped down the final few stairs and sailed past her mother. "I'll see you later. Don't wait up," she said breezily.

"Patricia Halliwell," Penny said sharply, enunciating each word.

Patty knew not to ignore that tone. She turned at the doorway, hand on hip. She tried to look brave, but her legs trembled slightly.

"I'm tired of this flippant attitude of yours lately," said Penny. "It's quite unbecoming. But besides that, Patty, you're a witch. You have access to many powerful things. It's a great honor, one that shouldn't be abused. I promise that it will come back to haunt you, if you do. I won't have my only child place herself in the face of danger. Okay?"

"Okay, Mom," Patty said.

"And I'll see you for dinner at seven thirty," added Penny.

Patty nodded. Then she was out the door and into the sunny San Francisco afternoon.

Penny rolled her eyes, taking a seat on the bottom step of the staircase leading to the second floor of Halliwell Manor.

"I can't *wait* until she has a daughter of her own someday," she said to herself, shaking her head.

PRESENT, ALMOST FORTY YEARS LATER

1

"I can't remember the last time we all sat around like this," said Paige Matthews as her sister Piper Halliwell poured some lemonade. "Remind me why we don't do this more often?"

"Very funny," said Phoebe Halliwell, Paige's other sister. "As if demons would allow *that* to happen."

"As if we could ever have anything resembling a normal life," added Piper. The oldest of the three, Piper had always been more reluctant than the others concerning all things Wiccan.

"Piper," said Phoebe. "We kissed 'normal' good-bye the minute we found out we were witches. How many times has Grams told you that?"

"How many times has everyone told her that?" muttered Paige.

"I know," said Piper, shooting Paige a look. "But I can still complain about it, can't I? Besides, Grams is a ghost. Who said ghosts are reliable?"

Phoebe just shook her head, rolling her eyes.

It was a lazy Sunday and the sisters, along with Piper's husband, Leo, and baby, Wyatt, were taking advantage of the downtime to relax and barbeque in the backyard.

"Actually," said Paige, "it's been remarkably quiet lately. Do you think we've scared evil away for a while?"

"Bite your tongue," said Piper. "You'll jinx it."

"Evil's probably just refueling before it comes back bigger and badder than ever," said Phoebe, spearing a pickle with her fork.

Just then there was a loud crash from inside.

"Speak of the devil," Paige said, jumping up.

"I'll stay here with Wyatt and orb him out if necessary," said Leo.

Piper, Paige, and Phoebe ran inside. They inspected the sunroom, but nothing looked out of the ordinary.

Then, suddenly, a man appeared behind Phoebe, having blinked in. He was tall, with dark hair, and had a birthmark in the shape of a crescent over his right eye. He grabbed Phoebe and held an athame to her neck. Phoebe gasped, clearly having a premonition.

"You want to save your miserable witch sister?" he asked. "Then do as I say."

"Athame!" Paige called, orbing the knife to her. Phoebe broke free, sending the warlock hurtling back with a spin kick. Yet he didn't fight back. Instead, as Paige hurled the athame at his chest, he began to recite Latin words that sounded to Paige like a spell.

"Thank you," he said, laughing, as he went up in flames.

"Thank you?" said Phoebe.

"And what was with the Latin?" said Paige. She looked at her sisters. "Are you thinking what I'm thinking?"

"Book of Shadows?" asked Piper.

"You got it," said Paige.

Once in the attic, the girls pored over the Book of Shadows with Leo. They frequently found themselves in this position, flipping through the pages of the book, which had been in their family for centuries, guiding their ancestor witches.

"There," said Phoebe, pointing to an entry. "That's him. Bartholomew Angus."

"He's part of the Angus family of warlocks," said Leo. "They have the power to resurrect past ancestors. By reciting a Latin incantation while being vanquished—but only during the actual act of being vanquished—the last known member of the family to die will be resurrected, with renewed strength."

"So we killed Bartholomew, but in doing so, resurrected his ancestor?" asked Paige.

"It's more complicated than that, actually," Leo said, sighing. "The ancestor is resurrected, but in his own time—so Bartholomew's ancestor was resurrected in the past."

"Aw, man," said Paige. "I knew that seemed too easy."

"Wait," Piper said, turning to Phoebe. "It looked like you had a premonition when he grabbed you. What was it about?"

Phoebe looked down. "It was another warlock. He also had that birthmark on his forehead. He was stealing Mom's powers and then killing her. With one of these." She held up the athame.

"Mom?" asked Piper. "But why would touching Bartholomew give you a vision of *her*? Unless . . ."

"Unless . . . ," Leo said, locking eyes with Piper.

"Could you share with the rest of us?" asked Paige.

"This resurrected ancestor," said Piper. "He must have come back during *his* time, not ours. And apparently, in an altered past, he's after Mom. Phoebes, how old did she look in your vision?"

"Young," Phoebe said. "Like, fifteen or sixteen."

"And do you see in here the warlock who had her?" Piper gestured toward the Angus entry in the Book of Shadows. Phoebe inspected it and then pointed at a young, handsome face.

"That's him," she said. "Simon Angus. He's our guy."

The sisters looked at one another. Their mother had died young, during a battle with the Demon of the Lake, and while they had been able to spend some time with her since—albeit mainly as a ghost—they still missed her terribly. Paige had been adopted as a baby, which made her miss Patty even more. The daughter of Patty and her Whitelighter, Paige had only met Piper and Phoebe after their older sister, Prue, died.

"We need to go save her," said Piper. She turned to her husband, who also served as the Charmed Ones' Whitelighter, a guardian angel who guided witches. "Leo, I need you to look after Wyatt."

"Of course, but you all need to think this through carefully before you go anywhere," said Leo.

"What are you saying?" asked Phoebe. "Leo, we need to get back there, and we need to get back there fast."

"Agreed," said Leo. "But these Angus warlocks aren't stupid. Take a few minutes to work out a plan."

"But he's after Mom!" Paige said. "We don't have a few minutes—this is urgent!"

"He's right," said Phoebe, trying to calm her younger sister. "Let's not do anything until we've figured out our attack."

"And then we go kick some Angus butt?" asked Paige.

Phoebe smiled. "And then we go kick some Angus butt. To save Mom's butt."

"And our butts," said Piper, looking at Leo and Wyatt. Then she turned to Paige. "You," she said. "You're on potion duty. Keep in mind that our powers will most likely be inactive, so we'll need some heavy-duty potions to replicate them, just in case. We'll also need a vanquishing potion."

"Got it," said Paige, saluting and heading downstairs.

"And you," Piper said to her other sister. "Can you write a vanquishing spell?"

"One warlock-vanishing vanquishing spell, coming right up," said Phoebe.

"And I'll figure out a way to get us back there," said Piper, taking a seat on an old settee in the attic. Leo sat down next to her.

"Be careful," he said.

"Always am," said Piper.

"I'm just not sure what you're up against with this one," he said. "Maybe I should go ask the Elders what they suggest."

"Because they've been ever-so-helpful in the past?" Piper asked sarcastically. "Leo, we know what we're doing." She picked up her husband's hand. "Please. Trust me."

Leo looked his wife in the eye. It had always been difficult watching Piper face the dangers she did on a daily basis, and now that Wyatt was in the picture, it was that much harder. But if anyone could handle a tough situation, it was Piper.

"Okay," he said. "I trust you."

An hour later the sisters regrouped in the attic.

"Potions?" asked Piper.

"Check," said Paige, holding up a selection of small vials filled with multihued liquids. "I got your exploding potion, your freezing potion, your orbing thingies potion, and your vanquishing potion right here . . . enough for all three of us."

"Good," said Piper, looking over at Phoebe. "Vanquishing spell?"

"Got it," said Phoebe, waving a piece of paper in the air. "We're going to send that warlock loser where the sun don't shine."

"Perfect," said Piper. "And I've got a spell that should take us where we need to go." She took a deep breath and held out her hands, motioning for her sisters to join her. They stood in a circle.

Piper held out the paper with the spell so that her sisters could read it with her. She knew their intent would guide them to the right place, but she was still nervous about the idea of interfering in their mother's and grandmother's lives, especially having to keep their identities secret. Piper took a deep breath, knowing what she had to do.

The Charmed Ones began:

Bring us back,
From whence we came.
To help our mother.
To save our name.

They looked up expectantly, as Piper mouthed the words "I love you" to Leo and Wyatt.

A moment later the sisters were engulfed in bursts of silvery blue light.

And just like that, they were no longer in the twenty-first century.

2

"Ow!" yelped Phoebe as Paige's elbow jabbed her in the ribs. The three had landed in a heap on the floor.

"Sorry," said Paige. She looked around. "Wait. Are we where I think we are?"

"Mother," came Patty's voice from the dining room. "All I'm saying is that I think we should share our magic."

"*OhmyGodthat'sMom,*" said Phoebe in a loud whisper, tugging on Piper's arm. "Listen to how young she sounds!"

"Just like you always told me to finish what's on my plate 'cause of all the starving children in the world," continued Patty. "I'm just trying to feed some people who are starving for a little magic in their lives."

"Patty, I really don't think it's the same thing," came the stern voice of Penny Halliwell.

"And that's Grams!" said Phoebe, sitting up and looking around.

"Shh!" said Piper. "Keep your voice down."

"Always the mommy," said Phoebe, shaking her head.

"Not quite. Our 'mommy' is in there," Piper said, gesturing toward the dining room. "Except she's currently, oh, about sixteen years old."

"Mother, why do you just disregard everything I say, as if I don't know anything?" Patty's voice carried through the Manor, slightly more raised than before. "Not only am I a witch, but I'm also practically an adult. Why can't you just treat me like one?"

"She's sixteen, all right," muttered Paige.

"Patricia," said Penny. "How many times do I have to tell you that I'll treat you like an adult when you show me that you deserve to be treated like one."

"Wow," said Phoebe. "I'm having a massive déjà-vu. I think Grams said the exact same thing to me when I was sixteen."

"I don't doubt it," said Piper. "At sixteen, you were a huge pain in the—"

"They're coming!" whispered Paige, disentangling herself from her sisters and pushing them behind a sofa in the living room. They peered around the corner so they could watch their mother argue with their grandmother.

"Are we going to have a repeat performance of this afternoon?" asked Penny. "I thought we'd gotten somewhere."

"Y'know," drawled Patty. "If Dad were here, he'd let me help Stacey."

"He absolutely would not," said Penny. "You know he feels the same way I do about abusing magic. And I told you, all Stacey needs is a little bit of self-confidence. No magic necessary."

"Fine," said Patty. "But I'm still going to ask Dad what he thinks when he gets back." She walked toward the stairs, stopping at the bottom and spinning around. "I'd like to be excused, so I can go take a bath. I'll certainly try not to abuse any magic on the way." She started up the stairs without waiting for a reply.

"You're asking for trouble, young lady," Penny called after her first and only daughter. She sighed and walked back into the dining room to clear the table.

Piper, Paige, and Phoebe looked at one another for a few moments before speaking.

"Whoa," Paige finally said. "This is wiggy."

"Totally," said Phoebe. "Mom's kind of bratty."

"She's a teenager," said Piper. "We've all been there."

"Maybe if we tell her who we are, and she sees how well we turned out, it would make her see things differently?" asked Paige.

"No," said Piper. "We can't tell Mom and Grams, or anyone for that matter, who we are. It could affect the future too much."

"But we've already affected the future, just by coming back here," said Paige.

"No, Piper's right," said Phoebe. "We came back to find Simon and save Mom. As hard as it's going to be, we need to stick to that agenda to try and keep who we are under wraps."

"Fine," Paige grumbled.

"So," Phoebe rubbed her hands together. "What's our plan of attack?"

"We need to figure out a way to approach Grams and Mom without freaking them out," said Piper. "And then we need to find Simon."

• • •

Which would turn out to be pretty easy, since Simon was closer than they could have imagined. He had been monitoring Patty via astral projection in order to strategize when would be best to make his move. In his astral state, he was invisible, but had the power of mind manipulation. Simon knew he had Bartholomew to thank for his renewed existence, and he also knew that now was his chance to kill the source of the most powerful line of good witches that had ever come to pass: Patty Halliwell, the future mother of the Charmed Ones. Not to mention steal her power to freeze.

He had yet to realize that the Charmed Ones themselves had come back to find him.

"So, who do you think this Stacey girl is?" asked Paige as the sisters made their way away from the Manor and down Prescott Street. They were headed to buy some clothes that would make them less conspicuous.

"I think Mom had a good friend named Stacey when she was in high school," said Phoebe. "I remember seeing her name in Mom's yearbooks."

"Well, whoever she is, Mom must really want to help her," said Paige. "I mean, if she's willing to cast spells."

"I don't know," said Piper. "I bet that any teenage witch has a hard time resisting the urge to cast spells to help out friends. I seem to remember another young witch we know casting some personal gain–esque spells when she first got her powers. . . ."

"Yeah," said Paige, "but I didn't know any better. And I learned my lesson. Maybe Mom just needs to learn hers."

"Maybe," said Phoebe. "But we can't have her drawing any extra attention to herself, especially with that Angus warlock lurking somewhere nearby." She shivered. "He could be anywhere."

"I know," said Paige, looking around. "And if we don't do

something soon, we can kiss the entire Halliwell line good-bye."

"Thank you," said Piper, "for looking at the bright side."

"No problem," said Paige.

Phoebe looked at her watch. "It's already almost eight o'clock. I say we try and buy some groovy threads and then crash for the night at a motel or something. We'll go see Grams first thing in the morning."

"Groovy threads?" asked Piper.

"What?" said Phoebe. "I'm just trying to be down with the lingo."

Back at the Manor, Simon, in his astral form, watched over Patty as she did some homework in her bedroom.

"Patty," he communicated via mind manipulation. "You need to tap into your magic. You're right to believe that you should be using it to help others. Your mother is just being overprotective."

Patty drummed a pencil against her notebook, staring out the window at a tree branch that was tapping gently against the side of the house. "I *should* use my magic," she said to herself. "I only want to help others."

"That's right," said Simon. "You're a good witch. Don't listen to your mother. Use your magic."

Patty looked behind her, sensing a presence in the room. A specterlike presence, almost like a spirit. She got up and looked under her covers, and then in the closet. No one was there.

Suddenly the tree branch slammed against the window pane, making her jump.

"Relax, Patty," she said to herself. "It's just the wind."

But she wasn't completely convinced.

The next morning the sisters were back on Prescott Street soon after the sun rose. They still didn't know where Simon was, but they did know that they needed to get cracking. They stopped a few houses down from the Manor and peered out from behind a hedge as Patty came down the front path. She held some schoolbooks under her arm and was looking around her, almost as if she was hearing voices.

"She looks seriously spooked," said Paige.

"Do you think we should follow her?" asked Phoebe.

"Wait," said Piper, pointing as their mother hurried down the street, meeting up with another girl her age at the corner. The girl had glasses with oval-shaped frames and wore clothes that were too big for her. She stood hunched over, tugging on her oversized cardigan. Patty put her arm around her and they walked away.

"Stacey?" asked Paige.

"Probably," said Piper. "I think Mom's safe for now. She's not alone, and we know where she's going. We can always track her at school. Simon won't attack there."

"So," said Phoebe. "Grams?"

"Grams," agreed Piper.

"You mean, Mrs. Halliwell," said Paige.

"Right," said Piper. "Mrs. Halliwell."

Phoebe looked at her sisters as they made their way up the walkway leading to the Manor's stained-glass front doors. "We lead very complicated lives."

"Tell me about it," said Piper.

They reached the front door. Phoebe took a deep breath. Then she knocked briskly. After a few moments there were footsteps inside and their grams's voice.

"Who's there?"

"Um," said Piper. "Mrs. Halliwell. We need to speak to you."

"Regarding what?" Penny asked.

"Regarding what?" whispered Paige.

"Regarding . . . ," stuttered Piper, "Regarding . . . your daughter."

Penny opened the door a crack, so that her granddaughters

could vaguely make out her form. "Tell me more," she said.

Phoebe leaned in. "Mrs. Halliwell," she said. "This is going to sound crazy, but please, just listen. We have reason to believe that there's a warlock who may be after your daughter."

Penny swung open the door, her eyes worried but suspicious. "Who are you?"

Paige smiled. "We're friends, Mrs. Halliwell. We're . . . um . . . practitioners, and we're only here to help."

"Who sent you?" asked Penny, still blocking the doorway, hands on hips.

"We, uh . . . ," began Phoebe. "We can't tell you that. You'll just have to trust us."

Penny shook her head and began to shut the door to the Manor. "I'm sorry, but that's not good enough—"

"Wait!" said Paige, sticking her foot in the door. "We know about your Book of Shadows."

Penny paused. "My what?"

"Your Book of Shadows," said Paige. "And we have information on a family of warlocks named Angus. We believe that one of them has recently been resurrected and is after Patty and probably you, too. He wants your powers, and he wants to wipe out the Warren witches."

Penny still blocked the doorway, but her stance had softened. There remained a trace of worry in her eyes. "Why us?" she asked. "Why now?"

"What warlock wouldn't want to get rid of some of the most powerful witches ever?" asked Phoebe.

Penny's eyes narrowed and for a moment the three sisters worried that their grandmother was not going to budge. But then she spoke. "While flattery won't get you everywhere, it will get you into my conservatory," she said, opening the door wider. "Come in."

Piper, Phoebe, and Paige followed Grams inside the house

and through the rooms of the first floor until they came to the conservatory.

"You have a lovely home, Mrs. Halliwell," said Paige as Phoebe jabbed her in the ribs.

"What?" Paige hissed to Phoebe. "She does! And we should know."

"Just play it cool, okay?" Phoebe murmured. She took a seat next to Piper by one of the windows while Paige sat in a chair facing Penny.

"Can I get you girls anything?" Penny asked. "Tea, perhaps?"

"Sure," Piper said. "Tea would be nice." Phoebe and Paige nodded as Penny went to fill the kettle.

They were silent for a couple of minutes but then couldn't stand it anymore. "This is so freaky," said Paige in a hushed tone. "I mean . . . that's *Grams*."

"It *is* bizarre," agreed Phoebe. "Don't forget, everybody—no mentions of our present. Or, I mean, the future—or—our past. Well, you know what I mean. Don't talk about us."

"Right," said Paige. "Future bad. No future."

"I wouldn't put it quite like that," said Phoebe. She looked over at Piper, who was staring distractedly out the window. "Hey. Lady. You okay?"

"Hmm?" asked Piper. "Oh. Yeah. I'm just thinking about Leo. And the baby."

"Baby?" asked Penny as she returned to the room with a tray piled with the kettle, four cups, and a small plate of pastries. "You have a baby?"

"Umm, yes," Piper said. "I do. A little boy. Wyatt."

"Wyatt," said Penny. "What an interesting name. How did you come up with it?"

"Oh, it's a long story," interrupted Phoebe, accepting a cup of tea from Penny. "Now, Mrs. Halliwell. We need to talk to you about this warlock. Simon Angus."

"Right," said Penny, but she didn't take the bait. "You know, you girls seem awfully familiar. Do you belong to a local coven?"

"No," said Paige, then she sipped her tea. "We're from far away."

"Far, far away," added Phoebe.

"Listen, Mrs. Halliwell," said Piper. "We're really sorry that we can't tell you more about us. Someday, you'll understand. But you have to believe that we only have the best interests of both you and your daughter at heart. If you'll check the Book of Shadows, it should corroborate our story about the Angus warlocks. They're capable of resurrecting past ancestors while being vanquished by reciting a Latin chant. We have reason to believe that Simon has returned from the dead."

"Past ancestors?" asked Penny.

"Yes," answered Piper.

"So, that means you'd be from another time?" asked Penny.

"Yes, we're from the future," said Paige. She looked at her sisters, surprised, her eyes widening.

"When in the future?" Penny asked Phoebe.

"Two thousand and—" Phoebe began before Piper slapped a hand over her mouth.

"What's in this tea?" Piper asked Penny.

"Oh, just a little truth serum I like to use once in a while," Penny said. "Nothing to worry about, it'll fade in an hour or so. Now, back to the future—"

"Mrs. Halliwell," said Piper. "Please. Yes, we're from another time. But please don't ask us any more questions. We're here to help. You've got to believe us."

Penny sat back in her chair. "I want to believe you," she said. "I really do. But you've got to understand my position. I need to be very protective of my daughter. You have no idea the kinds of things I see on a daily basis, the evil I need to ward away—"

"Trust us," said Paige, reaching over and putting a hand on top of her grandmother's. "We have an idea."

Piper stood up. "I think we should go. It's too dangerous for us to be here while the serum is in effect. We'll come back later. In the meantime please look up the Angus entry in the Book of Shadows."

"We'll help you in any way we can," added Paige. "We're friends."

"Here," said Phoebe, fumbling in her purse for a piece of paper and a pen. "We're staying nearby, at the Victorian Hotel. You can reach us there. Ask for room two-twelve."

As the sisters got up to go, Penny watched them with an expression that was a mixture of confusion, curiosity, and protectiveness. She didn't want to admit it yet, but she felt a strong pull to these young women, and she didn't sense any negative karma from them.

"Good-bye, Mrs. Halliwell," said Phoebe as she followed her sisters out of the conservatory. "We'll talk to you later."

Penny nodded and sat back in her chair, thoroughly confused by the wave of conflicting emotions washing over her.

Out on the street Piper was feeling both defeated and deflated.

"Great, we've been poisoned by our grams," she said.

"Oh, Piper," said Phoebe. "Grams didn't poison us. She just tainted our tea."

"I should have known she'd do something like that," said Piper.

"Can you really blame her?" said Paige. "Think about it. We show up out of nowhere with information that some warlock is after her teenage daughter. Then we refuse to tell her anything about ourselves. Plus, the woman fights demons daily. What is she supposed to think?"

"You're right, you're right," said Piper. "But the fact remains that we need a plan. Fast."

Back at the Manor Penny went up to the attic to take a look at the Book of Shadows. She thumbed through the pages until she came upon an entry marked "Angus."

"Hmmm," she murmured as she read it to herself.

Suddenly Simon Angus blinked into the attic. Penny looked up, startled, making eye contact with the warlock. His eyes narrowed, but before he could do anything, Penny raised her hand and, with two pointed fingers, telekinetically threw him against the far wall of the attic. He slammed into it and crumpled to the ground. Penny raised her arm again, but before she could send him flying, he blinked out, calling, "I'll be back. *Witch*."

Penny looked around her, breathing hard. Had she scared away some very important allies? She quickly made her way downstairs, where she picked up the phone and dialed.

"Hello," she said, after the front desk receptionist picked up at the Victorian Hotel. "Can you please connect me to room two-twelve?"

Penny tapped her foot anxiously as she waited.

3

"Patricia?"

Patty looked up from her desk at her history teacher, Mrs. Carter. She was standing with a tall boy with wavy dark hair that fell into his eyes.

"Patricia," Mrs. Carter continued. "This is Colin. He's new in town, and I was hoping that you'd be able to show him around school?"

Patty just nodded. She felt a strange pull toward the new student, but at the same time, there was something slightly off-putting about him. Colin sat down at the desk next to hers and smiled.

"It's hard being the new kid," he said. He had a trace of a British accent.

"Uh-huh," Patty said, nodding again.

"So, you'll help me out?"

"Uh-huh," Patty said. She felt a kick from behind and turned in her seat to see Stacey mouthing, "Who's that?" Patty smiled and turned back to Colin.

"So, where are you from?" she asked him.

"Oh, you mean my accent?" he asked. "Well, I have family all over the world but mainly England."

"Like the Beatles," said Patty. "So you moved here all the way from England?"

"No," Colin said. "I'm from closer than that. But I have relatives there. So, Patricia. What do people do around here?"

"It's Patty," she said. Then she shrugged. "I don't know. Not much."

Colin leaned in closer, and again Patty felt a strong attraction, but with a somewhat menacing undercurrent. She could feel his breath on her cheek.

"What say we skip out of here early, and you show me what you like to do for fun?"

"You mean cut class?" asked Patty.

Colin nodded, a smile creeping onto his face.

Patty's heart beat quickly while she heard her mother's voice in her head, its warning, disapproving tone ringing in her ears.

"Sure," she found herself saying to this new boy, who was really just a stranger.

Except . . . he wasn't a stranger at all.

Early that afternoon the Halliwell sisters entered the lobby of their small, nondescript hotel, after having decided their next step was to trail Patty so they'd be right there in case Simon showed up. They were on their way up the stairs to their room when a familiar voice stopped them.

"I thought you girls would never get back."

Paige, Piper, and Phoebe turned to see their grams standing in the corner of the lobby.

"But I thought—," Phoebe began.

"I was wrong," Penny said. "I apologize for not trusting you, but you can't really blame me, can you? I still don't know where—or when—you're from, but I don't care anymore. I received a little visit from a warlock after you left, so if you're still offering it, I'd love your help."

"We're still offering it," said Piper.

"Just no more spiked tea, okay, Mrs. Halliwell?" said Paige.

"I promise," said Penny. She walked over to them, shaking their hands one by one. "And please call me Penny."

"Okay . . . Penny," Phoebe said hesitantly, suddenly struck by a premonition as she shook her grams's hand. She saw, in black and white, a fleeting glimpse of their mother running toward a set of swings. And then she was back in the hotel lobby.

Penny looked at her, startled. "Are you all right, dear?"

Phoebe shuddered a bit, feeling the aftereffect of the premonition.

"Oh, she's got a little virus," said Piper, putting her arm around her sister. "Nothing to be alarmed about. Paige, why don't you stay here with, um, Penny. I'm just going to run upstairs with Phoebe to get her medicine."

"Medicine?" Phoebe asked, still a bit shaken.

"Yes, medicine," Piper said through clenched teeth.

"Oh, right," said Phoebe, smiling weakly. "I have medicine."

Piper swung her around, and they quickly climbed the stairs.

"What the hell was that?" shrieked Piper once they got into

their room. "I haven't been able to freeze or explode, and Paige can't orb anything. Why are you having premonitions?"

"Stop yelling!" said Phoebe. "I don't know. Maybe because it's a passive power? Or maybe because the psychic connection is so strong between us and Grams that it overpowered the whole 'no powers in the past' thing?"

"Hmm," said Piper. "Interesting. Okay. What did you see?"

Phoebe sat down on the edge of the bed. "I saw Mom again. At least, I think it was Mom. The whole thing happened so fast, I'm not sure."

"Where was she?" asked Piper.

"I don't know," said Phoebe. "All I could make out in the background were some swings."

"Swings?" asked Piper.

"Yeah, swings," said Phoebe. "You know, find 'em at a play-ground, kids like 'em, used to make you nauseous?"

"I know what swings are!" said Piper, glaring at her sister. "I'm just trying to figure out what Mom was doing near them. Could you see anything else?"

Phoebe shook her head. "Sorry. That's all I got."

"Okay," said Piper. "Swings . . . not much to go on, Phoebes."

"Hey!" said Phoebe. "I don't see you having any visions to help us out."

"Sorry," said Piper. She sighed. "Let's get back downstairs before Grams gets suspicious again."

"So, why did you move to San Francisco?" Patty asked Colin once they were outside the high school.

"I was looking for something," Colin answered. "And now, I think I've found it."

"Looking for something?" asked Patty. "What do you mean? You moved here just because you were looking for something?"

Colin shook his head. "It's not important. Tell me about yourself."

Patty shrugged as they walked alongside the perimeter of the school parking lot. "There's not much to tell."

"Really?" Colin's stare was piercing. "I can sense that you have secrets."

Patty flinched slightly. "Nope. I'm as regular as they come."

Don't let her know you suspect a thing, he thought.

"Sorry," Colin apologized. "I didn't mean to intrude. . . . I just sensed you were feeling bad about something, and I thought it might help to talk about it."

Patty searched his eyes. She wanted to tell someone the truth. But all she said was, "I'm just not getting along with my mom."

Colin nodded. "We're sixteen. We're not supposed to get along with our parents. It's totally normal. Maybe I can help? I'm a complete outsider. . . ." He was leading her farther away from the school, toward a more secluded part of the neighborhood.

Patty shrugged. "It's just that she won't let me do certain things that I'd like to do, you know?"

"It sounds like your mother is just being overprotective," said Colin.

Patty stopped walking and looked at him curiously. She'd heard that somewhere before. "What did you say?"

"I mean, most mothers are, that is," he backtracked. "Overprotective."

"Right," Patty said. She glanced around to make sure no one was close enough to see what she was about to do. Then she positioned her hands in front of her and froze Colin. She stared at him thoughtfully for a few moments. Something about him was so familiar, she felt like she already knew him. She liked being around him; it was thrilling. She tipped her finger toward him, and he unfroze.

"Listen, Colin," Patty said. "I'm going to get back to school. I promised my friend Stacey that we'd have lunch together. But maybe I'll see you later?"

Colin casually glanced at his watch, and then at Patty. *Don't let her slip away,* he thought.

"Wait," he said. "It's been so nice talking with you. . . . I'd love to take you out."

Patty smiled as she started walking away, but backward, so she was still facing him. "There's a dance tonight that you could ask me to," she teased.

Colin smiled. "Well, that would be smashing. Patty Halliwell, would you permit me to escort you to the dance tonight?"

Patty laughed. "Why, Colin . . . wait, what's your last name?"

Colin paused. "It's . . . Bartholomew," he said, in honor of the relative who had made his return possible.

"Okay, Colin Bartholomew," Patty said, now about twenty feet away. "I'd be honored to have you be my escort at the dance tonight. It's at the elementary school. I'll meet you there at eight?"

Colin nodded. "Eight o'clock," he agreed. "Don't be late."

"I won't," she said with a little wave. She smiled and started making her way back toward the high school.

Colin watched her for a bit, and then checked again to make sure no one was watching. *She froze me, the little witch,* he thought, glamouring back into himself. *New witches—always forgetting about time. Keeps on ticking, even when you're frozen. . . .*

"Just a matter of time, Patty Halliwell," he said, sneering. "Before the Charmed Ones are no more."

After school Patty returned to the Manor, still thinking about Colin. She couldn't shake the feeling that she knew him from somewhere.

"Patty?" Penny's voice called out from the living room as

Patty entered the foyer. "Could you come in here for a minute?"

"Okay," said Patty, dropping her books on a side table and walking into the living room. Three young women sat on one of the sofas, watching her intently. They, too, seemed somehow familiar, although Patty was sure she'd never met them before.

"Patty," Penny said. "This is Piper, Phoebe, and Paige. They're visiting from out of town."

Patty came closer but didn't sit down. The three strangers were staring at her, and it was unnerving. One of them looked like she was about to cry; another looked like she was ready to burst with excitement.

"We're witches too," said Paige.

"But just practitioners," said Piper. "We have nowhere near the powers that you and your mother have."

"Wait," said Patty. "You know about that?" She looked at her mother questioningly.

"Well, yes," said Paige. "We're here to help you."

"It's okay, Patty," said Penny. "We can trust them."

"So it's okay for you to welcome total strangers into our house, who could be after who knows what, but it's not okay for me to cast a simple spell to help a friend?" asked Patty, her voice rising.

"Patricia," said Patty tersely. "We have guests."

"Sorry," said Patty, making brief eye contact with the sisters. "Mother, I need to be excused." And without waiting for a reply, she ran upstairs.

"That went well," said Phoebe sarcastically, looking sadly after her.

"I'm sorry," said Penny. "Perhaps we shouldn't have talked to her all together—I'm sure she felt blindsided."

"What should we do?" asked Paige.

"I'm not sure," said Penny. "I don't want to scare her unnecessarily, but at the same time, I want to make sure she's more vigilant than ever. Maybe I should talk to her alone. Would you excuse me for a bit?"

"Sure," said Piper, getting to her feet. "We'll just go back to the hotel for a little while to give you and your daughter some privacy."

"Oh, you don't have to leave," said Penny.

"No, it's for the best," said Phoebe. "We'll come back a little later to help you keep an eye on Patty."

"Good luck," said Paige. "Let us know if you need us sooner."

They walked outside and down the front path, waiting until they were out of earshot to speak.

"That was hard," said Phoebe. "Poor Mom. Who wouldn't have been suspicious?"

"She's so pretty," said Paige. "It's really bizarre to see her so young."

"Yeah," said Piper. She bit her lip. "I'm worried."

"We have Grams on it now," said Phoebe. "She's not going to let anything happen to Mom."

"I know, but even Grams isn't infallible," said Piper. "Paige, when Phoebe and I were upstairs at the hotel, did she say anything else about the warlock who paid her a visit?"

"Just that he fit Simon's description, and that he looked surprised to see her in the attic," said Paige. "Oh, also that he looked pissed when she threw him against the wall, but that he blinked out before she could really wreck him."

"So Simon has staked out the Manor," said Piper. "But he most likely doesn't suspect that anyone has come back from Bartholomew's time to look for him."

"That's good, right?" asked Phoebe. "Do you think he has any way of knowing what we look like?"

"I don't think so," said Piper. "How could he? We haven't been born yet."

"Yeah, well, I hope we still *will* be born," said Phoebe.

"Bright side, girls, bright side," said Paige.

"Patty?" Penny asked after she knocked on the door to her daughter's bedroom. "Can I come in?"

There was a muffled reply in response, which Penny interpreted as a yes. She pushed open the door and went to sit next to Patty on her bed, pushing aside a few stuffed animals, remainders from childhood. Patty played with the tassels on her blanket, not ready to make eye contact.

"Darling," Penny said, pushing the hair out of Patty's eyes. "I'm sorry about surprising you like that downstairs. I should have given you more warning."

Patty was silent.

"But those women really are friends," Penny continued. "They're here because they're looking out for both of us."

"Can't we protect ourselves?" asked Patty.

"Well," said Penny. "Perhaps. But I've discovered that sometimes it's a good idea to accept help when it's offered, instead of letting pride get in the way."

Patty rolled her eyes. "I just don't like it that you've been so strict with me, but you get to do whatever you want. It feels hypocritical."

"When you've been a witch for a bit longer and you're on your own, then you can make more decisions," said Penny. "Look, Patty. We've been through this. Being a teenager is hard enough, but being a witch on top of it? That's even harder. I just want to make sure you're careful."

"Mom, how many times do I have to tell you that I always am?" asked Patty.

Penny smiled. "I know. Now. Have you seen anything out of the ordinary lately?"

Patty looked a little nervous. "Why?"

"Nothing, really," said Penny. "I don't want to scare you. But the women who were here before have reason to believe that there may be a warlock after us. He goes by the name Simon. Have you met anybody named Simon recently?"

Patty shook her head. "No."

"Okay, then it's probably nothing," Penny said, trying to appear calm. She stood up. "Do me a favor, though. Stay close to home for the next few days?"

"Mother," said Patty, "please . . ."

"Just humor your mother," said Penny. "I love you."

"I love you, too," said Patty. She watched as her mother left the room, shutting the door behind her. Patty got up to look at her reflection in the mirror, feeling torn between allegiance to her mother and the desire to rebel and prove that she could take care of herself.

"You don't need her protection, Patty," a voice spoke to her, seemingly from inside her head. "Your mother is just trying to get in the way of your independence. She's trying to get back at you for wanting to use spells for personal gain. But you won't let her. You're a good witch, a good and powerful witch."

Patty looked around her, but she was alone. She couldn't see Simon in his astral state.

"I *am* a good witch," she said aloud. "I know what I'm doing." She collapsed onto her bed, her hands behind her head. "I just wish Mom would accept that."

The sisters returned to the Manor that evening, hoping that Patty would be more receptive to them.

"Hello, girls," Penny greeted them. "I spoke to Patty about being more careful."

"Did you end up telling her about Simon?" asked Paige.

"Well," said Penny. "Sort of. I didn't give her too many details, but I asked her to be careful and stay close to home. She said she hasn't met anyone by that name recently. She's upstairs, resting. Actually, she's been resting since you left. She didn't even want to come down for dinner." She gestured toward the conservatory. "Why don't you have a seat inside and I'll go check on her."

The sisters nodded and went to sit down in the conservatory.

A few minutes later Penny hurried into the room, her face pale.

"Gr—Penny," said Phoebe, catching herself in time. "What's wrong?"

"It's Patty," said Penny. "She's not upstairs."

"Are you sure?" said Paige.

"Positive," said Penny. "I even checked the attic." She sat down on a chair, her head in her hands. "I knew I should have kept a better watch over her. I can't believe I—"

Paige went over to comfort her grandmother. "Penny, I'm sure she's fine," she said, although her eyes were equally concerned as she looked at her sisters. "Let's just go out and find her."

Penny nodded silently and got up. Paige kept her arm around her as Phoebe and Piper trailed a bit behind.

"What do you think?" asked Phoebe.

"Well," said Piper. "I think that Mom must still be alive. 'Cause if she wasn't, then wouldn't we have vanished by now?"

"Good point," said Phoebe. "We've got to find her, though. Before Simon does."

"Agreed," said Piper as they caught up with Paige and their grams.

4

A few minutes later the sisters stood on the front porch of a large home down the block from the Manor. Stacey's house.

"Stacey," called Penny as she rapped on the door. "Are you there?"

After a minute the door opened, and Stacey's face appeared.

"H-hi, Mrs. Halliwell," she said. "How are you?"

"Well, I've been better," Penny said. "Stacey, Patty's missing. Can you tell us where she is?"

"Missing?" asked Stacey. "You mean she's not at the dance?"

"Dance?" asked Penny.

"Yes, ma'am," said Stacey. "There's a school dance tonight. She was going to go with Colin."

"Colin?" asked Penny.

"Yes," said Stacey. "He's new, and he really likes Patty."

Penny looked perplexed. "How new?"

"Well, he just showed up today," said Stacey. "Kind of out of nowhere, actually. It was like one minute he wasn't there, and then the next, poof, there he was. . . ."

"Almost as if he appeared in the blink of an eye?" asked Penny, the truth of who Colin was slowly starting to crystallize in her mind.

"Sure," said Stacey. "I guess you could say that."

"Thank you, dear," said Penny. "You've been a huge help." She turned to the sisters. "Come on, we've got to get to that dance."

The foursome rushed over to the high school, running the whole way. But once they reached the school grounds, no one was there. The school was dark.

"Where could they be?" asked Penny, near frantic.

"This is crazy," said Piper. "Stacey did say there was a dance at the high school, didn't she?"

"No," said Phoebe. "She said there was a school dance. She

didn't say where." She looked at Grams. "Penny, this is going to sound crazy, but are there any swings nearby?"

"Swings?" asked Penny. "What do swings have to do with anything?"

"Please," said Phoebe. "Just trust me on this."

Penny thought about it for a moment. "There are swings at the playground behind the local elementary school. Do you think . . . ?"

Phoebe nodded. "Is it close?"

Penny grabbed Phoebe's hand and started to run. "Follow me."

At the elementary school the dance was in full swing. Colin and Patty stood at the edge of the dance floor, sipping drinks and talking.

"It's hot in here," said Colin. "Why don't we get a breath of fresh air?"

"Okay," said Patty, putting down a glass of soda.

They walked through the gym toward the back doors and out into a courtyard. Patty breathed in the crisp night air and smiled. She felt a bit bad about sneaking out of the house, but it was all worth it. She was having a great time.

Colin put his arm around her as she shivered a bit. "You look beautiful, Patty."

Patty blushed and looked away. "Thank you," she said.

"So, have I made you forget about everything that was on your mind?"

Patty nodded, turning to face him. "Yes. Thank you for that."

"You're welcome," said Colin. "Everyone deserves to escape sometimes." He looked out into the inky expanse of sky before them. "Is there somewhere that you like to go to escape?"

Patty felt an electric current of worry course through her, a warning. "No . . . not really."

"Not really?" Colin teased. "Come now, there must be some-place you like to go to be alone."

Patty shrugged. "We could go sit in the playground," she said. "I used to love it there when I was a kid. And it's not far."

Colin extended his hand before him. "Lead the way."

They walked toward the playground, away from the music and lights emanating from the school. With each step, they were plunged farther into darkness, so by the time they got there, Patty could barely make out Colin's features at all. They reached the swings, and Patty sat on one while Colin stood behind her and pushed.

"Having fun?" he called as she sailed high and then coasted back down to earth. Patty just nodded, feeling the wind whip her hair back and forth. She felt so free.

Suddenly she was pulled out of her reverie by a tight grip on her arm. Colin's face loomed above her, except it was no longer Colin's. It was an older man's, with a birthmark above his eye, in the shape of a crescent moon.

Patty opened her mouth to scream, but he clapped a hand over it.

"I've got you now," the man said. "It's been so lovely spend-ing time with you. My name is Simon. And I'll be killing you tonight."

He pulled back his jacket to reveal an athame. Patty managed to wrest one hand out of his grip and freeze Simon. She broke free and began running, tears streaming down her face.

"PATTY!" Penny's voice came ringing across the playground as she searched for her daughter.

"Mom!" Patty yelled, running into her mother's arms. They embraced, each crying, each talking at once.

"Oh, Patty, I'm so glad we found you. I was so worried when you were gone, and then when you weren't at the high school—"

"Mom, I'm so sorry I disobeyed you. You were right—there's a warlock after us, but I froze him. I'm so sorry—"

They clung to each other as the three remaining Halliwells watched, their own eyes tearing up. But after a minute, Phoebe realized something.

"Wait, Patty," she said. "You froze Simon, right?"

Patty nodded, her head on her mother's shoulder.

"How long do those usually—" Paige started to ask, but she was interrupted.

"Bingo," Simon said as he blinked in behind them. "Ah, what a lovely surprise. I get five for the price of one."

"That's what you think," said Phoebe as she leaped and kicked the athame out of his hand.

"Fine!" Simon yelled. "Go ahead and vanquish me!"

"No need to ask us twice," said Paige. She whipped out the vanquishing potion she'd made and got ready to hurl it at him.

"Wait!" said Piper. "We've been so worried, we forgot the most important thing about Angus warlocks. If we vanquish him, aren't we just going to release one of his ancestors?"

"You're right," said Phoebe. She turned to her mother. "Patty—freeze his mouth."

"Freeze his what?" asked Patty.

"Please, you've got to hurry! Trust her!" said Paige. Patty shrugged and froze Simon's face.

"We have a vanquishing spell," said Phoebe, unfurling it and pulling her sisters, mother, and grandmother close so they all could read it. Simon lunged blindly at them.

"Patricia, just freeze all of him," said Penny. "He's starting to irritate me."

Patty lifted both hands and froze Simon midlunge.

The five women recited the spell together:

You wanted our powers, but all for naught,
Your brand of evil just got you caught.
Past, present, future, all
The time has come for us to call
For the demise of all your kind:
We banish you, Simon, for peace of mind.

"Your time is up, warlock!" added Paige as she tossed the potion onto Simon for good measure. He went up in a huge explosion.

For a few moments, it was silent. All that remained were a few wisps of smoke and a pile of gray dust where Simon had stood.

Then Patty broke the silence. "Why did I have to freeze his mouth?"

"So he couldn't recite the words that would resurrect one of his relatives as we vanquished him," said Penny, and she looked at the three sisters and smiled. "Smart witches."

"Um," said Piper. "You mean, witch practitioners."

"Oh, right," Penny said. "Practitioners." But something in her eyes revealed that she knew there was more to their story than they were letting on. "Thank you for that spell. And the potion. You three were ready for action."

"Well," said Paige. "You never can be too prepared for those pesky warlocks."

"No, you can't," said Penny, hugging her daughter to her. "I won't ask you too many questions, but whoever you are, wherever you're from, thank you."

"It was our pleasure," said Phoebe.

Patty watched the three strangers shyly, almost in awe. "How did you know where to find me?"

Penny looked at Phoebe. "Yes, Phoebe," she said. "How did you know to look for swings?"

"Oh, it was just a sense I had," Phoebe said.

"A sense?" asked Penny.

"Must be that virus coming back," said Piper. "You know, fever-induced hallucinations."

"She gets 'em all the time," said Paige.

Penny just nodded, not content with the answer but deciding not to pursue it.

"We really need to be getting back home," said Piper.

"That's right," said Penny. "Your family is waiting."

"Right," said Piper. "Family. It's important."

"It certainly is," agreed Penny. She gazed at the sisters. "Will we see you again someday?"

"It may be a while, but I have a feeling this isn't the last time you'll be seeing us," said Paige. She went over to Penny and gave her a hug. "It was wonderful to meet you, Penny."

Piper and Phoebe came over and joined in the embrace, pulling Patty in as well. They stayed like that for a bit, until Piper released from the hug, her eyes wet.

"Good-bye, Penny," she said, clasping the hands of her sisters. The three walked deeper into the night, knowing they had to recite their spell alone. Patty and Penny stood and waved, overwhelmed by the events of the evening.

"They seem so familiar to me," Patty said to Penny as the sisters disappeared into the darkness.

"Are we far enough away?" asked Phoebe a minute later.

Paige craned her neck. "Yeah. They can't see or hear us over here."

"Okay, you know the drill," Piper said, taking a deep breath. Together the sisters chanted:

Bring us back,
No need to roam.
We saved our name.
Now send us home!

And in a constellation of silver light, they were gone.

When the sisters returned to the twenty-first century, they were in the attic, by the Book of Shadows. Leo and Wyatt were waiting, and they engulfed Piper in a bear hug as soon as she appeared.

"We missed you," Leo said, squeezing her to him.

"And I missed you," said Piper. "Terribly."

"Leo, how did you know when we'd get back?" asked Phoebe.

"Lucky guess," Leo said with a wink. Piper wanted to believe it was their emotional connection, but she suspected it had something more to do with the Elders. "You're still here . . . so everything's fixed?" he continued.

"You guys, look," said Phoebe. She was standing over the Book of Shadows. Once Piper and Paige joined her, she pointed down at the Angus entry, which now had some minor changes.

At the top of the page, in Grams's distinctive script, it said:
Sometimes, it takes the power of five. Blessed be, my darlings.
Piper, Phoebe, and Paige smiled and looked skyward.

"Blessed be, Grams," they said.

"You too, Mom," added Paige. "You too."

Witch Trap

Cameron Dokey

"Are you sure we're going the right way, Phoebe?" Paige asked. She leaned forward, gazing out the front passenger window of the Halliwell SUV. "Things are looking kind of . . . isolated. Maybe we should turn around."

From her position in the driver's seat, Phoebe shook her head. "No way," she declared. "In fact, this is exactly the sort of situation I was hoping for. Just think of all this"—she waved a hand at the landscape out the window, the hills of California's gold rush country—"as atmosphere for my article."

"I didn't know you were planning on writing a gold rush horror story, Phoebes," Piper remarked from the backseat.

"Ha ha," Phoebe said. "Very funny."

The entire car fell silent as Phoebe carefully negotiated a hairpin turn on the narrow, two-lane highway. *It's not that Paige doesn't have a point,* Phoebe thought. The area through which the sisters were currently traveling did feel remote, particularly now that they'd left Sacramento, the state capital, behind. South of Sacramento, the former gold rush towns were closer together, the country around them flatter and more settled. But to the north, things still felt a little . . . *wild,* Phoebe thought.

The Halliwell SUV was passing through tall, heavily wooded hills. The tops might still be in bright sunlight, but down in the valley, the shadows were growing deeper with every turn of the tires. Rills of fog lay in deep crevices, stretching down the hillsides like long white arms. Up ahead Phoebe could see one flung across the road. She gave an involuntary wince as they passed through it, thin and insubstantial as cotton candy. Beside her she felt Paige give a quick shiver.

Enough, Phoebe thought.

"Can't you just imagine the forty-niners coming along this windy mountain road? In a whole lot less comfort, of course," she remarked now. She made quick eye contact with Piper via the rearview mirror and was relieved to see her older sister give a nod of understanding.

Keep talking. Keep Paige's spirits up.

"Though, now that I think about it, there probably weren't any roads back then," Phoebe went on. "The forty-niners may have even created the original of this one themselves."

"Talk about hard work," Piper said at once.

"I can definitely imagine people traveling through this countryside," Paige admitted. "I'm just not so sure I can imagine why they'd want to."

"Well, that's easy," Phoebe said with a quick laugh. "Gold."

The trip to the gold-rush country had been Phoebe's idea, though, originally, she'd planned to travel alone. Inspired by how well her advice column was going, Phoebe was contemplating trying her hand at freelance feature writing. The newspaper for which she worked was planning a big section on California history. Writing about women in the gold rush had seemed like the perfect way for Phoebe to get her start.

But her plans for a solo trip had been put aside when Leo, Piper's husband, had learned of her expedition. He'd instantly suggested all three sisters go. The Charmed Ones had recently come through a close encounter with a particularly nasty demon, an encounter made all the more challenging by the fact that their own group dynamics had been off.

Believing she could handle things on her own, Paige had rushed in where witches should have feared to tread, without waiting for sisterly backup. The results had almost spelled disaster for them all. Leo was eager for the sisters to spend some quality, non-demon-fighting time together. Restore the family energy, the family connections so crucial to their success as the Charmed Ones.

Phoebe had been more than happy to have her sisters' company. All three had enjoyed the day so far. In the morning they'd stopped at the place where gold had first been discovered, and explored a town that had been restored to the way it had been in gold rush times and was now a state park.

Then, after a late lunch, they'd headed north. At first, the more rugged country had seemed mysterious and exciting. But, as the day wore on, it was clear that Paige was growing more and more uncomfortable. She squirmed in her seat, like a six-year-old in need of a bathroom break. She changed the track on the CD about twenty million times. Phoebe wasn't sure quite what was bothering her younger sister. Only that something very definitely was.

"Look!" she said now, pointing to a sign by the side of the road. "Williamstown is only another couple of miles. They're bound to have a coffee shop or something. We can take a break there, then head for home. How does that sound?"

"That would be great, Phoebe," Paige admitted. She was silent for a moment, staring out at the road. "I don't mean to spoil your trip—"

"Don't be silly," Phoebe interrupted.

"But something around here is just plain giving me the creeps," Paige finished up. "I know my instincts haven't been all that great lately—"

"Paige." Now Piper interrupted, her voice managing to sooth and provide a warning all at the same time. "That's not true. Your instincts about that demon were right on the money. The problem was, you tried to take him on alone. There's a reason for the Power of Three."

"Okay," Paige said. "You're right. I know. It's just . . ." She gave a sigh. "I was kind of hoping I was through making mistakes, at least witchy ones. Then I go and blow things, big time."

"You didn't blow things, Paige," Phoebe said supportively. "You just got in over your head, that's all."

"Hey, check it out!" Piper said, her voice perky. She pointed out the passenger-side window. "Williamstown bakery-café and antique mall. Plainly we have come to the right place. A caffeine break and retail therapy all rolled into one."

"I feel better already," Paige declared.

Sisterly support. It was a beautiful thing.

Phoebe was smiling as she took the exit into Williamstown.

"It looks like a movie set, don't you think?" she murmured to Paige, several moments later. Location: once prosperous town, fallen on hard times. Enter: the mysterious strangers, aka the Charmed Ones.

Williamstown looked as if it had sprouted at the base of the tall hill that reared up behind it. Houses clung like leeches up the steep hillside. The entire main street was shrouded in darkness. In fact, given the way the hills all around the town seemed to lean in, as if deliberately trying to cut the town off from the outside world, Phoebe had a hard time imagining the sun ever reaching Williamstown at all.

Great. Now I'm *getting the creeps,* she thought.

One side of the main street contained a bank, the post office, a gas station, and the combination that was the Williamstown bakery-café and antique mall. On the other side of the street, the hill fell suddenly away to reveal a rushing stream. *Probably the reason people settled here in the first place,* Phoebe thought.

"Sometimes you find real treasures in a place like this," Paige declared as the three entered the antique mall. "Though this looks like a movie set too," she whispered over the peal of the bell above the door.

The interior of the antique mall was dim. There was plenty of overhead lighting, but several bulbs seemed to be out. The air held that peculiar combination of the smell of old books and dust that seemed to be unique to secondhand stores. Underneath it was a tantalizing baking smell. To the right, about halfway along one interior wall, was a more brightly illuminated doorway, the entry to the café.

A figure appeared in the doorway. It was difficult to see features, just a female silhouette, outlined by the light. Then she came forward, and the outline became the pleasant face of a young woman not much older than Piper. She was dressed in jeans and a checked button-down shirt, both protected by a big, white apron.

"I thought I heard the bell," she said. "May I help you?"

"We'd just like to look around, if that's okay," Phoebe said.

The young woman smiled. "Of course. Make yourselves at home." She waved one arm in the general direction of the ceiling. "And I'm sorry about the lights. I keep meaning to replace them, but somehow . . ." She shrugged.

"Actually, I think it's kind of a nice effect," Phoebe said supportively. "Sort of increases the mystery, the thrill of the antique chase."

The owner laughed. "I wish I had more customers like you. Actually, I wish I had more customers. Welcome to Williamstown. I'm Ellen Stauber."

"Phoebe Halliwell," Phoebe said. "I thought things looked a little . . . quiet."

She could see Paige and Piper begin to wander out of the corner of her eye.

"Quiet," Ellen Stauber echoed. "That's a nice way of putting it. The word people use around here is 'forgotten.' Williamstown, out of sight and out of mind."

"You are kind of out in the middle of nowhere," Phoebe said, doing her best to sound supportive.

Ellen Stauber nodded. "True," she acknowledged. "But it's always seemed to me that it's something more than that." She smiled once more and shrugged. Her voice and face were both open and pleasant, but, even in the dim light, Phoebe thought she could detect a certain strain. Times were hard in Williamstown.

"One of these days I'm going to spend some time at the historical society," Ellen said. "I just know there must be a curse somewhere in our past."

"You're from here?" Phoebe inquired.

"Not originally," Ellen answered. "But my mother was. After she died, I discovered she'd left me this building. I'd always wanted to have my own bakery, so I decided to settle here and give it a go. The antique store just sort of came along for the ride."

Her voice trailed off as she shrugged once more. "Don't hesitate to let me know if there's anything you want to see," she called after Paige and Piper. "Most things are easy to get to, but some of the jewelry cases are locked."

"Do you suppose we could see this piece?" Piper's voice inquired.

Phoebe turned, surprised. While she'd been making small talk with Ellen, her sisters had made their way to a big, old-fashioned, glass-front counter.

"Ah!" Ellen said, the pleasure plain in her voice as she moved to where Piper and Paige were standing. Phoebe trailed behind. "I see you've discovered where the real treasures are. Some of these pieces are true finds. Which one would you like to see?"

Paige pointed.

"Oh, yes," Ellen nodded as she unlocked the case, and set the object Paige had indicated on a slightly dusty black velvet jeweler's display board. "That's a lovely old brooch."

The object that had caught Paige's eye was a brooch similar to one they'd seen a woman wearing just this morning, working in costume in the candy shop at the state park. It was large and oval-shaped, bore the miniature portrait of a woman, and was designed to be worn at the base of the throat, as if to help fasten a high-necked blouse.

"You have a good eye," Ellen Stauber complimented Paige. "Though it always makes me sad, somehow. There's just something about her expression. Sort of fierce and tragic all at the same time. I've always wondered who she was."

As she spoke, Ellen reached over and switched on a lamp sitting near the cash register on the counter. She swiveled the neck, so that the beam from the light fell directly onto the brooch. Phoebe caught her breath.

In the center of the brooch was the picture of a woman not much older than Phoebe herself. Her long hair was coiled around the top of her head, partly covered by a lace mantilla that was held in place by a decorative comb.

"She's beautiful," Paige said softly. "But I think I see what you mean."

It was the expression on the young woman's face that captured your attention. It was precisely as Ellen had described it: fierce and tragic all at the same time—as if she was engaged in some great struggle in which she knew she would fail, a fact that would never keep her from trying. Phoebe didn't think she'd ever seen such determination in anyone.

Around the image, the edge of the brooch was decorated in a raised pattern of twisting, intertwining lines. For the second time that afternoon, Phoebe caught her breath.

"You guys."

"I know," Piper said. "That's why—"

At precisely that moment a loud buzzing sound emerged from the doorway leading to the café. It sounded like a very large and angry wasp.

"That's the timer for my scones," Ellen exclaimed. "Will you excuse me for a moment?"

Without waiting for an answer, she stepped from behind the counter and crossed into the café. A moment later the buzzer went silent. There wasn't a sound in the antique shop.

"So," Phoebe said after a moment. "Any idea what's going on?"

"Your guess is as good as mine," Piper said. "But I think our coming here must be more than coincidence. The border on that brooch looks too much like the Triquetra on the front of the Book of Shadows."

"You mean we were supposed to end up here?" Paige inquired.

"You have been pretty squirrely all afternoon," Phoebe reminded her. "Maybe this is why."

"Okay," Paige said slowly. "I probably buy that. But does that make *her*"—she nodded toward the image captured in the brooch—"a good guy, or a bad guy?"

"My guess is we won't know till we find out who she is," Piper said. She leaned over the brooch, as if to examine it more closely.

Behind her, Phoebe leaned in too, placing a hand on Piper's shoulder. "Maybe there's some sort of inscription on the piece," Piper said. "A name or a date, or something."

With careful fingers she reached for the brooch. Her fingertips touched the decorative border.

There was a moment the likes of which Paige had never experienced before.

A moment completely without sound.

She could feel her heart, beating wildly within her chest. Feel her throat burn as she pulled a sudden breath into her lungs. Dust motes swirled frantically through the air in the light of the swivel lamp, so clear and individual she could have counted every single one. Her sisters stood, still as statues, Phoebe's hand on Piper's shoulder.

What is it? Paige thought. *What's going on?*

Then, with a *click* like the sound of a door shutting tight, the world snapped back. Everything was as it had been just a moment before. With one crucial exception.

Phoebe and Piper were gone.

Paige stood, staring down at the brooch resting on its cushion of black velvet.

Instincts, she thought. Apparently hers had been right on. The question was, what did Paige do now? Whatever had happened to her sisters, she had to figure they'd be better off together. The Power of Three. Pulling in a steadying breath, Paige reached for the brooch.

As her fingers made contact, she experienced that strange, soundless moment for a second time. But this time, she was completely in darkness. She had no sight. Could hear no sounds. Then, again, that sharp click, like a door shutting closed, tight. Paige found herself standing in the middle of a dense forest, the brooch clutched tightly in one hand.

What on earth? she thought.

In the next moment she felt desperate fingers clawing at her arm. With a cry Paige pulled back and swung around. The fingers released.

"Please," said a voice.

Paige stared, her heart pounding. In front of her stood a young woman not quite her age. She was wearing a long calico dress with an apron over the skirt and a shawl around her shoulders. Sturdy boots protected her feet.

"Please," the girl said once more. "Please, you must come with me."

"Who are you?" Paige got out.

But by now the girl was frantic, wringing her hands, casting desperate looks over her shoulder.

"Come with me, I beg of you," she said. "Or you'll be taken, just like the others."

"What others?" Paige asked a short time later.

At the girl's urging, Paige had followed her through the forest at a flat-out run. Just before Paige had thought her lungs might burst from the exertion, the dense trees had cleared to reveal a small cottage. The young woman had made straight for it, throwing open the door and beckoning Paige inside. For several moments the only sound had been that of their ragged breathing. Then, gradually, Paige had begun to get her breath back and take stock of her surroundings.

The cottage was spartan, but well cared for. Drying herbs hung from the low rafters. A cookpot on a tripod stood over an unlit fire. There was a well-scrubbed wooden table and several stools. Paige's rescuer moved to one of them and collapsed down upon it. Paige staggered to a nearby bentwood rocking chair and sank down.

It wasn't until she was seated that she realized part of the reason it had felt so difficult to run. Like her rescuer, Paige was dressed in a long skirt and sturdy leather boots that covered her ankles and laced up the front. Definitely not the clothing she'd selected when she'd gotten dressed in San Francisco that morning. In fact, unless she missed her guess, Paige was pretty sure the clothing she was currently wearing would have been worn during the time of the California gold rush.

Did touching the pin trigger some sort of time trap? she wondered. *The pin!* Paige thought.

She still had it, she realized, clutched tightly in one hand. She slid it into a pocket of her newly discovered apron, then covered the gesture by smoothing her skirt. Until she knew what significance the brooch had, it was safest to keep all knowledge of it to herself.

"What others?" she asked again now.

"There were two," the girl said, her words punctuated by her efforts to regain her breath. "I saw them. I was coming into town, walking along the road. Two women, in the trees. I don't know who they were. I'd never seen them before."

"What happened then?" Paige prompted.

"Men from the town," the young woman gasped out. "Coming back from the river. They saw. My brother was with them. He"—she drew in a quivering breath—"he insisted they be taken to the stockade at once."

"The stockade?" Paige echoed. "But why? What had they done?"

"They didn't need to do anything," the girl said, and now Paige could see that there were tears in her eyes. "William, my brother, believes that all strangers are evil. This place is remote. No one would come here unless they intended to hurt us."

"But that's crazy," Paige protested as she shot to her feet. "What about the gold?"

At her words the tears began to slip silently down the other girl's cheeks. "The gold," she whispered. "It is the gold that does us harm. But my brother does not see this. He thinks the gold is a blessing. I know it is a curse. The fever of it has taken him. He has so much, more than he ever dreamed of, more than anyone else hereabouts.

"He should be satisfied, but he isn't. All he can do is think of his gold. And now he sees harm behind every face, every gesture. I begin"—her voice sank to a whisper—"I begin to fear for his mind."

Even through her own emotion, Paige was moved by the other girl's words. If what she said was true, protecting Paige was putting her in grave danger.

"I haven't thanked you for saving me," Paige said. She went to kneel at the girl's feet and took her hands in hers. In spite of their run through the woods, the girl's fingers were icy cold. "It was a very brave thing to do, and I'm grateful for it. My name is Paige Matthews. What's yours?"

At Paige's words, the girl calmed. "I'm Marianne Olson," she said. "My brother is William Olson."

Williamstown, Paige thought. Apparently one of the things having the richest gold strike in the area meant was that you got to name a town after yourself.

"What will happen to the women in the stockade, Marianne?" Paige asked. "Do you know?"

Marianne's tears began to fall once more. Her fingers gripped Paige's as if they'd never let go.

"Evil," she whispered. "There is evil in this town, and I fear that it is William who brings it down upon us."

"What kind of evil? What do you mean?" Paige asked. She let go of Marianne's hands to grasp her firmly around the shoulders. Marianne began to weep uncontrollably, swaying back and forth. "He's killing innocent people," she finally gasped out. "You've got to help me. Please. You've got to help me find the way to make him stop."

Innocent people, Paige thought. All of a sudden, the strangeness of the day was beginning to make sense. Protect the innocent. It was the mission of the Charmed Ones.

"Listen to me, Marianne," Paige said. "I will help you; I will do all I can. But you've got to calm down. How can I get to the women in the stockade?"

"You can't!" Marianne blurted out wildly. "If you go, you'll be taken too."

"I *won't* be taken," Paige said firmly. "Not if you help me. The women in the stockade are my sisters. The three of us must work together to defeat the evil. I cannot do it on my own. There must be a way for me to speak with them. Think!"

"Yes, yes, there is," Marianne said with a nod. She pulled in a deep breath, and Paige quickly pulled over a stool and sat down beside her.

"How?"

"After dark," Marianne replied. "William and the townspeople, they are afraid of the dark. He says that is when evil is strongest. He will not even post a guard at the stockade. He cannot. No one would stay. They would be too afraid."

"All right," Paige said. "So we'll go after dark. What about in the meantime?"

"I must return to my brother's house," Marianne said. "He will grow suspicious if I am away too long. After nightfall I will come for you. I will take you to your sisters."

"You know," Phoebe remarked, "when I said I wanted to capture a little gold rush country atmosphere, this wasn't precisely what I had in mind."

"Capture," Piper echoed, from her position on the floor. "Very funny. Though strangely enough, I'm not laughing."

"Gee," Phoebe said, as she squirmed on her rough blanket, trying in vain to get comfortable. "I wonder why."

The stockade that the sisters currently occupied was definitely lacking in amenities. There weren't even any chairs, just a hard-packed dirt floor. Presently both Piper and Phoebe were sitting on blankets, with their backs against the wall. The little light there was came from a single candle. Phoebe supposed she should be grateful the men who'd brought them here had left them that much. The stockade had no windows. Without the candle, the dark would be pretty intense.

She gave a quick shiver and rubbed her arms.

"You okay?" Piper asked at once.

"Okay," Phoebe said. "Just a little cold. And I'll probably have some bruises to show for 'resisting arrest.'"

Piper gave a surprised chuckle. "You won't be the only one. You got a couple good kicks in."

"Before I tripped over my own skirts," Phoebe said morosely. She gazed down at them. "Which, by the way, I do *not* remember putting on this morning." She lifted her head to gaze at Piper. "What do you think is going on?"

"I'm not sure," Piper said. "But I do know this much: I'd feel a lot better if I knew where Paige was."

"Me too," Phoebe said. "Do you suppose she, er, followed us?"

"It's what I would have done, or at least tried to do," Piper said. "Particularly after that little Power of Three pep talk I gave her earlier."

"Okay," Phoebe said with a nod. "So we have to figure Paige is trying to get to us. Wherever we are. She's not in the stockade, not yet. That has to be a good sign."

"Assuming she's not being held captive somewhere else," Piper said.

"Hey—trying to think positive over here," Phoebe protested.

"Sorry," Piper responded.

Without warning the metallic rasp of a key sounded in the lock on the stockade door. Piper and Phoebe scrambled up off the floor and retreated to the far side of the room, determined to put as much space as possible between them and whatever might be coming. Phoebe tried not to think of this as running from a fight. *I'm just giving myself room to maneuver,* she thought.

The flame of the candle flickered wildly as the door opened, then closed. Two shadowy figures slipped into the room, their faces disguised by long, hooded cloaks. The first turned to secure the door, while the second pushed the hood back from its face.

"Paige!" Phoebe cried.

"Piper, Phoebe!" Paige said as she surged forward to throw an arm around each of her sisters' shoulders. "Are you all right?"

"We're fine," Piper said. "Just a little manhandled, and I do mean that literally."

As a unit the sisters retreated to the far side of the stockade. Marianne hovered by the door, listening for any movement outside.

"Who's your friend?" Phoebe asked in a low voice. "Does she know what's going on?"

"Her name is Marianne Olson," Paige explained. "Her brother, William, is the one who had you guys locked up. She definitely knows something, but I think there's more to what's going on than what she's said so far. She did say her brother is killing innocent people. She begged me to help her find the way to stop him."

"Uh-oh," Phoebe muttered.

"Yeah," Paige said, nodding. "Pretty much what I thought. I said we'd help, but I'm thinking there may be a problem."

"What?" Phoebe said sarcastically. "Only one?"

"Time travel," Paige said.

Piper nodded. "When those goons jumped us in the forest, I tried to freeze them. All I ended up doing was waving my arms around. We've definitely traveled back in time. Which means—"

"Which means no powers," Paige said soberly. "If we're in a time when we didn't exist, our powers can't exist. We can't even consult the Book of Shadows. Now isn't that just swell?"

"We do have two things in our favor," Piper said. "We're together, and we have a clue: the brooch. Do you still have it?"

Paige nodded. Plunging her hand into the pocket of her apron, she brought it out. Then she moved closer to the candle, the better to study it. Piper and Phoebe went with her.

"If only we knew who she was," Paige said. "Something tells me we'd be a long way toward solving the mystery of why we're here."

"Amelia's pin!" Marianne's voice suddenly cried.

Instantly the three sisters turned toward the door. They were just in time to see Marianne clap a hand across her mouth. Her voice had been loud. All four occupants of the stockade held their breaths. No sound came from outside.

"You recognize this?" Paige finally asked, her voice low as she gestured Marianne forward. "Marianne, these are my sisters, Phoebe and Piper. They've agreed to help, but you must tell us what you know."

Slowly Marianne nodded. She moved forward to stand beside the sisters. "That is Amelia's pin," she said in a voice that wavered ever so slightly.

"You know her?" Piper asked.

At this, Marianne's eyes filled once more with tears. "Amelia de la Cruz was my true friend," she said softly. "She was the first to die."

In a halting voice Marianne filled in the details of Amelia de la Cruz's story:

"William and I met Amelia during the voyage to California," she explained, "when our ship docked in Chile, in the town of Valparaiso. Our fathers had had some business dealings in the past. Amelia's father left her well off, but ours left us penniless. When we decided to join the gold rush, William wrote to Amelia, asking if we might meet her when our ship stopped for supplies.

"The first part of our journey had been very hard. Conditions on the ship were terrible, and I had developed a fever. William had all but given up hope, but Amelia nursed me back to health. She is, she was, skilled in herb lore. While I was recovering, she and William fell in love. Amelia wanted them to be married right away, but William convinced her to wait. He would send for her, he said, after he had established himself in California. After he had found gold. He didn't want to give anyone cause to say he had married Amelia only for her money."

Marianne pulled in a deep breath, as if steeling herself to go on. "William found a rich gold strike almost as soon as we arrived in this place. He was overjoyed. But there was trouble at once. When he went to file the paperwork that would stake his claim, he learned it already belonged to someone else: an old man named Paul Conrad. He had a daughter named Leanna."

"Uh-oh," Phoebe murmured under her breath. "Something tells me I can see the next part of this story coming."

Marianne nodded, with a glimmer of a grim smile. "Paul Conrad was an old man, as I have said. Not only that, he was dying. He wanted Leanna to be provided for before he died. He offered to relinquish his claim to the gold strike to my brother if William would take Leanna as his wife."

"But your brother was already betrothed to Amelia," Piper said softly.

Again Marianne nodded. "That is so. But I was the only one who found this situation to be an obstacle. For William, it was not. Leanna and the gold strike were here; Amelia was far away. I think, even then, that the gold fever had my brother in its grip. He thought of nothing but himself, and the gold.

"My brother accepted Paul Conrad's bargain. He married Leanna and instantly became the richest man for many miles around. He hired men not lucky on their claims to build Leanna and me a house in town. We lived there together while William worked the gold claim. Leanna was not a bad person. She was good and kind. But she was cowed by my brother, as she had been by her father. As for William, it seemed that he had forgotten all about Amelia."

"Don't tell me," Paige murmured. "She showed up, to surprise him."

"She did," Marianne confirmed. "But it was not a pleasant surprise for either of them. I do not know what was said between them when Amelia discovered that he was married. William refused, point blank, to speak of it. For the sake of our friendship, Amelia begged me not to. I think William assumed, even hoped, that Amelia would leave. But she did not. Instead she settled into the cottage where I took you, Paige. She continued to practice her healing skills, and she took in laundry."

"I've read about the women who did that," Phoebe interjected. "That was grueling, backbreaking work."

"Yes," Marianne said. "It was. Amelia did not need to stay here. She did not need to do such work. Her father had left her with enough money so that she could have gone wherever she liked. But she stayed. Even now, I'm not sure that I know why. Her presence was a constant . . . *disturbance* to William, like a thorn in a shirt seam, constantly rubbing against his skin. He became convinced that she stayed for only one reason: to do him harm."

"Okay," Piper said. "Now I'm the one who thinks she can see the end of the story coming."

"I think we all can," Paige said grimly. Piece by piece, things were starting to fall into place. "Let me guess," she said to Marianne. "Things started happening in the town. Bad things."

"Yes," Marianne said, nodding, her voice barely above a whisper. "Yes, you are right. Though, to speak the truth, at first they weren't all that remarkable. Gold towns are hardly known for their . . . good manners. There are thefts. Quarrels escalate quickly into fights. But then, *other* things began to happen. People began to fall ill. Once-rich strikes seemed to dry up overnight. This, in particular, terrified my brother. It did not seem to matter to him that we were already richer than we'd ever hoped.

"Then, his wife, Leanna, fell ill. I begged him to go to Amelia for help, but he would not. The bad things that were happening were all Amelia's fault, he said. She was trying to ruin him, to take her revenge for the fact that he had married someone else. I didn't take his words seriously at first. I'm not sure even William did himself. It was just wild talk. But then . . ."

Marianne's voice sank so low the three sisters had to lean in to hear it. "Leanna died. William seemed to change beyond all recognition, overnight. He was no longer the brother I knew and loved. He had become a stranger, bent on extracting his own revenge. On destroying his enemy before he could be destroyed."

"And he'd convinced himself that Amelia was his enemy," Paige said.

"Yes," Marianne said, her voice a little stronger. "That is so. He called a town meeting, and his words whipped the people into a frenzy. There was evil in their midst, William declared. Evil that must be rooted out and destroyed. He accused Amelia of being a *bruja,* a witch. This was the reason she had come to California, William said. She had been driven out of Valparaiso."

Just for a second Marianne closed her eyes, as if the memory of that day was too painful to remember.

"William was very clever," she continued after a moment. "He now revealed his engagement to Amelia, using it as proof that he, himself, had once fallen under her spell. Coming to California had cured him, William claimed, a fact that angered the witch, the *bruja.* For proof of his words, William told the people they need look no farther than Leanna's death. For who had been the witch's first victim? The woman who had taken her place, William's wife.

"'Any of you could be next,' William told the townspeople. 'None of you is safe. If the witch covets what you have, she will find the way to take it, or destroy you.' I tried to argue against him, but William was prepared. He claimed that I was still under Amelia's spell. He begged the townspeople to help him save me from her."

Here, at long last, Marianne broke down. As if the memory of what she was about to relate was almost too painful to remember, let alone speak of.

"He used me," she said. "My own brother used me as an excuse to condemn my friend, the woman he once loved. His words convinced the townspeople. Soon they were nothing more than a frightened, angry mob. They went to Amelia's house and dragged her from it. They were shouting, 'Kill the witch! Kill the *bruja!*' They took her to a sandbar in the middle of the river. There they erected a stake and built a pyre. Then they . . ."

Marianne pulled in a shuddering breath to continue, but Paige laid a hand on her arm. "You don't have to say it," she said. "We know what happened next."

Accused of witchcraft, Amelia de la Cruz had been tied to the stake and burned alive.

"Remind you of anything?" Phoebe queried in a low voice.

"Absolutely," Piper nodded. "The question now is—"

But before she could pursue her train of thought, the door to the stockade burst open. A man rushed in, holding a lantern above his head. After the dim light of the single candle, even this was enough to dazzle the eyes.

"Marianne!" the man cried.

"William," Marianne said. To Paige's astonishment the younger woman stepped in front of her, as if to shield her, cover her presence. "What are you doing here?"

"The question is, what are *you* doing here, Marianne Olson?" said a new voice. A second man now stepped into the stockade. He too carried a lantern in one hand. A group of men crowded in behind him. "You seek to aid our enemies, perhaps?"

"These women are not our enemies, Tom McKade," Marianne Olson said. Her words were strong, but Paige could hear the fear running through her voice.

She's right, Paige thought. The Charmed Ones were not the town's enemies, but Tom McKade was definitely someone to be afraid of. Tall and powerfully built, he looked like a man accustomed to getting his own way, regardless of the consequences to others.

"And just how do you know that?" McKade said, his voice growing deadly quiet. "Are they your friends, like the last witch was?" He took a step toward Marianne. She flinched back, accidentally exposing Paige. At once McKade stopped short. The men behind him gave a shout of astonishment and surged forward. McKade raised a hand and they fell back. William Olson remained silent, his expression grim.

"What have we here?" Tom McKade inquired. "A third witch?" Without warning, his free hand snaked out, seizing Marianne by the arm. He dragged her forward. "How did she get in here? Answer me! Did you bring her here so that she and her sisters-in-evil could plot against us?"

Out of the corner of her eye Paige saw Phoebe tense, as if preparing to go to Marianne's defense. Before she could move, there was a sharp *click*: the cocking of a gun.

"Let go of my sister, McKade," William Olson said. "Or I'll put a bullet in your gut."

For a moment nothing happened. Then, slowly, Tom McKade released his hold on Marianne Olson's arm. He smiled at William Olson, baring his teeth like a wolf. William pulled his sister to his side, but he kept his gun trained on Tom McKade.

"There is a simple explanation for my sister's presence," William said now. "You know she was affected by the first witch, Amelia de la Cruz. I explained this myself. Since that time, my sister's mind has not been strong. It's obvious what must have happened. This *witch*"—he made a gesture toward Paige—"this witch eluded us when the other two were captured. Now she has cast a spell on my sister, compelling Marianne to bring her here so that she might free these others, her partners in evil."

The other men began to murmur and nod their agreement.

"A good explanation," Tom McKade agreed, his voice a sneer. "One that clears your sister of blame very nicely. If it's true."

"Of course it's true," William Olson said.

"It is *not* true!" Marianne cried. With a sudden, unexpected movement, she yanked herself free from William's grip. At once she moved to stand beside Paige. "I came here of my own free will because I wished to help these women who have been wrongly imprisoned. If they are evil, then so am I!"

Her words struck the men in the stockade like a bolt of lightning. Paige heard someone, she thought it was William Olson, suck in a breath. Then the men all began to speak at once.

"She shows her evil!" one man declared. "She should be locked up here, with these others, while we decide what to do with them all."

"What we should do is obvious," the man beside him said. "We know what to do with witches. They should all be put to death, just like the first one was."

"Enough!" William Olson's voice abruptly cut across the argument. "This is not some stranger you are talking about. This is my sister. She is one of us. She would never seek to harm me. I am all she has in the world, her only brother. But you see how strong the spell cast over her is. She thinks its will is her will. She is totally in its control."

"Then she should be locked up, for her own good," Tom McKade said swiftly. "And for the safety of the town."

"I agree," William Olson said.

Bet that cost you something, pal, Paige thought. From the expression on William's face, agreeing with Tom McKade was the last thing he wanted to do.

"But not in the stockade," William went on. "My sister will not be locked up like some common criminal. Besides, removing her from the presence of these witches may weaken the spell's hold on her mind. If that happens, she may be able to reveal their evil plans."

"Where then?" the first man who had spoken asked.

"Let her be taken back to our home and locked in her room," William Olson proposed. In the light of the lanterns, his eyes glittered like dark stones as he gazed at his sister, their expression unreadable. "Then we will meet downstairs and decide what must be done."

"I agree with William's proposal," Tom McKade said swiftly, as if eager to make himself the spokesman for the town.

There's more to this than just the fear of some outside evil, Paige realized. A power struggle for control of the town was also going on, between Tom McKade and William Olson.

"Come with me, Marianne," William commanded. "If you don't come willingly, I will force you."

Marianne turned to Paige and her sisters, grasping Paige tightly by the hand. "Remember your promise," she begged.

"I will," Paige replied.

Without another word Marianne turned to her brother. "I am ready, but I will leave as I came in. Of my own free will."

Then she brushed past the men, her head held high.

"I hate to ask the obvious question," Phoebe said a few moments later. The Charmed Ones were once again alone in the stockade. "But I'm afraid it does seem appropriate."

"Let me guess," Paige put in. "Would it by any chance be: What do we do now? We can't use our powers to save ourselves, let alone Marianne."

"I think I have an idea," Piper said. "Though it may be a long shot. When we heard Amelia de la Cruz's story, I'm willing to bet we all thought the same thing."

"Absolutely," Paige nodded. "Melinda Warren. She was burned at the stake, just like Amelia de la Cruz. I'm not sure how that helps us, though."

"We don't have our powers," Piper answered slowly, as if she was still thinking her plan through. "But that doesn't mean we're power*less.* We still have ourselves."

"I think I'm following you," Phoebe said. "But I really want you to keep talking."

"So, we use that," Piper said simply. "The truth is, you could say all our power stems from the same source: who we are. And that comes from—"

"Blood," Paige said suddenly. "You're talking about Melinda Warren's legacy. We are witches of the Warren bloodline."

"More than that," Phoebe continued. "In a way we're the ultimate reason for Melinda's death. She could have used her powers to save herself. But she didn't. She died to protect her daughter, Prudence. So that she could live, and the Warren line could go on."

"Go on and eventually produce three sisters, the Charmed Ones," Piper finished up. "The most powerful witches of all time. Our other powers may not have survived the time trip. But not even being in a different time can change who we are. We still have the power that lives in our blood. I think we should use it to try and summon Melinda Warren."

"But how?" Phoebe inquired. "I hate to sound like the killjoy, but last time we did this, we had a focus point. We had Melinda's locket. We don't have that now."

"No," Paige said slowly. "But we do have this." She pulled the brooch containing the likeness of Amelia de la Cruz from her apron pocket.

"We're trying to summon Melinda, not Amelia," Phoebe said.

"I know that," Paige said. "But maybe Amelia can help us. I have a feeling she was like Melinda Warren in more ways than one. We all noticed the border on that pin, the one that reminded us of the Triquetra on the Book of Shadows. My guess is that Amelia really *was* a witch, though, like Melinda, she was falsely accused of doing wrong.

"Maybe we can use the pin as a focus point into the spirit

world. If we can get Amelia's attention, maybe she can—I don't know—deliver a message to Melinda, or something."

"It's worth a try," Piper said. "Not only that, it's the only plan we've got."

"Well, if you put it like that," Phoebe said. She held out one hand, palm upward. "I'm ready to give blood. You do the summoning, Piper. You're better at it than either of us."

"I'll do my best," Piper said. She gave Paige a nod.

Quickly Paige unfastened the pin on Amelia de la Cruz's brooch. She drew a thin line across her palms, then those of her sisters. She placed the brooch beside the single candle that was their illumination. Then she stepped back to join her sisters as they formed a circle, clasping hands tightly to mingle their blood. An unbroken chain of Warren heritage, Warren power.

"Okay," Piper said. "Here goes. Don't expect brilliant poetry, all right. I'm pretty much making this up as I go along."

Melinda Warren. Ancestress, strong.
Help us now prevent a wrong.
By our blood, and by our need,
Come to us. We summon thee.

"The candle. Look at the flame," Phoebe whispered.

"I see it," Piper said. "Well, at least I did something."

"Let's just hope it's the thing we wanted," Paige put in.

In the center of the circle, the flame of the candle was slowly turning bloodred. Above it, a twist of pale smoke was floating. In it, a face began to form.

"Look!" Paige suddenly cried out. "It's Amelia de la Cruz."

For several moments Amelia's fierce and tragic face stared out at the Charmed Ones. Then it turned away, as if focusing on something only she could see. Slowly a second face began to form.

"I think it's working," Phoebe said. "Oh, my God. It *is* working. That's Melinda Warren."

In the smoke the images of the two women faced each other. It seemed almost as if some sort of unspoken communication passed between them. Then Amelia's face began to fade away. The candle flared abruptly, its bloodred flame all but blinding.

"Don't let go!" Piper cried. "Maintain the circle."

As quickly as it had flared, the candle settled back to normal, the flame returning to its proper color. Paige blinked her eyes rapidly to make certain she wasn't seeing things.

In the center of the circle formed by the Charmed Ones' clasped hands stood a figure.

"Well done, girls," said Melinda Warren.

"It was Piper's idea," Paige said, a short time later. The Charmed Ones and their ancestor were having an emergency meeting of the minds. In their period clothing, the resemblance between the four young women was even more pronounced, though Melinda's dress and apron were from her own, colonial, time.

"She was the one who didn't get freaked about the no-powers aspect of the situation and encouraged us to remember the power that comes from just being who we are," Paige went on.

"But the idea to use Amelia's pin as the focus point was Paige's," Piper countered.

Phoebe held up a hand. "Guys. You are both incredibly brilliant. The judges all give you perfect tens. But could we change gears here and focus? In case you haven't noticed, we're running out of time. It'll be morning soon."

"I agree with Phoebe," Melinda Warren said. "Piper and Paige were brilliant to come up with the way to summon me"—she gave the two of them a slightly cheeky smile made all the more impish by her sober, colonial garments—"and Phoebe is right to remind us not to congratulate ourselves. There are still many things that must be done."

"Such as what, precisely?" Paige inquired. "Piper may be okay about the no-powers thing, but I admit, I'm still struggling. Things would be a whole lot easier if I could just grab Marianne and orb on outta here."

"Easier in the short run, yes. But maybe not better, particularly not in the long run," replied Melinda Warren. "There's something about this story you don't know yet. Something Marianne didn't know and so couldn't tell you.

"Before Amelia de la Cruz died, she cursed William Olson."

"Right on," Phoebe said, then found herself the focus of three pairs of eyes. "Okay," she said slowly. "Or do I mean, 'uh-oh'?"

"Both," answered Melinda Warren. "The irony of this situation is that Amelia de la Cruz did, indeed, have powers, as you figured out for yourselves. But she was innocent of any wrongdoing, just as I myself was. In spite of the terrible way in which he treated her, Amelia never stopped loving William Olson, in her heart of hearts."

"So why would she curse him?" Piper asked. "Aside from the obvious dying painfully part."

"Curses can be tricky things," Melinda said. "Once they are spoken, they can take on lives of their own. William Olson's actions broke Amelia de la Cruz's heart. And so, with her dying breath, she placed this curse upon him: 'Until you express remorse, nothing that you claim to love will prosper. Instead, it, and you, will dwell in darkness. Only by the breaking of your heart will the sun shine through. Only the breaking of your heart will save the Innocents from suffering.'"

"Wow!" Phoebe said. "That's pretty major stuff."

"Not only that," Piper said in agreement, "it explains a lot. The modern condition of Williamstown for one thing."

"And why we got sucked back through time for another," Paige put in soberly. "Marianne claims she and Amelia remained friends, right up until Amelia's death. If that's true, and I think it's safe to say it is, Marianne is the last person Amelia would want to suffer."

"Precisely," agreed Melinda Warren. "When you touched the brooch with Amelia's image, the power of her will was strong enough to bring the three of you back here, through time."

"To try and save an Innocent," Phoebe said. "Specifically, an Innocent Amelia loved: Marianne Olson."

"But what do we *do*? How do we save her?" Paige cried, her frustration clear as day, even in the dark stockade. "*We don't have our powers!*"

"Paige," Piper murmured, moving to wrap an arm around her shoulders. "Calm down."

"How can I calm down?" Paige asked. "Unless we do something, Marianne is going to die tomorrow morning. And we won't be far behind. I'm not freaking. Honestly I'm not. I just genuinely don't understand how we can save her without using our powers."

"By using the powers you still possess," said Melinda Warren. "Just like you did when you summoned me. Even without your extra abilities, you are still the Charmed Ones. You have powers William Olson does not dream of, though he needs them desperately."

"I don't suppose you'd like to be a little more specific as to what they are, would you?" Paige asked.

"You have the power of your own hearts," replied Melinda Warren.

There was a silence, while all three sisters digested this.

"I'm sort of with Paige on this one," Phoebe admitted after a moment. "I really like the sound of that, I'm just not sure how to turn it into an action item."

"I know this is difficult for all of you to understand," Melinda said, her voice quiet. "But the obvious, clear-cut action is not always the right one. Not in the long run."

"Such as, for instance, someone with powers using them to save herself when there's someone she needs to protect," Piper ventured. "A daughter."

Melinda gave her a slow smile. "That's it precisely, Piper. Not all courses of action are easy to see. Sometimes they take many years to unfold. And sometimes, much as we might like to deny it, sacrifices are required."

"I understand what you're saying too," Paige said. "But I'm not prepared to sacrifice Marianne Olson."

"Neither am I," said Melinda Warren.

"So what do you suggest?" Phoebe inquired.

"I suggest we consider coming up with a—what do you call it—Plan B," Melinda said.

All three sisters grinned, but it was Paige who spoke.

"Now you're talking like a Charmed One."

"I think they're coming!" Phoebe whispered. Quickly she left her position by the stockade door, where she had been listening for the approach of the townspeople, and rejoined her sisters and Melinda Warren. "We're all clear about the plan, right?"

"Right," Paige confirmed. "I'll go help Melinda get set up."

The two hurried to the far corner of the stockade. There Melinda dropped to the dirt floor. Paige covered her with the blankets the townspeople had left behind for Phoebe and Piper. Then she stepped back, checking out the effect.

"This is going to work," she pronounced.

In the dim light of the stockade, it was impossible to tell there was a person concealed beneath the blankets. When their captors removed Piper, Phoebe, and Paige, Melinda Warren would be left behind. The Charmed Ones were taking one big gamble: that, with their prisoners in their possession, the townspeople would see no reason to lock the stockade. This would leave Melinda free to slip away, to serve as Plan B backup.

This is going to work, Paige told herself silently, once again. *I just wish I felt better about it.*

Although she, her sisters, and Melinda had discussed the situation virtually all night, Paige still felt dissatisfied. Intellectually she understood that holding back could be considered a course of action in and of itself. But that wasn't the same as saying it was a course of action in Paige's comfort zone.

It's just not the way we're supposed to operate, she thought. *We're supposed to do things. We're the Charmed Ones.*

Although even Paige had to admit that doing something didn't always bring about the desired, positive result. Her last demon encounter had certainly proved that. Her precipitous actions had almost destroyed them all.

So she would wait, to see if events unfolded the way Melinda believed they might.

As it happened, she didn't have to wait very long.

With a great crash the door to the stockade was flung back. Pale sunlight streamed in, then was cut off as Tom McKade stepped through the door.

So that's the way things are, Paige thought. It looked like McKade was winning the battle for control of the town.

"Bring the witches," he said in a hard voice, as his followers began to crowd in behind him. "Let them learn for themselves what we do to those who would bring evil to our town."

At his words, Piper, Phoebe, and Paige were seized by rough hands and hurried from the stockade into the main street of Williamstown.

Oh, no! Please, no! Paige thought. In the center of the main street stood a tall wooden pole. At its base were piled bundles of straw and pieces of wood. Torches, just waiting to be lit, were thrust into the ground nearby. It was a scene to chill the blood, and it could have but one purpose.

I wonder which one of us will be first, Paige thought.

As she watched, Tom McKade strode purposefully to stand as close to the stake as the materials around its base would allow. For a moment he simply stood, surveying the crowd. On his face was a mixture of anticipation and triumph.

"Let Marianne Olson be brought forward," Tom McKade called in a loud voice.

At first nothing seemed to be happening. Then the crowd began to part. William and Marianne Olson appeared, side by side. Their appearance was striking.

Gone was the William Olson whom Paige had first encountered yesterday. The one who seemed powerful and in control. In his place was a man who looked as if he was on the edge of a nervous breakdown. His shoulders slumped. His face had a gray, unhealthy pallor. His eyes shifted nervously from side to side.

William Olson looked spent and broken. By his side Marianne walked calmly, her expression fixed and purposeful. Her stride firm and strong. Even when the pair came in sight of the stake, Marianne did not falter. If anything, she lifted her chin a little higher. Paige felt an emotion she'd never thought to experience on this morning: hope.

Slowly Marianne and William continued walking, until they stood beside Tom McKade.

"You see before you William and Marianne Olson," McKade addressed the crowd. "Last night, in the stockade, Marianne was discovered attempting to aid the strangers in our midst, strangers her brother, William, himself declares to be evil.

Strangers I know we all believe came here with just one purpose, just as the last stranger did: to bring harm to our town."

A ripple of assent moved through the crowd of townspeople. Paige felt the man who was holding her tighten his grip on her arms.

"William would have you believe that the strangers have used their dark powers to take control of his sister's mind. It is for this reason that she tried to help them. Marianne insists she tried to aid them of her own free will. So who do we believe? Marianne Olson, or her brother?"

A second murmur passed through the crowd, more agitated than the first. People looked to one another, as if trying to gauge what each believed before declaring themselves.

"I will tell you what *I* believe," Tom McKade said, his voice rising. At once the crowd fell silent. Every single eye was fixed on Tom McKade.

Here it comes, Paige thought.

"I believe Marianne Olson. I believe she aided these strangers of her own free will, just as she claims. Which means there is only one conclusion that can be drawn: Marianne Olson is a witch, just as they are. She must be put to death before her evil can spread and infect us all. But before this can be done, you must tell me what *you* believe."

"Kill her! Kill the witch! Kill them all!" the crowd began to roar.

"No!" William Olson protested desperately, his voice all but drowned out by the crowd. "You must not do this. It is wrong."

"It is the will of the people," Tom McKade said. At the sound of his voice, the crowd began to calm. "Marianne Olson must die. Evil that attacks us from outside is bad enough, but an evil that grows in our very midst is worst of all. It cannot be allowed to grow. It must be stamped out. But perhaps there is still some goodness in Marianne."

"What do you mean?" gasped William Olson.

"In olden times there was a tradition," Tom McKade said. "Those condemned to die at the stake were given a chance to confess before their bodies were given to the fire. If they did, they were put to death before the flames could claim them. They never had to feel the horror of the fire.

"We are also prepared to show this mercy. If the evil has spread beyond Marianne, if she knows of others in our town who are infected, let her confess it now. It will not save her life. Nothing can do that. But it can save her from dying in agony."

The way Melinda and Amelia died, Paige thought.

"Yes, yes, I will confess," Marianne's voice suddenly rang out. "I know who the true evil-doers are in this town, and I am not afraid to name them."

Tom McKade's face flushed with triumph. *That's what this is really all about,* Paige thought. *McKade doesn't believe in witches. He just wants to control the town.* And the only way to do that was to put an end to William Olson's power. What better way than to accuse his sister of being a witch?

Marianne turned to face the crowd. "I will tell you who the true evil-doers are," she said again. "Here are their names. Tom McKade. Jeremiah Whitlock." Paige heard the man beside her cry out in fear and astonishment as his name was called.

"Hugh Matthews. William Olson. I accuse each and every man and woman in this town. Every single one of you is guilty of the same evil. You fear strangers for no reason other than that they *are* strangers. In your fear you condemned Amelia de la Cruz; you let an innocent woman die. You are the evil that infects this town, not I. Your own actions this morning prove it."

Nice going, Marianne, Paige thought.

All around her she could feel agitation swirling through the crowd. It seemed clear to Paige that many townspeople had misgivings about the action they were about to take. But they were afraid to speak out. Anyone who did so ran the risk of suffering Marianne's fate.

"Enough!" Tom McKade shouted in a harsh voice. "You see how far gone the witch is. Nothing can save her now. Let her be put to death at once." Quickly he seized Marianne and led her to the stake. Marianne did not struggle as McKade began to tie her bonds himself. "Light the torches," he commanded. "What are you waiting for?"

"No!" William Olson cried. He sank to his knees, his face buried in his hands.

Looks like it's time for Plan B, Paige thought. She only hoped Melinda could create a frightening enough diversion to disperse some of the crowd. That way, Paige and her sisters could get to Marianne.

His terrible task complete, McKade jumped from the pyre and seized one of the torches.

"No!" William Olson cried once more. Without warning he surged to his feet, as if to grapple the torch from McKade's grasp. Tom McKade stumbled back, the two moving dangerously close to the flammable material surrounding Marianne.

For a few breathless seconds the two struggled together. Then a sudden gust of wind blew the flame of the torch straight into Tom McKade's face. With a scream he dropped the torch. It fell directly onto the pile of straw and wood. At once the fire roared up. Marianne Olson called out.

"Marianne!" William shouted. "I was wrong. Forgive me."

With that he dashed straight into the hungry flames. They flared up, so bright Paige was compelled to shut her eyes.

They were gone when she opened them again. She was standing in the antique mall, her sisters beside her. Amelia de la Cruz's brooch rested on its cushion of black velvet in front of them.

"Do you see what I see?" Phoebe asked.

"We're back where we started," Piper said.

Phoebe shook her head. "Not just that. Look at Amelia's expression."

"I see what you mean," Piper said.

Amelia de la Cruz no longer looked fierce and desperate. Instead, she was smiling.

Old Family Recipe

Diana G. Gallagher

"Please, Piper," Darryl pleaded. He dropped to one knee in the front hall of the Manor and clasped his hands.

"Oh, all right!" Piper threw up her hands in surrender. "I can't stand watching a grown man grovel."

Darryl stood up with a devilish grin. "If begging hadn't worked, I was ready to call in some of the favors you owe me."

"I do owe you a few," Piper said. She and her sisters owed Darryl Morris more than a few favors. She had lost track of how many times the detective had saved the Charmed Ones from death, exposure, jail, or losing an Innocent.

"Right." A mischievous twinkle brightened Darryl's brown eyes. "So I have another request."

Piper's eyes narrowed. "More than wanting me to make something for the Police Precinct Bake Sale?"

"I love homemade apple pie," Darryl said. "I mean, I really *love* homemade apple pie."

"Is that so?" Piper smiled. Darryl's wife was a great cook, but Sheila didn't bake. Period. That's why he had asked her to contribute to the bake sale. "How many?"

Darryl shrugged. "Three?"

"You got it," Piper said.

"Great." Darryl turned to leave, then swiveled back. "And no funny stuff, right?"

"I don't use magic to bake pies." Piper followed Darryl to the door and called out as he trotted down the front walk. "When is the big event?"

"Saturday," Darryl called back. "I'll pick the pies up at nine A.M. sharp."

"No problem," Piper muttered, closing the door. She continued talking to herself as she headed to the kitchen. "It's only Thursday night. Leo can watch Wyatt while I shop and bake all day tomorrow, *if*—"

"Leo's still reading bedtime stories to Wyatt," Phoebe said as she and Paige came down the stairs.

"Uh-huh." Preoccupied, Piper marched into the kitchen.

"Problem?" Paige asked Piper as they filed in behind her.

Phoebe sighed with mock resignation. "Okay, Piper. How many demons do Paige and I have to vanquish before we can go to the movies?"

"Relax." Piper grabbed the teakettle and filled it with water. Hot tea helped her think. "It's a pie problem."

Paige frowned. "Pi as in a problem that can't be solved because the number is *never* evenly divisible after the decimal point?"

"No, pie as in apple." Piper turned on the stove burner and sank into a chair. "I promised Darryl I'd bake three apple pies for the Police Precinct Bake Sale this Saturday."

"Ahhh." Phoebe nodded knowingly. "And apple pie isn't one of your favorite things to bake."

"Because apple pie is a bad witch thing," Paige said.

Piper and Phoebe exchanged a glance, then turned quizzical stares on Paige.

"Apple pies, wicked witches, poison spells," Paige said,

shrugging as though the logic should be obvious.

Phoebe laughed. "Only in fairytales."

"And Hollywood," Piper added. She didn't laugh, even though Paige's association was funny. "But that's not why I don't bake apple pie unless I absolutely have to."

And a specific request from Darryl definitely qualifies as a 'have to,' Piper thought. He rarely asked them for anything.

"Trust me," Phoebe said. "Grams's apple pie was harmless."

"And the best we've ever tasted." Piper dropped her chin in her hands. "So if I can't bake Grams's apple pie, I don't want to bake any apple pie."

"I don't understand the problem." Paige folded her arms, and her eyes clouded with confusion.

"Grams always made it from memory," Piper said. "The recipe's been in the family for ages, but—"

"It wasn't written down?" When the kettle whistled, Paige stepped to the stove and turned the burner off.

"Grams assured me it *was* written down," Piper went on, "but she died before she told me where."

"Or what the secret spices are," Phoebe said. "We've searched the house looking for it, but we've never found it."

"Are you sure it's in the Manor?" Paige's gaze flicked around the kitchen.

"Pretty sure." Phoebe dropped her bag on the counter and opened a cabinet door. She took a stack of dishes out and lifted the shelf paper to peer under it. "How badly did you want to see *Warrior Winter,* Paige?"

"I can wait for the DVD." Paige started her search with the silverware drawer.

Piper and Phoebe had scoured the kitchen for the recipe before, but Piper kept quiet. She didn't want to dampen her sisters' enthusiasm for the hunt. Besides, things often turned up in places that had already been searched. Despite that, Piper ignored the cook books and recipe files, because she had turned every page and flipped through every loose paper and card many times. She hadn't been as thorough with Grams's other books, photo albums, and framed pictures.

Tea can wait, Piper thought as she left for the living room. Grams wouldn't have told her the recipe was in the Manor if it wasn't in the Manor. She didn't care if it took all night, she was going to find it.

Hours later the three sisters had searched all the obvious places one might find a recipe. They had also looked in, through, over, and under Grams's personal belongings—except what was stored in the attic.

"We probably should have looked up here first," Paige said as she trudged up the stairs. "Maybe Grams thought the attic was the most obvious place."

"We've thought of that." Phoebe opened the door and flicked on the light. "But looking for one piece of paper up here is a daunting task."

"You could say that." Piper's resolve slipped as she scanned the century of accumulated stuff stored in the attic. Halliwells didn't throw anything out—ever. From prized possessions to old clothes, they hauled it to the top floor of the mansion and stashed it. Piper didn't know where to start.

"This is an old *family* recipe, right?" Paige asked.

"Right." Piper's gaze settled on several stacks of old magazines. "Grams never said who made the original pie, but her mother and her mother's mother all used the recipe."

Piper walked over and picked up a copy of *Hearth and Home* dated Fall 1981. It was addressed to Penelope Halliwell. When they were children, Grams had let them pick recipes out of magazines to try. Could she have put the family pie recipe inside a magazine and forgotten?

"Where did we put that box of Grams's old handbags?" Phoebe lifted a stack of frayed towels to read the label on the box underneath. "Maybe she kept it in an old wallet."

"Or maybe she stuck it in the Book of Shadows," Paige suggested. "It *is* a family thing with secret ingredients."

"Thought of that, too—" Piper looked up as Paige pulled a yellowed paper out of the leather lining on the inside of the front cover. "What's that?"

Phoebe dropped the towels and dashed over to look.

"We'll see." Paige carefully unfolded the old piece of paper. The sheet was linen stationery and didn't tear.

Piper's heart fluttered when she read the precise script at the top of the page. "That's it! 'Apple Pie.'"

Phoebe studied the page. "The words are still legible, but that's not Grams's handwriting."

"Grams didn't say *who* had written it down. Only that it *was* written down." Piper grinned as she took the paper from Paige's hand. Finally she could bake the traditional, family-tested-and-approved apple pie the Warren witches had enjoyed for generations.

"Have you got everything?" Piper asked as Leo shouldered the diaper bag. He was taking Wyatt to the park so she could bake her pies without being distracted. Phoebe was still at the newspaper, and Paige was working a temp job downtown.

"Everything except the kid." Leo kissed her on the cheek and grinned. "I'll pick up pizza on the way home."

"Have fun." Piper smiled as Leo took Wyatt from his playpen. They were, in that instant, the image of domestic bliss and contentment. When the door slammed behind them, she got down to business.

Piper had made a duplicate recipe to protect the delicate original, which she would put back in the Book of Shadows later, after the pies were done. Since the first direction said to follow the directions exactly as written, she checked to make sure she had copied the recipe to the letter. How various seasonings blended for taste could depend on the order they were added to a mixture.

Piper began with the crusts. Rather than shortcut the process with packaged pastry dough, she preferred to make her own from scratch. She mixed, kneaded, and rolled the dough, then inserted and trimmed bottom crusts in three nine-inch disposable aluminum dishes. She put a fourth crust in a glass dish for the family and placed all the dishes in the refrigerator. After she portioned the dough for four top crusts, she tackled the filling.

"Exactly as written," Piper murmured as she read through the directions. Ordinarily, she liked to experiment with recipes to refine tastes and aromas. This time she reined in that instinct. The old family recipe couldn't be improved.

"Soak an apple blossom in apple-cider vinegar and set aside." Surprised by the token Wiccan ingredient, Piper rolled her eyes, but she did as the recipe said.

The apple blossom wasn't the only ingredient found in the potion-supplies cabinet. The recipe also called for a sprinkling of dragon's blood, a resin drawn from the fruit of an Indonesian tree, often used in spells to enhance potency. In folk medicine it alleviated chest pains, healed bruises, and stopped bleeding. Piper assumed that the unknown witch ancestor who had created the apple pie recipe had used the unusual ingredient to enhance the flavors of the other, ordinary spices.

The use of cinnamon, rosemary, and vanilla made Piper shake her head too. In folk remedies and charms, these three seasonings represented some aspect of love. Piper wondered if the apple blossom, a catalyst for love in spells, had modified Halliwell taste buds to accept *no* substitutes for this particular apple pie. She smiled at the whimsical thought. She wouldn't put it past a proud Warren-line witch to make sure her mark on the family was never diminished or forgotten.

Piper peeled, cored, and cut sixteen crisp apples into slices. She took one of the pie plates out of the refrigerator and rolled a top crust to have it ready. Then, following the directions exactly, she combined the ingredients for the apple pies one by one.

She cleaned up while the first two pies baked, then relaxed with tea and a magazine until the second batch came out of the oven. The finished pies went into disposable plastic pie containers she had purchased at the grocery store. She set three on the counter for Darryl and hid the fourth in the pantry. Grams's apple pie deserved to follow a meal with more class than pizza. She'd surprise the family with it tomorrow night, for dessert after a proper dinner.

"What smells good?" Leo deposited an empty glass in the sink, on his way to hug Piper as she stood near the stove. "Where's Wyatt?"

"Paige is changing him. Don't!" Piper glanced over her shoulder as her adorable, but sweaty, husband raised his arms. Paige had volunteered for baby duty, and Leo had spent the entire Saturday afternoon trimming shrubs and mowing the lawn. Piper playfully warned him away with a wooden spoon. "Shower before cuddles. I'm cooking."

"The chef's wish is my command." With a flourish of his hand, Leo bowed and backed off.

"Works for me." Piper grinned and reached for the ringing phone as Leo headed out. "I need that hug, so hurry! Hello?"

"Hey, Piper. It's Darryl. Just wanted to let you know that your pies were a big hit with the local police."

"I'm assuming that's a good thing." Piper set the oven temperature. Fifteen minutes after she popped in the dinner rolls, her family would be sitting down to crisp green salad, hot bread, Yankee pot roast, and Grams's apple pie.

"Completely," Darryl said. "When Captain Hoyt saw me grab one of your pies before the sale even started, he bought one too. Angie Shore snapped up the third one."

"Is she a cop?" Piper asked out of curiosity.

"A rookie who's getting married next month." Darryl chuckled. "But Angie's cooking experience is limited to pouring milk on cereal and putting frozen dinners in the oven. After seeing those pies, she couldn't wait to treat her fiancé to some home cooking . . . even if the cooking was done in someone else's home. You should be honored—both Angie and the captain are eating your pies tonight!"

"Well, I'll look forward to hearing what they thought! And you enjoy too!" After hanging up, Piper finished setting the table.

Based on the tangy aroma when the pies had come out of the oven yesterday, Piper was sure Darryl would love it. Leo and Paige would too. It was Phoebe's critique that had her on edge. Nobody but Phoebe had eaten Grams's apple pie before.

"Dinner's ready!" Piper called out.

"Great." Phoebe rushed downstairs ahead of Paige and Wyatt. "I'm so famished, sautéed shoe leather would taste like perfect prime rib."

"You'll have to settle for pot roast," Piper said.

Phoebe wasn't the only member of the family who had worked up an appetite that afternoon. Every speck of salad and every dinner roll crumb disappeared off every plate. Even Wyatt, who had to have everything cut into tiny, easily swallowed pieces, cleaned his dish. Although Piper didn't want to spoil the surprise, she had to confess she had pie for dessert when Leo and Phoebe asked for seconds.

"I knew you'd make one for us." Phoebe beamed with expectant pleasure when Piper set the pie and dessert plates on the dining-room table.

"Had to," Piper said as she cut into the flaky, golden brown crust. Grams had taught her one cooking secret: to baste the top crust with milk and sprinkle it with sugar. Now she knew that the secret had been passed down with the old family recipe. She handed Phoebe the first slice. "I've missed having apple pie."

"It sure looks good enough to eat." Paige took the second slice and cut a bite with the side of her fork.

"Bigger for me," Leo said. "Please."

Piper cut a larger portion for Leo and handed him the plate. Then she noticed Wyatt rubbing his eyes. "Did Aunt Paige wear you out today?"

"Eh." Wyatt banged his shoe against his high chair and lifted his capped milk glass to fling it.

"Whoa there, Wyatt." Leo swallowed as he took the cup from Wyatt's hand. Wyatt started to cry. "C'mon, guy. It's okay."

"Maybe I'd better put him to bed." As Piper bent over to unfasten Wyatt's safety straps, she glanced at Phoebe. "Well?"

"Let me just taste this again." Phoebe took another bite and chewed with thoughtful concentration.

"Absolutely great." Leo nodded vigorously and took a second bite.

"Very good," Paige agreed.

"But—" Phoebe hesitated, obviously reluctant to voice her opinion. "It's good. Better than most I've tried, but—"

"It's not as good as Grams's?" Piper asked as she lifted Wyatt out of his high chair.

"I'm not sure 'good' is the right word, Piper," Phoebe said. "It's just not quite the *same*, you know?"

"Yeah." Piper shrugged. "I wonder what I did wrong?"

"Not a thing." Leo grinned. "See? I'm almost done."

Piper smiled as she turned to leave. Later, when she was over her initial disappointment, she'd sample the pie to see if she could figure out her mistake.

"I'll help you with him in a minute, Piper." Leo jabbed his fork into the pie. "As soon as I finish this."

Paige drained her water glass and frowned at the lipstick smudge on the rim. "And I'll do the dishes. Seems only fair since you cooked, Piper."

"In that case, I'm going to relax," Phoebe said. "If there's nothing interesting on TV, I've got a new thriller I've been dying to read."

Before Piper reached the first landing, Leo was taking Wyatt from her arms. He knew she was bummed because the pie, although tasty, had fallen short of her goal.

"Why don't you lie down for a few minutes, Piper." Leo smiled at Wyatt. "I'll give Wyatt a bath and put him to bed."

"That's an offer I won't refuse."

Parting ways with Leo and Wyatt at the bedroom door, Piper flopped on her bed and immediately dozed off. She awoke an hour later to see Leo tiptoeing out of the room. "Leo?"

Leo flinched. "Sorry, Piper. I didn't mean to wake you."

"Where are you going?" Piper yawned, but she felt better after the nap.

"Wyatt seems a little restless tonight," Leo said. "I just thought I'd sit with him for a while."

"Okay." Piper smiled, pleased that Leo lavished his son with time and attention. Besides, they couldn't be too careful where Wyatt's safety was concerned. Too many evil entities wanted to steal or control their son's powers.

Rested and awake, Piper went downstairs to sample the pie. She had followed the directions as written. So why didn't her pie taste like Grams's pie?

She walked into the kitchen expecting to find the sink full of pots and pans. Paige always let them soak when she did the dishes—except tonight.

"Wow." Piper stopped just inside the kitchen doorway. Not only was the sink pots-and-pans free, all the stains had been scoured away. The counters were clear, and the dishwasher hummed along in midcycle. Paige wasn't around, but Piper had to be sure to thank her for doing such a great job tomorrow.

As Piper stepped into the pantry to get the leftover pie, she noticed the disposable pie case in the trash. Suspecting the worst, that Phoebe and Paige had accidentally dropped or polished off the pie, she opened the dishwasher. The glass pie plate was inside.

"No pie, no pots, no problem!" Free to do what she pleased, Piper poured a glass of ginger ale and went into the front hall. As she turned to go upstairs, a scream sliced through the quiet. She jumped back to look into the living room. Phoebe was stretched out on the sofa, watching an old horror movie.

"It was so hideous!" A blonde girl on the TV screen sobbed into her hands. "I'll see that awful face until the day I die!"

"Which might be today . . ." The gravelly voice rose from a foggy, moonlit swamp and was followed by a chilling laugh.

"What are you watching, Phoebe?" Piper asked.

"'Monsters and Mayhem Movie Weekend,'" Phoebe said.

"Why?" Piper didn't understand her younger sister's addiction to horror movies and thriller fiction.

"Because this is what came up when I turned the TV on." Phoebe looked back with a disapproving frown. "Shhh!"

"Sorry." Piper hurried up the stairs and peeked into Wyatt's room. Leo had fallen asleep in the rocking chair by the crib. She decided not to wake him. For the next hour, all she wanted to do was relax in a hot bubble bath.

Piper hummed an original tune by one of P3's new weeknight bands as she spooned pancake batter onto a sizzling skillet.

"Finished with those?" Paige asked, pointing to the measuring cup and spoons Piper had used to make the batter.

"They're all yours." Piper flipped the last flapjacks. She wasn't always this perky at breakfast, but Leo was doing Daddy duty, and Paige had designated herself as the morning Merry Maid, scrubbing away at the dishes as fast as Piper could dirty them.

Piper didn't know how long Paige would try to keep the perfectly clean kitchen perfectly clean, but she wasn't about to question her motives or stop her. The dishwasher had been emptied before she came down this morning, and the trash was outside.

"Look, Wyatt!" Leo exclaimed. Wyatt rode on his shoulders, holding on to fistfuls of daddy hair. "Pancakes! Your favorite."

"Pa-tah!" Wyatt giggled.

Leo winced when the exuberant boy yanked his hair. "Let's grab a seat, okay?"

"This is good to go." Piper scooped the final pancakes onto the serving platter and carried it to the table.

"I'm just about ready." Paige ran a sponge over the counter to wipe up drops of spilled milk. She rinsed the spatula Piper had just finished using and put it in the dishwasher. Then she stood by the stove, drumming her fingers.

Leo stabbed a pancake and sausage for Wyatt and began to cut them into baby chunks. When Wyatt pointed impatiently, Leo fed him a bite of pancake dripping with maple syrup.

"Did I forget something?" Piper asked Paige.

"No." Paige shook her head. "I'm just waiting for the pan to cool down so I can wash it."

When were clean pans ever Paige's most pressing priority? Piper asked herself. *Weird. She's been cleaning like a maniac since last night.*

"Not too fast, Wyatt." Leo wiped syrup off the boy's chin, then fed him another bite. "There's plenty."

"He likes to feed himself, Leo," Piper said.

"But then he gets so messy." Leo made a face.

"I'm pretty sure that's *why* he likes to feed himself," Piper pointed out. Leo, however, wasn't listening. He had the baby fork loaded with sausage and poised, waiting for Wyatt to open his mouth for more.

"Where's Phoebe?" Piper turned and shouted. "Phoebe!"

"Don't bother," Paige said. "She won't answer. *Blaze of Gory* is on, and it's her favorite horror-movie spoof."

"What time did she go to bed?" Piper asked, but she anticipated Paige's reply.

"She didn't." Paige turned on the hot water and shoved the skillet under the tap. Water sizzled and spat as it hit the hot metal. As soon as the shallow pan was clean and dry, she put it away and came to the table.

Piper used Paige to test the theory working in her head. "Are you doing anything special today, Paige?"

"I don't have much to do, really . . . just some more work around the house." Paige buttered three pancakes and poured blueberry syrup over the stack. "Do you have any idea how much china and glassware we have in this house? I might not be done washing it all before I have to get back to work!"

Paige's words jolted Piper back to the realization that something sudden and totally unexpected had affected everyone's behavior except hers.

"You could probably use a break from feeding Wyatt, Leo." Piper set her fork on her plate and reached to take Wyatt's silverware from his hand. "I can take over now."

Leo jerked his hand back and scowled. "I've got it."

"Fine." Piper wasn't mad. Leo's attitude only confirmed her

suspicions. Something weird was going on. As she stood up, she picked up her plate to carry it to the sink.

"Put it down, Piper," Paige said. "I'll take care of the dishes."

"It's no trouble, Paige," Piper objected. "I'll just—"

"I said 'put it down'!" Paige snapped, her voice tight with warning.

Piper dropped the plate and whirled to leave. Neither Leo nor Paige tried to stop her as she stomped into the living room. Wyatt had his father's undivided attention, and Paige was completely focused on dirty dishes. Now that Piper had identified the problem, she was only one test subject away from isolating the cause.

Phoebe didn't look away from the TV screen when Piper stopped at the end of the sofa. "Can I talk to you a minute, Phoebe?"

"No! Can't you see I'm watching television?" Phoebe asked. Just in case Piper hadn't gotten the message that she didn't want to be bothered, Phoebe picked up the remote and raised the volume.

Piper went straight to her room and locked the door. Her family's belligerence might get worse, and she needed time and quiet to think.

It wasn't hard to figure out what had triggered Leo, Paige, and Phoebe's sudden obsessions. They were unwaveringly focused on the things that had captured their attention immediately after they had eaten Piper's pie, which was obviously no simple apple dessert—it was bewitched. She and Wyatt hadn't ingested the magically tainted dessert, so they weren't affected. However, her baby boy couldn't help her figure out how to reverse the effects.

Piper paced, trying to organize a dozen relevant thoughts. Except for the hostility when she interfered with the objects of their interest, the family's obsessions were harmless and confined to the Manor. At least, for now.

Piper came to a dead halt when she suddenly realized the calamity was much wider in scope.

Three other pies had sold at the Police Precinct Bake Sale yesterday!

Piper rummaged in her bag for her cell phone and speed-dialed Darryl at home. His wife, Sheila, answered. "Can I please speak to Darryl?"

"No, he's playing computer games, and I don't want to be yelled at again." Sheila barely paused for breath. "I can't talk to you right now, Piper. I'm pulling everything out of my garden that doesn't match my new patio furniture. Bye!"

Piper stared at the phone when the line went dead. She didn't think Darryl and Sheila's obsessions would get them into serious trouble, but what about Captain Hoyt and the soon-to-be-married rookie Angie Shore? They were both cops, who might develop career-ending or dangerous fixations. And any obsession could get out of hand if left unchecked. . . .

Since Darryl was too focused on his computer games to talk, Piper had no quick way of finding the other affected police officers. Her only hope of insuring that no one came to harm was to find a reversal spell for the pie. Immediately.

When she heard the downstairs door close, Piper looked out the window. Leo was putting Wyatt in the car. How could she stop him when Leo interpreted everything as an attempt to separate him from his son? As soon as Wyatt was safely secured in his car seat, she froze Leo. From the street, it looked like he was still strapping Wyatt in.

"I'll just have to think of something on my way to the driveway."

By the time she reached the front door, Piper knew she

wouldn't be able to concentrate on the magical problem if she was worried about Leo running off with Wyatt. The solution was to keep husband and child where she could watch them while she worked on the spell. To accomplish that, she simply took Wyatt to the attic, unfroze Leo, and waited for him to arrive.

"Calm down, Leo." Piper jumped back when Leo stormed through the attic door. As planned, he headed straight for the baby playing on the carpeted floor. She closed and locked the door behind him. "Wyatt wanted to surprise you."

"Gah!" Wyatt held up a plastic dinosaur, one of several scattered around him. Then he picked up another and offered it to his father. "Pa-tah!"

Piper had been buying toys and clothes for Wyatt to grow into since she found out that she was pregnant, whenever she found something on sale that was too good to pass up. Today had been a good day to break open one of the bags.

And, to her great relief, Leo's raging-bull demeanor changed back to docile daddy the instant he saw Wyatt's happy face. On her way up to the attic with Wyatt, she had checked on her two obsessed sisters. Paige had been hand-washing Grams's crystal goblets while the dishwasher mechanically cleansed the everyday glasses. Phoebe was still on the sofa, locked into the TV and a sappy vampire saga called *Dreams to Die For.*

"You know what these dinosaurs need?" Leo asked Wyatt now.

Wyatt stared at his father without a clue.

"They need some plastic people to trample."

"That sounds like fun," Piper quipped as she sat down in the rocker. Although, she wasn't sure crushing play people was a good game to teach a boy with enormous powers.

"Isn't there a bag of toy soldiers up here?" Leo asked. "Phoebe used them in a school history project."

Piper reached behind the rocker for another bag of plastic

toys. "How 'bout some creepy crawly things instead."

"Snakes!" Leo took the bag and ripped it open. "And frogs and lizards. Cool, huh, Wyatt?"

Piper smiled, watching them. The spell just emphasized the very real and deep love Leo felt for his son. It was, however, a good thing she hadn't eaten the pie too. If she was obsessed with getting Grams's apple pie recipe right, she wouldn't be aware of the spell or the need now to reverse it.

Except she hadn't made Grams's old family recipe for apple pie. She had made someone else's recipe, and that someone was a Warren witch whose motives weren't merely culinary. Only a member of the family could have hidden the recipe spell in the Book of Shadows. And the only Warren witch she knew about who had turned evil was P. Russell.

Piper frowned, remembering their brief encounter with P. Russell—and wondered again why she'd never found out the woman's first name. Back in the 1920s P. Russell had broken with her cousins, P. Bowen and P. Baxter, when she fell for an immortal warlock named Anton. With P. Russell playing for the evil team, Anton knew it wouldn't take long until her good-witch cousins killed her—so he gave her a protective amulet. Of course, the good cousins killed her anyway.

The only clue Piper had was the handwritten recipe. Since she'd once met P. Russell, she knew it was possible that the long-dead cousin had stashed the recipe in the Book of Shadows as a prank before she'd turned evil, and while the book was still receptive to her. It was a long shot, but since the spell had been left in the Book of Shadows, maybe the reversal spell was somewhere in the Manor too. She didn't have any other ideas.

Piper retrieved the recipe spell, the blueprints for the house, and the scrying crystal. Holding the handwritten piece of linen stationery to guide the crystal, she held it over the diagram of the Victorian house. In less than a minute the crystal dropped, pinpointing a cabinet inside the pantry.

"Are you two going to behave if I leave for a few minutes?" Piper asked Leo.

"We're having a great time." Leo twined a plastic snake around a plastic T. rex. "Oh, no! He got me!"

"Gah!" Wyatt squealed and clapped when Leo made the dinosaur fall over.

"What's this?" Leo stood the dinosaur up again. "The dinosaur lives to fight . . . a giant frog!"

Satisfied that Leo and Wyatt were enjoying their dino duels too much to leave the attic, Piper hurried down to the kitchen. Paige was standing in front of the dishwasher, waiting for the drying cycle to finish.

"Finally," Paige exclaimed, when the dial clicked into the off position. She opened the dishwasher, removed a glass, and held it up to the light. "Spots," she muttered, scowling.

"How ever will we cope?" Piper quipped as she walked by toward the pantry.

"Like this," Paige said with a look of determined resolve.

Piper tensed. She had once made the entire Manor disappear during a cleaning frenzy induced by a witch doctor's hex. Since anything was possible under the influence of an unintentional, and thus unpredictable, spell, she prepared to freeze the glass in midair if Paige decided to trash it. She relaxed when Paige pulled a clean dishtowel from a drawer and rubbed the dried splatters off the glass.

After holding it up for a second sunlit inspection, Paige set the glass on the counter and took another out of the dishwasher. She wiped that one too.

"Missed a spot," Piper said as Paige started to put the glass down.

"Where?" Paige stooped to study both glasses.

Piper ducked into the pantry, stricken with a pang of guilt about the insensitive joke. Paige's single-minded effort to make the family dishes sparkle was a constructive endeavor, and Leo was spending quality time with Wyatt. Phoebe was just losing sleep, getting eyestrain, and numbing her brain on old B movies. The harmless obsessions were amusing, but there wasn't anything funny about magically altering her family's behavior.

"Even though it was an accident," Piper muttered as she opened the corner cupboard on the left.

The shelves were crammed with empty canning jars, cookie tins, and other kitchen paraphernalia. Since scrying wasn't an exact magical discipline, the crystal hadn't pinpointed where the counterspell or antidote to the toxic pie was hidden.

Piper took everything out of the cabinet, then ran her hand under the shelves and over the sides, top, and bottom. The wooden surfaces were smooth, with no loose panels. Curbing a rising alarm, Piper started to close the door. The yellowed page from an old magazine that was tacked to the inside of the door caught her eye. The apple tart recipe had been there as long as she could remember, and she usually just glanced past it. Today she took a closer look.

The publication date at the bottom of the magazine page was October 20, 1920.

Phoebe's evil predecessor, P. Russell, lived in the Manor with P. Bowen and P. Baxter in the early 1920s, Piper thought, frowning. P. Russell was a flirtatious tart; the poison pie was a kind of apple tart; and the scrying crystal had matched the recipe with the cabinet. Although the connections were a stretch, she doubted they were a coincidence. In the Charmed universe, coincidence was rare.

Piper removed the rusted thumbtack at the bottom of the page, but the paper had been on the door so long, it stuck to the painted wood. She went back to the kitchen for a knife, then loosened the edges of the aged clipping. A folded piece of linen stationery embossed with the name P. Baxter fell into her hand. Piper carefully opened the paper. Inside, written in her great-grandmother's elegant script, was the spell to neutralize the black magic in P. Russell's apple pie.

Piper wondered if Grams had left the clipping undisturbed because her mother had tacked it on the cupboard door or if she had known it masked a hidden spell that might be important someday.

"Maybe both," Piper said as she returned to the kitchen.

Paige had been too busy wiping smudges off glasses to notice when Piper took the knife. However, she zeroed in when Piper brought it back. "I'll take that, Piper."

Piper didn't argue. She just handed Paige the knife and sat down.

"What's that?" Paige asked as she dropped the knife in the dishwasher basket.

"The reversal spell for vengeance pie," Piper said. "Great-grandma Baxter left it in the pantry."

"That's nice." Paige began putting the spotless glasses back in the cabinet.

"Uh-huh," Piper said as she read the brief explanation contained in P. Baxter's note. She wanted to know why the pie recipe had been written and hidden in the Book of Shadows. Paige wouldn't care why some long-dead ancestor's spite pie had bewitched her until *after* she was cured.

According to the note Piper found, P. Russell had concocted the cursed pie when a lover jilted her for a mortal woman. Playing the good soldier, she offered the recipe to the woman, claiming it had always been his favorite. After eating the pie, the man ignored his new love and became obsessed with alphabetizing all the books in his extensive library. When P. Baxter discovered what her cousin had done, she quickly devised and administered an antidote, and then demanded that P. Russell turn the recipe over to her. Of course, P. Russell refused, so Piper's great-grandmother, P. Baxter, had put the antidote on the cupboard door to protect innocent descendants who might stumble upon the recipe and accidentally bake an enchanted apple pie.

After a quick read through of the reversal spell, Piper began assembling the ingredients. The herbs and spices in the antidote were as common and—on the surface—as harmless as the seasonings P. Russell had used in the pie. The proportions and the order that the ingredients were combined endowed the mixtures with magical properties.

"What are you doing?" Paige asked when Piper set several jars and sealed bags of dried herbs on the counter.

"Mixing a potion." Piper pulled a pestle and mortar out of one cabinet and took ordinary measuring spoons from the utensil drawer. She set a cutting board and knife beside them, poured a half cup of water into a pan, and set the pan on the stove. She set the burner on medium heat, then pulled three sprigs of dried clove out of a bag.

"How long will this take?" Paige hovered behind Piper.

"A few minutes." Piper tried to ignore the obsessed sister peering over her shoulder as she cut the flowery tops off the clove sprigs. When she set the knife aside, Paige's hand shot out.

"Mine now." Paige snared the knife with the swift accuracy of a frog snagging a fly.

Piper was quicker. Her hand clamped over Paige's wrist, pinning it to the table. "I'm not done with that yet."

"But it's dirty," Paige protested.

"It doesn't matter," Piper said. "I'm mixing everything together. You can have it as soon as I'm finished. Promise."

"Whatever." Paige let go of the knife, but she didn't move away. She watched as Piper crushed the clove flowers in the mortar, measured one-half teaspoon—exactly the amount called for on her great-grandmother's antidote recipe—and added the clove to the half cup of water simmering on the stove.

The instant Piper set down the measuring spoons, Paige orbed them into the sink.

"Hey!" Piper complained. "I still need those!"

"Oh, all right!" Exasperated, Paige threw up her arms and stomped over to the sink. She washed and dried the measuring spoons and handed them back in a huff.

"Thank you." Piper inhaled deeply to calm herself. She figured she needed nine doses of the vengeance pie antidote potion. So far, she knew her sisters, Leo, Darryl, and Sheila had eaten the pie—and assumed Captain Hoyt, his wife, Officer Angie Shore, and Angie's fiancé had sampled it too. But right now, she only needed one dose to solve the Paige problem. If Paige was working with her instead of against her, they could whip up the remaining eight batches in less time with a lot less hassle.

"Will you *please* finish so I can clean up this mess?" Paige asked impatiently.

"I'll hurry, if you'll sit over there until I'm done." Piper pointed to a stool by the counter.

Paige hesitated. "Then will you let me finish washing the dishes?"

"Yes," Piper agreed. "You can clean all the dishes you want—*after* you taste-test this herbal tea. It's an old folk remedy for stress." She picked up a balm of Gilead leaf, which was often used in folk tonics to reduce tension.

Paige peered at the assortment of herbs, wrinkled her nose, and then shrugged. "Okay. I have been a little strung out today."

"A little." Smiling, Piper waved Paige over to the stool.

Ignoring her sister's intense but silent scrutiny, Piper crumbled the dry leaf in the mortar. She added powdered elecampane root to eliminate the angry, violent impulses associated with vengeance and combined the two herbs with the pestle. On the cutting board, she crushed a eucalyptus seed, chopped a dried apple blossom, and mixed them together to restore emotional balance. After she scraped everything into the simmering brew on the stove, she added a dash of dragon's blood to activate the potion and stirred vigorously for exactly thirty seconds.

"Ready!" Piper poured the antidote into a cup. The acrid aroma stung her nostrils as she handed the cup to Paige. "I guarantee, you'll feel terrific after you drink this."

Paige didn't look convinced. She cautiously sniffed the warm liquid and took a small sip. Her whole face contorted with disgust. "It's bitter."

"Trust me," Piper said. "The effects are worth it."

Paige paused a second, then chugged the tea. She shuddered with another look of disgust as she set down the cup. "How long before I mellow out?"

"Instantly, I hope." Piper glanced at the empty cup. Paige was obviously in no hurry to put it in the dishwasher.

"I don't think it's working." Paige grimaced. "The aftertaste is so foul, I feel like throwing things."

"But do you feel like washing more dishes?" Piper raised an expectant eyebrow, but she already knew that the potion had worked.

"Actually, no." Paige glanced at the soiled utensils on the counter.

"Good. Okay, I'll explain," Piper said as she rinsed the pan and dishes, "while I make potions for Phoebe and Leo."

"What are they cleaning?" Paige didn't offer to help. She just watched.

"Nothing." Piper measured a cup of water into the pan and set the pan back on the warm burner. "Phoebe's watching old movies on TV, and Leo is playing with Wyatt."

"How did I get stuck with marathon KP duty?" Paige asked, annoyed.

"You volunteered." Piper glanced at Paige with a mischievous twinkle in her eye. "At least we know the antidote works," she continued as she cut the tops off of six sprigs of clove.

"Antidote to what?" Paige asked.

"I'll explain while you help me make more tea," Piper replied.

Piper had a large supply of ingredients, so she could afford to experiment now that she knew the potion worked. If a double batch proved to be effective, they could cut the prep time in half and get to her other victims twice as fast.

"This is ready," Piper said as she finished stirring the second batch. She divided the bitter tea into two cups and handed one to Paige. "Phoebe first."

Phoebe was stretched out on the sofa, engrossed in a classic 1950s murder mystery.

"I brought you some tea, Phoebe," Piper said. "It might help you stay awake."

"Thanks." Phoebe's gaze didn't drift from the screen as she sat up and took the cup. She was so mesmerized by the black-and-white film, she drank the antidote down before the stench and the taste registered on her senses. When the potion hit her stomach, she snapped out of her obsessive daze in a fit of coughing. "Are you trying to poison me, Piper?"

"No," Paige said. "She already did that with the pie."

"Why did you poison Grams's apple pie recipe?" Phoebe asked, stunned.

"I didn't," Piper explained. "There are apparently *two* old family recipes for apple pie. I baked the pie that makes people fixate on the first thing that grabs their attention after they eat it."

"So I watched TV all night instead of reading my book." Phoebe used the remote to turn off the TV.

"At least you don't have dishpan hands like Paige," Piper offered as solace.

"Maybe next time you'll both listen when I warn you," Paige said. "Witch plus apple pie equals evil spell. It's like the worst kept secret in the magic world."

"Can we talk about this later?" Phoebe asked, yawning. "I need a nap."

"No time for sleeping now." Piper grabbed Phoebe's hand and yanked her upright. "Darryl and two other cops bought my pies at the bake sale yesterday."

Paige winced. "That can't be good."

"Darryl's playing computer games and Sheila's working in her garden," Piper said. "That's probably not a major problem, but we don't know what effect the pies had on everyone else."

"Who just happen to be *cops*," Paige added.

Exactly, Piper thought. Captain Hoyt and Angie Shore could be focused on some harmless after-dinner chore or entertainment. *Or they could be locked into a law enforcement imperative to arrest criminals, endangering themselves and maybe even innocent bystanders.*

"Leo's in the attic with Wyatt." Piper waved Paige and Phoebe toward the stairs. "Go give him the cure while I start making more antidote. He needs to be thinking rationally to babysit while we go clean up my magical mess."

"You didn't bake bewitched pies on purpose, Piper," Paige said.

"I know, but—" Although Piper hadn't meant to put anyone in jeopardy, nothing could change certain cold, hard facts. "If anything bad happens because of the pies, it will be my fault."

Forty minutes later Paige orbed the Charmed Ones into Darryl's garage. They had planned to cure Darryl first, but a commotion in the yard diverted their attention.

"I don't care if your husband is a cop, Sheila," a man said loudly. "If you touch my shrubs, I'm going to have you arrested."

Piper, Phoebe, and Paige looked out the back door. A chubby, middle-age man dressed in a Hawaiian shirt and shorts stood between Sheila and a row of bushes that grew along the boundary between yards. The bushes were in full bloom with bright orange flowers.

"But your shrubs clash with my new patio furniture!" Sheila countered. A woman of impeccable taste who usually dressed with refinement, she was wearing jean shorts, a T-shirt streaked with dirt, and sneakers. Clumps of hair escaped the clasp perched high on her head. She gripped the long handles of a pruning tool in gloved hands. "My furniture print is pink, lavender, and green on white. No orange. Your flowers have to go."

The three witches all glanced toward the gardens around Darryl's screened-in patio. All the plants with yellow, red, or orange blooms had been pulled out by the roots and piled in heaps. One of Sheila's new chairs propped the door open.

"She's right," Phoebe said. "Orange flowers don't go with that color scheme at all."

Piper knew that in her right mind, Sheila Morris would never instigate a hostile showdown with her neighbor, not even if he had painted his house iridescent chartreuse.

"I'm warning you, Sheila—" Sheila's neighbor pulled his cell phone out of his pocket to dial. He was completely caught off guard when she bolted past him toward his shrubbery with the pruning blades to cut the offensive orange flowers off the bushes.

Piper didn't want to contemplate what might happen if the

man got in the way of Sheila's determination to color-coordinate his landscaping with her chaise lounge.

"No! Don't!" he yelled as Sheila's pruners started to close around a brilliant orange flower. He dropped his phone and leaped to tackle his crazed neighbor.

Since the situation was a magical emergency, the Charmed Ones could use their powers as long as no one noticed. Piper sprang through the garage door and froze the man just as he hit the ground—before his hands closed around Sheila's ankles. If a neighbor was watching, it looked as though he needed a moment to catch his breath.

"Sheila!" Phoebe yelled.

Sheila ignored the call, but the pruners turned to glittering light just as she snapped the blades closed. The orange blossom remained attached to its stem with a split second to spare. Furious, Sheila turned and stormed toward them. Piper released the neighbor as the orbed pruners materialized in Paige's hand. He looked a little stunned as he rubbed his grass-stained knees, but since Sheila had broken off her attack on his shrubs, he beat a hasty retreat into his house.

"What are you doing here?" Sheila demanded.

"We came to see your new patio furniture," Phoebe said.

"And to ask you to try this." Piper uncapped one of the antidote vials and handed it to Sheila. "It's something new I'm testing for P3."

When Sheila hesitated, Paige held out the pruners as a bribe. "If you drink it, I'll give these back. Otherwise, there's no telling where they might end up."

"Okay, fine." Anxious to get back to her gardening, Sheila swallowed the bitter potion and instantly reverted to her normal persona. "Please, tell me I didn't just threaten my neighbor with my pruners."

"You didn't," Paige said. "You threatened his flowers."

"I'm sure you can smooth things over, Sheila," Piper said. "But right now, we need to get Darryl to try this."

"Good luck." Sheila rolled her eyes. "He threatened to cut up my credit cards if I interrupted his game again. And—no offense, Piper, but what is that drink? Wheatgrass? It's horrible!"

The Charmed Ones found Darryl sitting at the computer in his den. An intricate maze populated with cartoon monsters and traps filled the screen. Darryl was concentrating on the game and didn't hear them come in.

"Come on," Darryl mumbled to himself. "If I can just get past that last shark—"

"Break time," Paige announced as she pulled the cap off another vial.

Crash-and-burn sounds blared from the computer speakers.

"What!" Darryl stared at the monitor for a moment before he slowly turned around. His eyes were wide and manic. "I've been trying for *hours* to get past that level. One more minute and I would have had it."

"Drink this, and believe me"—Paige held out the vial—"you won't care."

"Not care?" Darryl jumped up and kicked the desk in a fit of fury. "Do you have any idea how hard it is to get past level eighteen? It's practically impossible, and I was this close! This close—"

"Sorry, Darryl, but we don't have time for this." While he ranted, his mouth was open just wide enough for Phoebe to pour the potion in. Darryl froze, then swallowed, sputtering. "Gross does not even begin to describe how vile that stuff tastes. What was it?"

"A potion to reverse the effects of my pie," Piper said.

"Effects?" Darryl asked, frowning. "What effects?"

"Obsessions," Paige answered. "I bet you decided to relax with a computer game right after dinner last night."

"Yeah, I—" Darryl's puzzled expression changed to panic. "Captain Hoyt and Angie. They bought your pies too."

"And if they ate them, they're obsessing about something too," Piper said. "That's why we came to you first. We don't know where the captain and Angie live."

"Let's start with the captain," Darryl said, adjusting to the bizarre circumstances without hesitation. He grabbed his jacket off the desk chair and hurried toward the door. "I don't know where Angie lives, but Captain Hoyt probably does."

"That's what we're counting on," Paige said.

Darryl paused to level Piper with an accusatory glance. "I thought you said you didn't need magic to bake pies."

"I don't!"

"It wasn't Piper's fault, Darryl," Phoebe interjected. "She didn't know that old family recipe was a vengeance spell."

Darryl nodded. "Too bad. That was good apple pie."

"We have to orb, Darryl," Piper said. "We can't take the time to drive."

Captain Wayne Hoyt and his wife lived in a town house a few blocks from the precinct. Mrs. Hoyt, a stout woman in her late forties with a round face and short dark hair, answered the door. She looked frazzled and upset.

"Inspector Morris," Mrs. Hoyt said, clutching Darryl's arm. "I'm so glad you're here. Wayne wouldn't let me call anyone, and I didn't know what to do."

"Call anyone about what?" Darryl asked calmly. The woman was near hysteria, and he didn't want to tip her over the edge.

"He's been downstairs working out since dinner last night." The woman whispered, as though that would diminish the problem. "He brought an apple pie home from the bake sale, and he wanted to work off the two pieces he ate for dessert."

"Did you eat any?" Piper asked.

Mrs. Hoyt shook her head. "Pie isn't on my diet."

"Why don't you sit with Paige and Phoebe for a few minutes, Mrs. Hoyt," Darryl suggested. "Piper and I will check on Wayne."

Piper followed Darryl down the stairs into a paneled recreation room. Captain Hoyt was hunched over the handlebars of an exercise bicycle, barely holding on, pedaling at slow speed. Sweat trickled down the sides of his face. The man was too exhausted to talk, but his weary eyes begged for relief.

"Your wife said you were trying to break some kind of record," Darryl said, giving the cop an acceptable explanation for his compulsive behavior. "I brought a high-potency vitamin booster to replenish your energies—if you want it."

Captain Hoyt managed a weak nod.

Piper took the cap off another vial and gave it to the tired man. He drank it, then slid off the bike onto the floor.

"Are you okay?" Piper asked as the captain dragged himself to an old sofa.

"I'll—be fine," Captain Hoyt rasped, struggling to catch his breath as he curled up. "I just need some . . . rest."

"First I need to know where Angie Shore lives," Darryl said. When his boss didn't respond, Darryl shook the man's shoulder. "Captain?"

"Forget it, Darryl," Piper said. "He's asleep."

Darryl stood up with a resigned sigh. "I don't want to alarm anyone at the department by calling there for her information. . . . It might raise gossip."

"Maybe Mrs. Hoyt knows where we can find Angie?" Piper suggested.

As Piper followed Darryl back upstairs, she couldn't shake a sense of dread. So far nothing awful had happened. Captain Hoyt had taxed his physical limits and Sheila had almost come to blows with her neighbor, but no permanent damage had been done. The odds did not favor an equally benign outcome for Angie Shore.

"I don't have Angie's phone number," Mrs. Hoyt said. She thought for a moment, and then her face lit up. She pulled an envelope from a stack of mail on the counter. "But I have her address on the wedding invitation RSVP. Will that help?"

"May I?" Phoebe took the envelope from Mrs. Hoyt's hand. Her expression blanked when she touched the paper.

A vision, Piper thought, tensing. She diverted Mrs. Hoyt's attention so she wouldn't notice the sudden change in Phoebe's demeanor.

When Phoebe emerged from the trance, she drew everyone aside. "Angie has a gun, and she's threatening to shoot a man who's cleaning her apartment."

"That's probably her fiancé," Darryl said. "He's a neat freak, which drives her crazy, but she loves him." Noticing Piper's strange look at him, he added, "What? I talk to her a lot at work. Or, I should say, *she* talks to me a lot."

"We've got to get over there," Phoebe urged. "Now."

"You guys go," Darryl said. "I'll stay here to make sure Wayne doesn't develop any delayed complications. He's not in bad shape for his age, but nobody's heart is indestructible."

"Thanks, Darryl. Talk to you later." Piper and her sisters raced to the front hall. Armed with information from Phoebe's vision, they orbed into Angie's apartment behind the bedroom door.

"Put those back, Robert!" Angie's voice rose in anger. "My bills are none of your business."

"It'll be my business after we're married," Robert countered hotly. "How do you know what you've paid and what you haven't? They're just tossed here in a heap."

"I know, okay?" Angie retorted. "I don't want you organizing my stuff. I want you to talk to me!"

Piper quickly deduced that Robert probably kept his desire to organize Angie's apartment under control. Then P. Russell's pie had unleashed his compulsion.

"What are you going to do?" Robert asked. "Shoot me?"

"If that's the only way I can get your attention," Angie said. "Then yes, I'm going to shoot you."

The Charmed Ones didn't need to confer before acting. Piper stepped into the open doorway and froze the couple before they saw her. She noticed that the half-eaten apple pie was on the counter, covered in plastic wrap. There was no doubt that the bewitched dessert had caused the lovers' spat.

The couple had been yelling when Piper froze them, so their mouths were open wide enough for Piper and Phoebe to pour in the antidotes while Paige pried the gun from Angie's grip. She removed the bullets, then slid it back into the officer's hand. When they returned to the bedroom, Paige positioned herself so she could watch the young couple without being seen.

When Robert unfroze, he swallowed and fell to his knees, gagging.

Angie's first inclination was to spit out the bitter liquid that had mysteriously appeared in her mouth. Paige orbed it back in twice before the young policewoman finally swallowed it.

"What happened?" Leo asked when the three sisters orbed back into the Manor sunroom. Wyatt was asleep in the playpen.

"We managed to get the antidote potion into everyone," Piper explained. "But I don't think we'll know if any real harm was done until later." She cast a glance around the room, thankful that all her loved ones were back to normal. "Okay, then! Who wants dinner?"

Piper spent the afternoon in the kitchen, fixing her family's favorite dinner dishes. She wanted to keep busy so she wouldn't worry about the aftereffects of P. Russell's spell. Besides, she owed her family a special treat for accidentally bewitching them.

"That was a fantastic dinner, Piper," Paige said, leaning back with a satisfied sigh. "Thanks."

"Ham with pineapple raisin sauce is my favorite." Leo wiped the sticky, sweet glaze off Wyatt's chin and fingers. "You like it too, huh?"

"I loved the au gratin potatoes made from scratch." Phoebe reached for the bowl to help herself to seconds.

"You might want to wait on that, Phoebe," Piper said. "I made—" The ringing phone cut her off.

Paige orbed the cordless phone to the table. "Sorry, but I'm too full to get up."

"You're forgiven this time," Piper said as she answered. Darryl was calling to report.

Paige leaned forward as Piper hung up. "Are we busted?"

"Not this time," Piper said with relief. "Captain Hoyt *is* worried about staying fit. He thinks he just got carried away trying to work off the extra calories from his second helping of pie, but he doesn't want anyone to know he overreacted. He swore Darryl and his wife to secrecy."

"What about Angie and Robert?" Phoebe asked.

"Angie called Mrs. Hoyt while Darryl was still there," Piper said. "Angie and Robert broke off their engagement."

"Is that our fault?" Paige asked.

Piper shook her head. "Apparently they had both been having second thoughts. Robert really didn't want to marry someone who can't cook and clean, and Angie really didn't want a man who thinks a working wife *should* cook and clean."

"That's good then." Leo put another dab of pineapple sauce in Wyatt's bowl. Wyatt dipped the tip of his finger into the sweet goo then stuck his finger in his mouth. "What about Sheila? Did she make amends with the neighbor?"

Piper nodded. "Darryl told him that Sheila was really mad at him for playing computer games all weekend. And, since he brought the magic pie home from the bake sale, he promised to help her replant the gardens she tore up."

"Well, that could have been worse," Phoebe said.

"For sure," Paige agreed. "Shouldn't we get rid of P. Russell's recipe before some unsuspecting descendant decides to try the famous family apple pie?"

"I tore up the recipe for vengeance pie," Piper said, "but I still wish I had the *real* old family recipe."

"You know," Phoebe said. "I'm not sure Grams's apple pie tasted as great as we remember, Piper. I think we just like to think so because we loved her so much."

"Could be," Piper said as she stood up.

"I won't argue that," Paige said, frowning. "I vote for no more apple pie in this family ever. It's obviously the dessert of choice for evil witches everywhere."

"Well, I sure hope no evil entities have a claim on this." Piper carried a covered dessert stand from the sideboard to the table.

"What is it?" Paige asked with a wary look.

"My second favorite dessert," Piper said as she removed the cover. "Boston cream pie."

"Are you sure it's safe?" Paige asked, teasing.

"Positive," Piper said. "It's cake."

Family History

Laura J. Burns

"I thought we were supposed to have a relaxing weekend!" Paige Matthews yelled.

"What?" her half sister Phoebe Halliwell called back. "I can't hear over the tornado!"

Paige rolled her eyes. The tornado was the whole problem. On a normal relaxing weekend, there wouldn't be a tornado in the living room. She took a deep breath and prepared to yell louder. "I said—"

"It's changing." Piper Halliwell, Paige's other half sister, spoke in her usual steady, quiet voice. Miraculously that worked better than the yelling. "It's taking form."

Paige squinted into the wind from the ministorm. The funnel cloud reached from the rug up to the ceiling, but now it was starting to squeeze in on itself. Through the dark, swirling air she could make out the beginning of a form—kind of human . . . kind of not.

She shot a questioning look at Piper. "Any ideas?" she asked in her own normal voice.

"Nope," Piper replied. "It's not orbing, and it's not shimmering. So we can rule out Whitelighters and all the usual demons."

"What kind of demon storms in?" Phoebe asked. "Or should I say 'twisters' in?"

Paige shrugged. "A wicked witch?"

The wind stopped abruptly, and with it the loud rumbling sound of the ministorm. Paige caught her breath. This was always the most interesting moment—the first sighting of a new magical enemy. She'd known for a couple of years now that she was a Charmed One, a member of the most powerful trio of witches in history. She'd gotten used to fighting various demons and monsters and warlocks. But it was still a trip every time a new one showed up—scary and exciting all at once.

This one blew them all away.

She was tall, at least eight feet. Her humongous body was covered in gleaming silver armor, form fitting enough to show that she had the body of a human woman. Well, a really gigantic human woman. But her head was anything but womanly. It was the head of a bull, complete with sharp, curved horns.

"Holy cow," Phoebe cracked.

The bull demon's nostrils flared in anger.

"Uh, I don't think she has a sense of humor," Paige said. "Anyone recognize her?"

Her sisters shook their heads. This particular monster didn't look familiar to Paige, either, and she'd spent a lot of time studying the various demons in the Halliwells' Book of Shadows, where her ancestors had kept all their notes and stories about the demons they'd fought. *Maybe she's not a demon,* Paige thought hopefully. *Maybe she's friendly, and she's just under an enchantment or something.*

The bull demon lifted one armor-plated hand and shot a lightning bolt at Piper. Piper leaped out of the way just in time and held up her hands to freeze the demon. But the bull demon simply aimed again and hurled another bolt of energy at Piper.

"Okay, she's not freezing," Piper gasped, jumping out of the way of the second bolt. "A little help, anyone?"

Paige frowned. Not freezing was bad. Piper had the power to freeze all but the most powerful demons. Which meant that this particular demon must fall into that category.

"Can you blow her up?" Phoebe asked.

Piper shook her head. "If I can't freeze them, I can't blow them up either."

The demon's hand raised again, forming another lightning bolt. "Then I guess it's my turn," Paige cried. "Lightning bolt!" The stream of electricity orbed away from her sisters and toward Paige's outstretched hand. Before it could hit her, she orbed it back at the bull demon. The shock hit the intruder, ran up and over her silver armor, and centered on her head, burning brightly. Paige held her breath. Would it do the trick?

The bull demon gave a little shimmy and the current ran back down her body, obscuring Paige's view. When the energy hit the floor again it went out, leaving behind a tall, astonishingly beautiful woman.

Phoebe's mouth dropped open. "What happened to the cow-monster thing?" she asked, climbing over the armchair to join Paige and Piper near the doorway to the foyer.

"I don't know," Piper replied helplessly.

"She is *gorgeous*," Paige murmured, studying the amazon who now stood where the bull demon had been. The woman was still eight feet tall. But now she was dressed in a skimpy sarong that showed off her voluptuous body. Her face was so beautiful that all Paige could think to do was stare.

The woman lifted her arms and hurled a lightning bolt at them.

"Whoa!" Phoebe cried, pushing Paige in one direction and Piper in the other. She threw herself to the floor just as the stream of energy crackled through the air where they'd been standing.

"Okay, I've had enough of this," Piper said angrily. She glanced over her shoulder toward the playpen in the corner of the room. Her son, Wyatt, was watching the fight with wide, frightened eyes. Paige knew they didn't have to worry about Wyatt. He had his own strong powers, and if this amazon demon tried to go anywhere near him, he'd put up his protective shield.

"How do we vanquish her?" Phoebe yelled.

The amazon threw back her head and laughed, a sound like thunder. Phoebe put her hands over her ears to block it out as it bounced off the walls of the living room. Wyatt began to cry.

What can we do? Paige thought frantically. Her powers wouldn't vanquish this demon and neither would her sisters'. She racked her brain for any information she'd heard about giant, loud, lightning-throwing bull-women. Nothing. Paige nervously reached for the amulet she had begun wearing on a chain around her wrist. She'd found it in the attic a few months before and a little research in the Book of Shadows had revealed that it belonged to an ancestor of hers, Prudence Warren. It was a protection amulet given to baby Prudence by her mother, Melinda, and Paige had a superstitious belief that it would protect her, too.

It was gone.

"My amulet," she cried.

"My baby!" Piper shrieked.

Paige whirled toward the playpen. But it wasn't there. The playpen was gone, and so was Wyatt.

"What happened?" Phoebe demanded, stalking toward the amazon. "Where is my nephew?"

The woman, still laughing her earsplitting laugh, lifted her hands to throw another bolt at Phoebe. Piper had gone momentarily catatonic, staring at the place where Wyatt had been.

This was getting seriously out of control. Paige knew she had to do something, and fast. She grabbed Piper's hand and yanked her toward Phoebe. "Power of Three," she yelled. "We need to get her out of the Manor."

Phoebe nodded and grabbed her hand. Together they recited the spell to rid Halliwell Manor of evil:

When in the circle that is home,
Safety's gone and evils roam,
Rid all beings from these walls,
Save us sisters three.
Now heed our call.

The amazon's lovely face twisted into an expression of shocked outrage, and then she vanished into thin air.

Paige was breathing hard, still clinging to her sisters' hands. Had they vanquished the demon? It was hard to tell.

A little whimper escaped Piper's lips. Paige turned to find her sister staring at the corner of the room. The playpen was still gone, and so was Wyatt. Even if they had managed to vanquish the demon, they still hadn't reversed whatever magic had taken the baby.

Phoebe put her arm around Piper's shoulders. "We'll find him," she murmured. "We know evil can't harm him, so he's fine. We just have to find him."

At Phoebe's words Piper seemed to snap out of her daze. "Leo!" she yelled.

Instantly their Whitelighter—and Piper's husband—orbed into the room in a swirl of bright light. "What?" he cried, casting worried eyes around the room. "What happened? Where's Wyatt?"

"That's what we want to know," Piper said. "He's gone. We were fighting a demon and he just vanished."

"What demon?" Leo said. "No demon should be able to touch him."

"That's the weird thing," Paige put in. "She didn't touch him. As far as I can tell, she never even looked at him."

"You're right." Phoebe bit her lip. "Wyatt just disappeared in the middle of the fight, but he was never involved in the fight at all. The demon didn't seem to be after him."

"He's not the only thing that vanished," Paige told them. "My amulet disappeared too. And the demon didn't touch that, either."

"What kind of demon was she?" Leo asked.

Piper shrugged helplessly. "We didn't recognize her. She started out having a bull's head, and then she changed into a beautiful woman."

"A giant beautiful woman," Paige added. "With a really loud laugh."

"Let me check with the Elders," Leo said. He squeezed Piper's hand. "I'll be right back."

As he orbed out of the room, Paige noticed that Phoebe was looking a little ill. "Phoebes? You okay?" she asked.

"No," Phoebe whispered. "I'm having visions." She sank onto the couch. Paige and Piper exchanged a worried glance. Phoebe's premonitions didn't usually make her sick.

"Visions, plural?" Piper asked. "As in *many* visions?"

Phoebe nodded. "It's hard to make them all out. I can't even tell . . . I think it's from the past. I see Grams and Mom."

"What are they doing?" Paige asked.

"There's someone else. I don't recognize her," Phoebe went on. "That one's in the future, I think. But there's one in a long dress, too. That's the past."

"She sounds delirious," Piper said, worried.

"No, I'm okay," Phoebe said weakly. "There are just so many visions all at once." She raised her tired brown eyes to her sisters.

"Everyone is fighting that demon," she murmured. "Most of them are in the Manor." Phoebe's eyes rolled back in her head and she passed out.

"Okay, what is going on?" Paige cried. "What happened to Phoebe?"

The room filled with white light again as Leo orbed back in. "It's an ancient demon. So ancient that she used to be considered a god," he said in a rush.

Piper narrowed her eyes. "What god?"

"Her name is Astarte," Leo said. "She once ruled ancient Sumeria. She led the people to believe that she was a goddess of war and also of fertility. She enslaved them all."

"Well, that explains the armor and the bodaciousness," Paige said. "I still don't get the bull head, though."

"She's a force of evil," Leo told them. "As far as the Elders were aware, she'd been out of commission, slumbering for thousands of years now."

"Well, it looks like somebody woke her up," Piper said. "But why did she come after us? And where's Wyatt?"

"And what's wrong with Phoebe?" Paige demanded.

Leo sat on the couch next to Phoebe and took her hand. He frowned as he concentrated on healing her. Finally he shook his head. "It won't work. There's nothing wrong with her, really. She's just overwhelmed with visions."

"She said she was seeing other witches, our ancestors maybe, and that most of them were fighting Astarte here in the Manor," Piper said.

Leo's eyes went wide.

"Uh-oh," Paige murmured. When Leo got that panicked expression, it meant things were *really* bad.

"That's what's so dangerous about Astarte," Leo said. "She's not bound by one dimension, so time has no meaning to her. She can exist in the past, present, or future."

"So you think when we got rid of her, she went to the past?" Paige asked.

"That's just it," Leo said. "She can exist in different times *simultaneously*. She could be in 1962, or 1654, or 2040, or all of those times at once. Right now. Attacking your ancestors or your descendants all at the same time. That's what Phoebe's seeing. All the Halliwell witches, of all times, fighting for their lives."

Piper paced up and down in front of the couch. Leo and Paige watched her with worried eyes. She knew she must seem a little crazy—she'd been pacing for ten minutes straight. But Phoebe was still passed out on the couch, and Wyatt was still gone. They were no closer to figuring out how to deal with this demon, or god, or whatever she was.

"So we think Astarte is attacking our ancestors right this very second," Piper said.

"And probably your descendants, too," Leo replied.

"Maybe we should go back to the past and help them fight her," Piper suggested. "We're more powerful than any of our ancestor witches. They didn't have the Power of Three."

"Um, I don't think *we* really have it right now either," Paige pointed out. "Phoebe is completely out of commission."

"Anyway, your powers won't work in the past," Leo said wearily.

"Right." Piper kept pacing. The mirror on the wall vanished. That was the third strange thing that had happened in the past ten minutes. First Phoebe's hair had suddenly become long. Then the grandfather clock in the hallway, which had been blown up more than it had kept time, started bonging. Now the mirror. "What is going on?" Piper demanded.

"I think it's a time issue," Leo said. "Astarte is attacking the other witches. If something happens in the past, it affects the present."

"So you think Astarte forced one of our ancestors to fix the grandfather clock in the past?" Paige asked skeptically.

"No, it's not that simple," Leo said. "Every single action we take, no matter how tiny and insignificant, has an effect on the future. For all we know, that grandfather clock got broken in a fight between your great-great-grandma and a demon. But if Astarte hurt or killed your great-great-grandma at a point in the past *before* the fight, then the grandfather clock never got broken."

"And the demon never had to deal with our great-great-grandma," Piper finished. "So now there's one more demon in the world."

"I'm not saying that's exactly what happened. It's just a guess," Leo told her.

But Piper knew that her husband's guesses were usually pretty accurate. He'd been around long enough to understand how things worked. "But what about Wyatt?" she demanded. "What does any of this have to do with him?"

"I don't know." Leo looked as helpless as she felt. "Astarte must have changed something, somewhere, that resulted in Wyatt being wiped out of the timeline. When you say he simply disappeared, it sounds to me as if he just ceased to exist. Like the mirror on the wall."

"Do you think that's what happened to my amulet?" Paige asked. "If Astarte managed to get to Melinda Warren before she ever gave the amulet to her daughter, then the amulet never would have been in the Manor for me to find."

"If Astarte killed Melinda Warren, none of us would be here," Piper argued. "She's the witch who started our bloodline here in America." As the words left her mouth, their meaning sunk in. That was the idea. That was Astarte's plan—to erase the Charmed Ones from existence, just as she'd erased Wyatt.

She stopped pacing and whirled around to her husband and

her sisters. "She's trying to get rid of us," she cried. "The Power of Three worked against her, so she has to kill us some other way. And she's going to do that by attacking *all* of us—every witch of the Warren bloodline, from Melinda on down!"

All the color drained from Paige's cheeks and she nodded. "Astarte is attacking everywhere at once—well, every *time* at once—because it's easier than attacking us directly."

"It's impossible to pick one single event in the past that led to the three of you being born," Leo said. "But if she attacks all the other witches, past and future, chances are that she'll make enough changes in the time line to get rid of you. Maybe things will change so that your mom only had two daughters. Or so that one of you became evil . . ."

"There are so many ways she can ruin the Power of Three," Piper murmured. "The only reason we're still here right now is that we're lucky. She hasn't killed the right Warren witch yet."

Paige stood. "No. We're still here because all the other witches are fighting. Our ancestors and our descendants are at war with this evil demon right now. We have to help them."

Piper glanced around the room. The wallpaper had changed to a black and white toile. She knew that minor changes like that were going to keep coming. But they had to help their family witches before *major* changes happened. "Okay," she said. "Phoebe's visions showed that most of the other witches were fighting Astarte here in the Manor."

Paige ran toward the kitchen. "Protection spell," she called over her shoulder.

"Exactly." Piper grabbed a pad and a pen and quickly began writing a protection spell. She knew Paige was making a sage-and-apple mixture to spread around the outside of the house. By the time her half sister came back in from making a circle around the Manor,

Piper was ready. She and Paige joined hands and read:

For every witch, in every hour,
Send us now the greatest power.
Brick and mortar, wood and stone,
Protect our center, protect our home.

Nothing changed. The mirror was still gone and the grand-father clock still ticked in the hallway. But Phoebe slowly opened her eyes.

"Ugh," she said. "That sucked."

"What happened?" Piper asked.

"It was one vision after another," Phoebe said, her voice tired. "Sometimes they blurred together. All the witches fighting Astarte."

"How do you know her name?" Paige asked. "You passed out before Leo told us."

Phoebe gave her a half smile. "Grams figured it out in one of my visions." She slowly sat upright on the couch. "Why do you think I had such a rush of visions?"

"Probably because they were all happening in the same place," Leo said. "Right where you're sitting, just in different time periods."

Phoebe nodded. "I heard your spell. It banished Astarte in all the different times. But I don't think she's vanquished."

"I don't think so either," Leo agreed. "She's no ordinary demon. I'm going to go talk to the Elders. Maybe they have some idea of how to destroy her."

"What about Wyatt?" The question was burning in Piper's mind. She was concerned about all the other witches, of course, but nothing could take precedence over her worry for her baby.

"I'll ask the Elders that, too," Leo said. "I'm hoping that once we vanquish Astarte, the time lines will go back to normal. All the changes that have happened will reverse. Including Wyatt."

"You're *hoping*?" Piper repeated. That wasn't good enough.

"Piper, we'll get our little boy back," her husband promised. "Or Astarte will answer to me." Then he orbed away.

Piper turned to her sisters with a sigh. "How long do you think the protection spell will last?" she asked.

"Who knows?" Phoebe replied. "That is one strong bull-headed woman. I have a feeling she'll find a way to break the spell. Plus, some of our ancestor witches are still vulnerable. Melinda Warren lived on the East Coast. The protection spell around the Manor isn't going to help her."

Piper bit her lip. "I was kinda hoping it would work to put a shield around all the homes of all the witches, not just around Halliwell Manor."

Phoebe sighed. "I could try to make myself see into the past and make sure," she said. "But not yet. I'm still on vision overload."

"Why do you think she's after us?" Paige asked. "We never did anything to her. We didn't even know she existed!"

"Good question," Piper said. "Maybe it's not us she's mad at. Leo said she was slumbering for centuries."

"So she's grumpy because she's still half-asleep?" Phoebe joked.

"I don't know," Piper said. "But I do think we should figure out who woke her up."

"I'm way ahead of you," Paige said, heading toward the stairs. "Let's ask the Book of Shadows."

"Um, Paige?" Phoebe croaked. "A little help?"

Piper studied her sister. Phoebe really did look too exhausted to climb three floors to the attic. "At your service," Paige said, coming over to take Phoebe's hand. Piper grabbed on, and Paige orbed them upstairs.

"I'm going to try scrying," Piper told her sisters. She took a crystal off a hook on the wall. "With a twist."

The Book of Shadows lay on its pedestal, closed. Piper lifted her arm, letting the crystal dangle on its chain over the book. She concentrated on the crystal, forcing her thoughts of Wyatt out of her mind. Usually scrying was done over a map, and the crystal would land in the spot where the demon or warlock or other evil being was at that moment. But Piper had a feeling that the Book of Shadows could help her scry through time instead. She gazed into the lights reflecting off the crystal and focused on Astarte. Where was she? *When* was she?

Suddenly the book flew open. The old pages crackled as they turned quickly, blowing through page after page even though there was no wind. Piper kept her focus on the crystal and waited for the pages to finish turning. They stopped just as suddenly as they'd started, and the crystal thunked down onto the book.

Paige and Phoebe crowded close to see the results of Piper's scrying. She let her thoughts leave Astarte, and looked down at the Book of Shadows. It lay open to a page entitled "The Enemy at Home." And the first thing Piper saw was a drawing—a picture of her ancestor, P. Russell. An evil witch.

"I don't care how tired I am, I'm the one who's going," Phoebe insisted. "Our great-cousin Russell was *my* past life."

"Great-cousin?" Paige repeated, wrinkling her nose.

"Whatever. Great-grandma's cousin," Phoebe said. "It was me, my past incarnation. She's the one who woke up Astarte. So I'm the one who's going back there to find out why."

"But you're still tired from all the visions," Piper said, her voice filled with concern.

"I know, and that's why I have two talented sisters to help me do the time-travel spell," Phoebe said. "Nineteen twenties, here I come."

Piper sighed. "We know that P. Russell was killed in 1924. So she couldn't have woken Astarte after that. But she could've done it anytime before then. We don't even know what year to send you to."

"We can do a spell to follow the trail of evil," Paige suggested.

"Good idea," Piper said. "And then we'll all go back together."

Phoebe opened her mouth to protest, then closed it again. She *was* exhausted. And the idea of going back to face her own past life was daunting. It would be a relief to have her sisters with her.

Before she knew it, Paige and Piper had set up a magic circle on the attic floor and lit all the candles. Phoebe joined them and recited the time-travel spell.

Then everything went white and she couldn't see a thing. There was a strange, peaceful feeling of weightlessness. *I could get used to this,* Phoebe thought. And then . . . chaos!

They were in the Manor, still in the attic. But everything was different. The stained glass in the window was cleaner, for one thing. The rest of the attic, though, was a disaster. Furniture lay upended on the floor, pieces of broken china and scattered remnants of herbs and potions were strewn about the room. In one corner the floorboards were scorched black from an obviously recent fire. The air was filled with smoke.

At the top of the stairs stood two witches, arms raised.

"Don't shoot!" Phoebe yelped, ducking. "Or freeze, or put me in slow motion."

One of the witches narrowed her eyes. "How do you know what our powers are?" she demanded.

"Um, I met you guys once when I was in the body of my past life," Phoebe explained. "Your cousin Miss Russell?"

The witch raised her hands again. "You mean our cousin who just almost got us killed?"

"No!" Piper stepped in front of Phoebe. "That was a past life of Phoebe's. Now she's a good witch, and she's my sister." She smiled at the witch. "And you're our great-grandmother."

Phoebe held her breath. When she'd inhabited the body of her past life, these two witches had killed her. Would they do it again?

Slowly the witch lowered her hands. "I'm not even married," she said.

"I know," Piper told her. "And I'm not supposed to tell you any of this . . . but our lives are at stake, so screw the rules. You'll be married, and you'll have a daughter who's our grams. Your last name is Baxter, right?"

The witch nodded. "I'm Miss Baxter, and this is my cousin Miss Bowen."

The other woman grinned at them. "Now that you mention it, I can see the resemblance," she said. "So you're from the future? That's a kick!" She glanced around the room. "Sorry it's such a mess in here. We had a big battle right before you showed up."

"Is that why you're here?" Miss Baxter asked. She still seemed suspicious of them, while Miss Bowen was all smiles.

"Yes," Phoebe said. "There's a powerful ancient demon on the loose. She's attacking our family in lots of different time periods all at once."

"We think she was awakened here," Paige put in. "In your time."

Miss Baxter nodded. "She was. About an hour ago."

"Do you want some tea?" Miss Bowen put in. "Or a little giggle water?"

"Um, no thanks," Phoebe said, wishing she'd had time to brush up on her 1920s slang before coming here. "We're in a bit of a rush."

"Where's Miss Russell?" Piper asked. "She's the one who awakened the demon. We think so, anyway."

Miss Baxter frowned. "She's gone. Astarte killed her."

Phoebe felt a rush of fear. P. Russell wasn't supposed to die until 1924, and she was supposed to be killed by these two witches, not by an ancient evil goddess. Already the normal time line had been messed up—who could tell what repercussions this would have in the future?

"Can you tell us what happened?" Paige asked the cousins. "Why did she wake up Astarte?"

Miss Bowen rolled her eyes. "You have to know her. She'd been getting more and more balled up lately—interested in all kinds of dark magic. She got it into her head that Aparte—"

"Astarte," Miss Baxter corrected her.

Miss Bowen shrugged. "Sorry. She thought that Astarkay was the real McCoy, and that if she awakened her, she could steal her powers. Apparently there were some old Somoleans—"

"Sumerians," Miss Baxter corrected.

"Who thought Astupay was the goddess," Miss Bowen went on. "And she thought they were right."

"So your cousin Miss Russell wanted to be a goddess," Piper said.

Miss Baxter sighed. "She has a new fella. He's a bad influence on her. Lately all she wanted was more power."

"She didn't tell us about the Aparke spell," Miss Bowen put in.

"Astarte," Phoebe corrected her.

"Right," Miss Bowen said. "We only found out about it because we heard a ruckus up here. We came into the room and our cousin was already fighting with Aspartay."

Phoebe gave up on correcting her pronunciation. "What were they fighting about?"

"Miss Russell was trying to take Astarte's power," Miss Baxter said. "And Astarte was offended that a mortal would presume to steal from her. She said she was going to teach our cousin a lesson—by wiping her bloodline off the face of the earth."

"Great," Paige said. "That's just what we were afraid of."

"Are you dolls the ones who stopped her?" Miss Bowen asked. "I was ready to cast a kitten, but then we felt a magic wind and Atarpay disappeared."

Paige shot Phoebe a confused look. Phoebe shrugged. Miss Bowen's conversational style was hard to follow.

"Do you mean Astarte almost killed you, too?" Piper asked.

"And how!" Miss Bowen said. "But something stopped her."

"We put a protection spell around the house," Piper explained. "But we don't know how long it will last against Astarte."

"How are we going to fight a demon who can attack our entire family tree at once?" Miss Baxter asked.

"I don't know," Phoebe told her great-grandmother. "But we'll find a way."

Paige breathed a sigh of relief as the strange feeling of time travel ended and she found herself back in the attic—their own attic, in their own time. Leo was waiting for them.

"You have a visitor downstairs," he said, glancing at Paige.

"Who?" Piper asked.

"And why are you looking at me that way?" Paige added. His eyes were filled with concern.

"I'm not sure you should meet her, Paige," Leo said. "Maybe you ought to wait in the attic."

"Why?" Paige demanded. "Who can't I meet?"

"Me," said a voice from the doorway.

Paige turned to see a petite young girl peeking into the attic. She had light brown eyes and full lips, and something about her looked familiar.

Leo sighed. "Paige, this is your granddaughter Posie. And for the record, it's a bad idea for you to meet her."

"Why?" Phoebe asked. Paige knew that she should be the one asking the questions, but she was too blown away to speak. Her *granddaughter*? This girl was her granddaughter? The ramifications of that were mind-boggling. It meant she would have a child someday. Maybe more than one. Maybe she'd be married. Maybe—

"Because if Paige finds out too much about her future, she could accidentally do something to change it," Leo said. "It's never a good idea for people to know about their own future lives."

So much for finding out all about my husband and children, Paige thought with a sigh.

"Sorry, Grams," Posie said.

"Okay, never call me that again," Paige told her. "Or not until I'm old, at least."

Posie nodded. "Right. Sorry. Should I call you Gigi?"

Paige stared at her blankly. "Why would you call me Gigi?"

"Oh, well, that's what Great-aunt Phoebe's grandkids call her," Posie said. "You know, for 'Gorgeous Grandma.'"

Phoebe gave a little shriek and covered her ears. Leo's frown grew deeper.

"You know what, just call me Paige," Paige said quickly, taking the girl's hand. "And let's go back downstairs before Leo has a fit."

"Right. Sorry." Posie shook her head, frustrated. "I don't really know what I'm doing here. I'm brand-new at all this magic stuff."

"How old are you?" Paige asked.

"Seventeen," Posie told her. "I've been studying with my mom, you know? But I've never had to do anything on my own."

"How did you get to this time?" Piper asked as they all tromped down the stairs to the wrecked living room.

"Mom did the spell to send me here," Posie said, tears filling her eyes. "She was hurt real bad, so she couldn't come herself. I'm scared that when I get back, she'll be—"

"Don't think like that," Paige interrupted. "Your mom will be fine. We're going to fix everything."

"That amazon demon was too hard to fight," Posie said. "Mom is a strong witch, but that demon had her beat. Then all of a sudden she disappeared."

"We did a spell to protect the Manor," Phoebe explained.

Posie nodded. "That's what Mom said. She figured only the Power of Three was strong enough to fight that demon."

Paige had to force her jaws to stay closed. Everything that Posie said made her more curious. So her daughter was a strong witch, and she knew about the power of three, and she was teaching her own child the craft—

"What's her name?" Paige blurted out. "Your mom?"

"Pandora," Posie said.

Piper snorted, and Paige felt a blush creep up her cheeks. She was going to name her daughter Pandora? That was just asking for trouble.

"But she calls herself Dora," Posie added.

"Can we stop talking about the future, please?" Leo begged.

The floor in the foyer suddenly became covered in ceramic tile. Paige shot a worried look at her sisters. "The floor changed."

Piper nodded. "That's not good."

"Astarte must've gotten through the protection spell in one of the other times," Phoebe said worriedly.

"We need a plan," Piper said. "Paige, you take Posie and whip up some more sage-and-apple potion. Maybe you can give the protection spell a power boost. Phoebe and I will try to figure out a way to vanquish Astarte."

"Okeydokey. C'mon, kid." Paige led her granddaughter into the kitchen and pulled out a small packet of dried sage. "I used up the fresh herb making the potion earlier," she said. "So we're stuck with the dried stuff."

"Is that bad?" Posie asked.

"It's not as powerful when it's dry," Paige replied. She studied

Posie's sweet, innocent face. "How long have you been studying the craft?"

Posie bit her lip. "About a month," she said. "I guess you can tell that I don't know much, huh?"

"Have you ever made a potion before?" Paige asked.

"Oh, yeah. Mom taught me how to do a potion that would make a rose go from bud to bloom instantly."

Paige smiled. "How did that go?"

"Not too good," Posie admitted. "I was supposed to use a pinch of ragwort and I used too much. The rose turned into a cabbage."

"How much did you pinch?" Paige asked.

"I scooped up a bunch in my fingers. But how am I supposed to know how much a pinch is? Everybody pinches differently, don't they?"

Paige heard frustration in the girl's voice. But that was the least of her problems right now. "It does take some getting used to. Usually when the potion calls for a pinch, it means you should just pick up a tiny bit between your thumb and your forefinger." She handed Posie an apple peeler. "I'd love to teach you, but since we're in a rush, I think you'd better stick to the easy stuff."

Posie grinned and grabbed an apple from the bowl on the counter. "That's more my speed, anyway."

By the time she and Posie had recircled the Manor with the protective potion, Phoebe and Piper had come up with a plan.

"Leo got an ancient parchment from the Elders," Piper explained when they all gathered back in the living room. "It's in Sumerian, but a medieval monk translated it. It tells how to vanquish Astarte."

Paige's mouth dropped open. "That's perfect!" she cried. "What are we waiting for?"

"We're not sure it will work," Phoebe told her. "It's impossible to know who wrote the instructions."

"It's all guesswork," Leo said. "Astarte is extremely old, and the different groups of people who followed her told stories of her having a wide range of powers. It's hard to tell which powers she really has and which ones are myths."

"Well, we know she can throw lightning," Phoebe said. "And we know that sometimes she's a babe and sometimes she's an armor-plated bull. That's enough for me."

"Okay, so the parchment contains a vanquishing potion and a spell," Leo said. "It says that first the spell, then the potion must be used in order to forever vanquish Astarte."

"If these instructions come from ancient Sumeria, then why is she still around?" Paige demanded.

Piper sighed. "Apparently the spell and the potion never worked," she said. "The parchment states that Astarte can only be vanquished by witches with 'untroubled hearts' who are willing to give those hearts to the cause of getting rid of Astarte."

"And since her followers thought she was a goddess, they might have been conflicted about whether or not they should fight against her," Leo said.

"Or else Astarte just zapped people with lightning whenever they tried to vanquish her, which seems more likely to me," Phoebe said. "That's why we need to make her weak before we do the spell, to keep her from fighting it."

"Okay." Paige thought the plan seemed a little vague. But it was the best chance they had. "How do we weaken her?"

"We borrow her own idea," Piper said. "We're going to use the same weapon she does."

"A lightning bolt?" Posie asked.

"No, the power to be in all times at once," Piper said. "Since Astarte can be in different time periods, we're going to attack her in all of them at the same time."

"How can we do that?" Posie asked, wide-eyed. "Are you guys

powerful enough to be everywhere at once the way Astarte is?"

"I wish." Paige grinned. "The Power of Three is strong, but not that strong."

"We'll need help," Phoebe agreed. "And we know where to get it."

"All of our ancestors, and whatever future Halliwells we can find"—Piper smiled at Posie—"all together, we'll summon Astarte. She'll be fighting us all at the same time, using up a lot of energy. If we all keep her busy, her strength will start to wane."

"Then, when she's weak, we'll all say the vanquishing spell together, and we'll all throw the vanquishing potion together," Phoebe finished. "If we hit her at the same instant in all the different time periods, she won't be able to escape or to fight."

"We'll send you back to your own time. Your mom can help you make the potion," Piper told Posie.

Posie nodded, still frightened.

"Okay, sounds like a plan," Paige said. "But there's one problem: How are we going to tell all the other witches?"

Phoebe relaxed into the strange, wonderful feeling of the time-travel spell. She knew it wouldn't last long, and she intended to enjoy every delicious second of it. All too soon, the usual sensations came rushing back to her body and she had to deal with reality.

She opened her eyes in the Manor. The calendar on the wall told her that the year was 1967.

Her mother and her grandmother stared back at her from the other side of the kitchen table. Grams looked the same as Phoebe remembered, but with dark hair and fewer lines on her face. Phoebe's mother, Patty, wore her long hair parted in the middle and hanging straight down. She had on a gauzy halter top and a peasant skirt that reached the floor. A peace sign was drawn on her cheek. Phoebe couldn't believe it—her mom was a teenage hippie! "We've been waiting for you," Patty said. "We knew someone would come to discuss Astarte—we could feel powerful good magic putting a protective spell around the Manor."

Phoebe raced across the room and flung herself into her mother's arms. Patty pulled away, surprised.

"Oh. Sorry." Phoebe forced herself to release her mom. "Um, it's just that I . . . I know you."

"You're a witch of our line, come from the future," Grams said.

Phoebe nodded, suppressing the urge to give Grams a big hug too. "Yes. I'm your—"

"Don't!" Grams barked. "It's dangerous for us to know about our own futures. You could tell us something that would accidentally change the way we behave. You could cause us to step onto the wrong time line."

"That's what Leo, our Whitelighter, said," Phoebe told her. "But why does it matter? Astarte has already disrupted the time line. We're fighting to restore it to normal. So what if we mess it up a little more along the way? When we vanquish Astarte, everything will go back to the way it's meant to be."

"I agree," her mother said. "We're already dealing with strong magic. Why not be honest with one another?"

"Because it's irresponsible," Grams muttered. "Even if we manage to restore the time line to normal, there's a chance we'll remember what happened along the way. We may remember what she tells us about our own futures, and it would change our actions."

Patty rolled her eyes. "My mother has no faith that things will work out the way they're supposed to," she said.

"I don't believe that magical things always turn out for the best," Grams retorted. "You throw caution to the wind when it comes to magic."

"I trust my instincts," Patty argued.

Phoebe didn't know what to say. She'd known her mother and her grandmother didn't always see eye to eye, especially when it came to their magical destinies. But it was still strange to see these two women, whom she loved, arguing like . . . well, like a mother and daughter.

"Um, sorry to interrupt," she said, "but I need to tell you guys something."

Patty turned to her and studied Phoebe's face intently. "You're my daughter," she murmured.

"Yes. I won't be born for another eight years." Phoebe smiled. "It's amazing to see you, especially so young."

"Please don't say anything else," Grams interrupted. "You've already told us too much."

"Oh, don't listen to her," Patty said. "She's too conservative."

Phoebe thought about it. Maybe Grams had a point. It was so tempting to warn her mother about the demon who was going to kill her in 1978. That way Patty could avoid being killed, and Phoebe could grow up having a mom. But she knew that changing the time line could have disastrous results. For all she knew, having her mother around would have changed their lives so much that they never would have accepted their powers. Or maybe if her mother hadn't been killed, she and her sisters would have evolved into different people than the ones they were right now. Maybe they wouldn't have wanted to accept their destiny as the Charmed Ones.

And besides, magically traveling back in time to save her mother's life would definitely count as using her powers for personal gain. Phoebe knew better than to do that. As hard as it was, she had to do what Grams said. She had to stop herself from telling them about the future.

"I think you're right, Grams," Phoebe said.

Grams's face softened when she heard the name.

"Oops, I mean Penny," Phoebe corrected herself. "We shouldn't talk about the future. We should talk about Astarte. She's trying to wipe out our entire family, and she can exist in all times at once."

Her mother and grandmother exchanged a worried look. "Wow, that's really bad," Patty said. "We thought she was just a time-traveling demon, not that she could be in more than one time at once."

"*You* thought that," Grams replied. "I told you she was more powerful than we realized."

Patty rolled her eyes again. "Fine, Mom, you're right," she said. "You're always right. I guess I shouldn't even bother having an opinion of my own."

"Don't be so dramatic, Patty—," Grams started.

"Stop!" Phoebe interrupted. "No more bickering! Let's stay focused on Astarte. My sisters and I came up with a plan to vanquish her."

"Your sisters?" Patty asked. "How many sisters do you have?"

Phoebe bit her lip. *Whoops. Shouldn't have said that.* She forced herself to look into her mother's eyes. "I shouldn't tell you about that," she said. "I'm sorry."

"Oh. Okay, I guess," Patty said.

Phoebe hated to see her mother's face look so sad. This visit back in time was turning out to be harder than she'd expected. When she, Paige, and Piper had agreed to split up the trips to see all the ancestor witches, Phoebe had thought she was getting the best assignment of all—a visit to her mother and grandmother. But she hadn't realized it would be so hard.

"Let me just tell you the plan and then I'll leave," she said in a rush, eager to get this over with before they started fighting again. "We're going to fight Astarte with her own weapon—the ability to be in all times at once. We'll summon her in our time.

Other witches will summon her even further in the future, and in every other time period we know about."

"And then we vanquish her," Grams said.

"Exactly," Phoebe told her. "The summoning starts at six o'clock tonight. Are you two ready to help?"

"Of course we are," Patty told her. "As long as we don't kill each other first."

Piper looked around the large, empty hallway. The time-travel spell had taken her somewhere, that much was certain. But she'd been expecting a house on the other end of it—and a witch. Great-great-great-aunt Brianna, to be specific.

"Hello?" Piper called. Her voice echoed off the marble floors and down the long hall, but nobody answered.

"Aunt Brianna?" she tried again.

Nothing.

Piper started down the hall. Occasionally there was a bench, and paintings hung on the walls. Maybe it was a museum. She spotted a door with a glass doorknob. *Might as well check it out,* she thought, reaching for the knob.

"Do not go in there," a voice said from behind her.

Piper froze. She hadn't heard anyone come up.

"That room is not protected," the voice continued. A barefoot woman with thick red hair stepped up to her side. "Only the hallway."

Piper stared at her. She was thin, with a lined face and a few strands of gray in her hair. "Are you Brianna Warren?" Piper asked.

"That I am."

"Where are we?" Piper asked.

"In the national museum in Sevastopol," Aunt Brianna said.

"I'm Piper Halliwell. I'm a descendant of yours," Piper told her. "I come from one hundred and forty-four years in the future."

"I see." Aunt Brianna didn't sound very surprised. In fact, she didn't even sound interested. She turned and began walking down the hall. Piper followed.

"When I didn't see you, I was afraid Astarte had succeeded in killing you," Piper said.

"No." Aunt Brianna glanced at her. "She tried. But a spell came and stopped her."

"My sisters and I put up a protective wall around the homes of all our ancestor witches," Piper explained. "At least, we tried. I wasn't sure it would work at any building other than our own house."

Aunt Brianna shrugged. "It worked here. I consider the museum home, even though I'm only the maid. It's why I can go unseen—I know the building well. I was simply behind the column yonder, watching to see if you were friendly."

"I don't understand," Piper admitted. "Do you live here?"

"I sleep here often," Aunt Brianna said. "In the room back there."

"But you said it wasn't protected," Piper cried.

"My bed is in that room, but my heart is in the halls of the museum, with the art," Aunt Brianna said. Finally some emotion had crept into her voice. "This is my true home."

"Huh," Piper said. Her spell had worked even better than she'd expected. It not only protected witches outside the Manor, it also protected witches in places that weren't traditional homes at all.

Aunt Brianna was lost in thought, staring at a painting of a pastoral scene. Piper knew she'd seen the piece before, but she didn't have a clue who the artist was. Her great-great-great-aunt seemed to have forgotten she was there.

"I've come to ask for your help," Piper told her. "Astarte is attacking all of our family, in many different time periods at once. She's very dangerous."

"Yes." Aunt Brianna didn't take her eyes from the painting. "Do you see the brushstrokes?" she asked dreamily. "Short, careful strokes. Just the tiniest dab of the brush to convey all the greatest passions of the human spirit."

"Um . . . sure," Piper said. She was getting the feeling that Aunt Brianna didn't quite live in reality, whatever her particular reality was. She barely seemed aware that there was a powerful demon out there who needed vanquishing.

"Aunt Brianna, do you remember Gabriel, the Lord of War?" Piper asked. "I know that you once separated him from his weapon."

"Yes."

"Even though he was the strong and evil Lord of War," Piper went on.

"Yes," Aunt Brianna said. "He brought violence here, to the museum. He led soldiers here to loot and burn. The paintings were in peril."

"Oh." *So that's why she'd attacked him,* Piper realized. *Not because he was evil, just because he had threatened her precious art.* "I've come to ask for your help," Piper said. "My sisters and I are gathering as many witches from our line as we can. We're going to pool our powers to vanquish Astarte. Will you join us?"

Finally Aunt Brianna tore her eyes away from the painting. "Why should I?"

"Because it's your family," Piper said. "Astarte is trying to kill us all."

"I have no family," Aunt Brianna told her. "Only one sister, and she's gone to America. I care nothing for these battles of magic. I care only for the art. My job is to take care of the paintings in this hallway, to keep them clean and make sure the sunlight doesn't enter to fade their colors. I care for nothing else."

Piper didn't know what to say. Aunt Brianna didn't seem fanatical, or unhappy, or even particularly unfriendly. But it was obvious that she didn't care for human life, even the lives of her own relatives. All she cared about was art.

"We're doing a spell tonight," Piper told her. "One spell to summon Astarte, another to vanquish her. And there's a potion." She lay two pieces of paper on the bench, one with the spell, another with the recipe for the vanquishing potion. "Aunt Brianna? Will you help?"

Aunt Brianna had moved on to the next painting, a still life with fruit. "Hmm?" she said.

"Will you help us vanquish Astarte?"

"Oh . . . possibly," Aunt Brianna replied vaguely. "If I finish dusting the paintings in time."

Piper had a bad feeling she knew what that meant—that Aunt Brianna would forget all about them. They couldn't count on her.

Paige gritted her teeth and waited for the bizarre, weightless feeling of the time-travel spell to end. She knew they had no choice but to talk to their ancestor witches face-to-face, but she really hated that tingly, antigravity feeling. Finally it was over. She opened her eyes.

The sun hung low in the sky over a tree-covered hill, and the thick glass in the window made the light look shimmery and warped.

"Where did ye come from then?" asked a frightened voice behind her.

Paige turned to see a teenage girl and an older woman huddled together near the fireplace of the tiny room. The girl clutched at an amulet she wore on a piece of leather around her neck.

"Melinda?" Paige asked.

The girl's green eyes widened, and she gave a little cry.

"I asked a question," the woman said, raising her chin.

"I came from the future," Paige told them. There was no way to explain it any more than that. "Are you Melinda Warren?"

The girl gave another little cry and hid her face in her hands. The woman frowned at Paige. "The one who intrudes in our home uninvited should be the first to introduce herself," she said, eyeing Paige's tight jeans with distaste.

"Right. Sorry. I'm Paige Matthews. I'm a descendant of Melinda Warren." She held out her hand to the woman. "And you are?"

"Melinda's mother," the woman replied. She didn't shake Paige's hand.

"Charlotte," Paige said. "That's your name, right?"

She noticed Charlotte's look of surprise, immediately hidden. Obviously Paige had gotten it right. The teenage girl had to be Melinda. She was still hiding behind her mother. These were seriously terrified people.

"The year, is it 1684?" Paige asked.

"Of course it is," Charlotte said suspiciously.

"Right. Good." Paige glanced around the room. It was lit only by the fire and a large candle set on the table. "There's been a demon here, hasn't there? A very tall woman, maybe with the head of a bull."

"How can ye know such things?" Melinda gasped.

"She's a demon," Paige went on. "She's trying to kill us, all of us, from the two of you right down to my granddaughter."

Slowly Charlotte relaxed. "Yes, she was here. I thought at first that she was the goddess, but then she attacked my daughter. The true goddess would never turn on one who honors her as we do."

"Mother," Melinda cried.

"It's all right, child," Charlotte said. "This lady won't be visiting Reverend Rossiter, I reckon. She's a witch like we are."

"Yes," Paige told Melinda. "My two sisters and I are all witches. And you're the one who predicted that we would be the most powerful witches of all time. You're the first Warren witch." She didn't mention that Melinda was destined to be burned at the stake in the Salem witch trials some years later. It was hard to imagine this scared young girl facing down her accusers and willingly allowing herself to be executed in order to save her daughter. Right now Melinda seemed like a frightened little rabbit.

"There, child, stop hiding," Charlotte said gently. "Miss Matthews is here to help us, I think."

"Actually, I'm here to ask for your help," Paige admitted. "You were right about one thing—that demon *is* a goddess. Unfortunately she's an evil one."

Melinda shuddered. "Her laugh was loud as thunder. I feared she would burn down our cottage with her lightning."

"I know," Paige said. "My sisters and I did a protection spell to keep her from our home. We hoped that it would work to keep her from your home too."

"And that it did," Charlotte replied gratefully. "We are in your debt, Miss Matthews. Had it not been for your spell, we would surely be lost."

"It was only a temporary fix, though," Paige said. "Astarte will keep coming after us, all of us. We have to vanquish her once and for all."

Charlotte nodded, but Melinda still looked frightened.

"It won't be easy," Paige went on. "My sisters and I have a plan, but it requires summoning Astarte into your home again. You have to be brave enough to face her, and fight her." She looked into Melinda's eyes. "Do you have the courage?"

• • •

Phoebe paced nervously up and down the length of the kitchen. "There are only a handful of us left," she muttered. "Who knows how many other ancestors and descendants Astarte has killed?"

"I know of at least six," Leo said from his perch on one of the stools.

"Thanks a lot." Phoebe shot him a frown. "That doesn't help me feel better."

He shrugged helplessly. "I'm only telling the truth. And your silverware just changed patterns." He held up an ornately carved silver spoon, still dripping from the tea he'd been stirring. "That means the protection spell has failed again in another time."

A whirring sound filled the room as Paige appeared. She shuddered, as if trying to shake something off her body. "For the record, I hate time travel," she announced.

"Did you find Melinda Warren?" Phoebe asked.

"Yup, I talked to her and Charlotte, her mother." Paige sighed and sat next to Leo. "Charlotte is ready to help us, but I'm worried about Melinda. She's only a kid, and she was terrified of Astarte."

"Do you think she'll chicken out?" Phoebe asked, worried. It was bad enough that she couldn't count on her own mom and Grams to make it through the summoning spell without fighting so much that they forgot what they were doing. If they had worries about Melinda Warren, too, they were in bad shape.

Another whirring sound came as Piper appeared from the past. She didn't look happy.

"Uh-oh. What happened?" Phoebe asked.

"Great-aunt Brianna is a total bust," Piper cried. "She doesn't even care that we're being attacked by Astarte. All she cares about is the artwork in her precious museum!"

Phoebe couldn't believe her ears. *Another* unreliable ancestor? "What are we going to do?" she asked. "Things keep changing— Astarte is still out there attacking other members of our family."

Piper examined the new silverware. "This is bad," she said. "We need the help of the others. If I don't see Wyatt again soon I'm going to go crazy."

Leo slipped his arm around her shoulders. "Try not to worry," he said. "As long as you can vanquish Astarte, Wyatt will be back. I'm going to check in with the Elders and see what I can find out about the rest of your ancestors. Maybe there are others whom we haven't talked to yet who will be more willing to help us." He gave Piper a kiss and orbed out of the room.

"I have an idea," Paige said. "We've talked to the other witches in person, but maybe we need to do the spell together for real."

Phoebe frowned. "What do you mean?"

"I've been working with a rare crystal called Indochine tektite. It strengthens communication between loved ones. I'm thinking we can use it to set up some kind of magical conference call," Paige suggested. "If we summon all our ancestor witches while drawing on the power of the crystal, we can all be here in the same place at once. That way we can keep an eye on all the ancestors we don't trust."

"That's perfect," Phoebe cried. "First we'll summon our ancestors—"

"And Posie," Paige put in.

"Right," Phoebe agreed. "And then, all together, we'll summon Astarte."

Suddenly a bolt of lightning arced through the kitchen window. Phoebe ducked just in time as the electricity passed over her head. "I don't think we have to summon Astarte," she said grimly. "She's already here."

"The protection spell can't hold her much longer," Piper said. "Everyone into the living room. Paige, let's get your magic conference call going. We can use the spell to summon our matriarchs."

"Right." Paige placed the huge crystal on the living-room

floor. She, Phoebe, and Piper arranged themselves in a rough circle around it and recited:

> *I call forth from time and space*
> *Women from the Warren line,*
> *Mothers, daughters, sisters, friends,*
> *Our family's spirit without end,*
> *To gather now in this sacred place*
> *To help bring this demon to disgrace.*

One by one they appeared, the other Warren witches. They filled out the circle around the tektite crystal. Melinda cowered behind her mother. Aunt Brianna frowned and glanced about as if she were looking for an escape route—or maybe for her precious artwork. Grams reached out to fix a strand of Patty's hair, and Patty brushed her arm away in annoyance. Miss Bowen appeared alone, a deep burn on her arm.

Phoebe met her eyes. "Miss Baxter?" she asked.

Miss Bowen shook her head. "She's gravely hurt. Astarte managed to get through the protective circle and into the Manor."

Phoebe forced herself to push down her panic. Miss Baxter was their great-grandmother. If she died before her time, Phoebe and all her sisters—not to mention Grams and Mom—would never exist. Astarte would succeed in wiping out their line. They had to vanquish her *now*.

Posie appeared last, her eyes rimmed with red from crying. *Her mom must've succumbed to her wounds in the future,* Phoebe thought sadly. *We have to vanquish Astarte before we lose any more witches—and any more of our time line.*

"Okay, everybody, listen up," Piper called. "We're going to do this together, all of us here right now. Astarte is already attacking."

"I thought we were supposed to summon her to all our separate times," Grams said.

"Where is my museum?" Aunt Brianna demanded. "You never mentioned me having to leave my museum."

"If Astarte wins, you'll never see your museum again," Piper snapped. "She's trying to kill you!"

Aunt Brianna raised her chin stubbornly, but Phoebe cut her off before she could say anything else. "If you get killed, who will take care of the paintings?" she asked.

Slowly, understanding filled Aunt Brianna's eyes. "You're right," she said.

A lightning bolt blew down the front door, and Astarte appeared in full armor, her bull's head terrifying with its red eyes and flaring nostrils. Phoebe could swear she was five feet taller than she'd been before.

She raised her arms to strike.

"Now!" Phoebe cried. "Begin the spell!"

They all spoke together, voices mingled in a chorus of past, present, and future.

Earth, water, fire, air,
See Astarte standing there.
Draw our power to do your work,
Vanquish her forever from this earth.

Astarte staggered backward, her fingertips crackling with electricity.

"It's working," Phoebe cried. "She's getting weaker!"

But Astarte just shimmied, changing her shape to that of the amazon woman. She raised her hands and shook them in the air. Tiny lightning bolts shot from her fingers like sparks, then went out. Satisfied, she raised her eyes to the circle of witches.

"That spell didn't vanquish her," Patty pointed out.

"What should we do?" Phoebe asked. "Throw the potion?"

"I don't think that will work either," Piper said. "The truth is, neither the spell nor the potion has ever worked." She raised her voice. "Leo!"

Leo appeared in a swirl of light. "Our translation was wrong," he said immediately. "The Elders figured out that the ancient parchment was mistranslated in the middle ages. You're supposed to say the spell and throw the potion simultaneously, not one at a time."

Astarte strode forward, looking as strong as ever. With one flick of her wrist, she sent a ball of lightning rolling across the floor toward their circle. Melinda gave a little shriek and leaped out of the path of the lightning, breaking the circle. The ball of fire careened into the center of the room, crushing the tektite crystal with its force.

"No!" Paige cried.

Phoebe saw the faces of the other witches, horror and fear in their eyes. Then they vanished, all at once. She and her sisters stood alone in the Manor. And Astarte began to laugh.

Piper felt as if the thunderous laughter might split her head in two. But even through the confusion and noise, her memory of Wyatt kept her thinking straight. Astarte was incredibly powerful, but she and her sisters had faced other powerful entities before.

"We need to get her out of here," she said, grabbing Phoebe's hand. "Even if it's only for a minute or two so we can think."

Paige grabbed her other hand, and they quickly recited the spell to rid the Manor of evil. Astarte vanished, still laughing.

"Thank God," Phoebe murmured, rubbing her ears. The air still vibrated with sound.

"What are we going to do?" Leo asked. "That spell got her out of the Manor, but she'll just come right back as soon as she can."

Paige was examining the tektite crystal. "It's crushed," she said. "We won't be able to use it again."

"Can we contact the other witches in a different way?" Phoebe asked.

"I doubt it," Piper said. "We probably don't have enough time, anyway."

"Well, they all heard the plan," Paige put in. "Say the spell and throw the potion at the same time. So chances are that all of them are making the potion right this second. When Astarte attacks again, they'll throw the potion and say the spell."

Paige bit her lip. "If Posie's making the potion, she's going to put in way too much oak bark. The recipe only calls for a pinch, but she thinks that means a handful."

Piper thought about that. "Okay, then we'll make the potion without any oak bark. Maybe that will compensate for Posie."

"What about Miss Bowen, then?" Phoebe asked. "With Miss Baxter hurt, Miss Bowen's the one who'll be doing the spell."

"And?" Piper asked.

"And she can't pronounce Astarte's name to save her life," Phoebe said. "Literally."

"Hmm." Piper remembered her ancestor mispronouncing "Astarte" in a ton of different ways. "We can't just say the name wrong because Miss Bowen never said it the same way twice."

"Maybe we can reword the spell to account for that," Paige suggested. "So it will cover Astarte by any name."

"Okay," Piper said. "Phoebe, start rewriting. Paige, whip us up a batch of oak barkless potion." Her sisters took off to get started, and Piper turned to her husband. "There's one other problem," she told Leo.

"What?"

"Aunt Brianna is reluctant to help us, Melinda Warren is

scared of her own shadow, and Phoebe said Mom and Grams were constantly arguing."

Understanding filled Leo's blue eyes. "And the instructions for vanquishing Astarte called for witches with untroubled hearts."

Piper nodded. "And witches willing to give their hearts to the cause."

"So how are we going to get them all on board?" Leo asked.

Piper thought back to how Aunt Brianna had acted in her museum. She hadn't necessarily been unwilling to help; she'd just been distracted by the art. "Aunt Brianna can't think of anything other than her paintings," she mused. "She's obsessed with them. It's like she doesn't even notice anything else as long as she has a painting to look at."

Leo smiled. "So you have to take away her paintings for a few minutes. Then she'll be able to concentrate on vanquishing Astarte."

"Especially if she thinks Astarte is responsible for taking the artwork," Piper agreed. "That's why she fought Gabriel, the Lord of War. He was threatening her paintings." She grabbed a match and lit one of the white candles that stood on the mantel. Gazing into its flame, she pictured the museum hallway and its famous paintings. The words came into her mind, and she softly murmured the spell:

> Oils and canvas, masterpieces
> Hide yourselves from witch's eyes.
> Only when Brianna has spoken
> May you reveal yourselves and return her prize.

A sense of power filled her body, and in her mind's eye she saw Aunt Brianna, in the marble hallway, watching in astonishment as the paintings vanished. Nothing but empty walls were left.

Piper glanced up at her husband. "I think it worked. What about Melinda?"

"Her mother wasn't afraid," he said. "We might not have Melinda's help, but we'll have Charlotte's. That will just have to be enough."

Paige came back in from the kitchen. "Okay, here's the new-and-improved potion. Is Phoebe done with the spell?"

"Yup," said Phoebe, running down the stairs from her room.

A bolt of lightning crashed against the living-room window, bathing the room in sinister blue light.

"I took care of Aunt Brianna," Piper told her sisters. "But what about Grams and Mom? If they're fighting, the spell won't work."

"How can we fix that?" Paige asked desperately. "We don't have time to travel back there and referee."

"Even if we did, it's the emotions that matter," Phoebe said. "We might be able to stop them from bickering, but if they're feeling angry and distant from each other, the spell still won't work because their hearts are troubled."

Piper looked at her sisters, their faces etched with worry. "It's okay," she said suddenly.

Paige and Phoebe stared at her, confused.

"You're right, Phoebes, it's the emotions that matter," Piper explained. "Right now, Wyatt is gone. He never existed. But I still love him with all my soul, and I'd do anything for him. He's my child. That's how Grams feels about Mom. It doesn't matter how much they fight, Grams loves her—so deep down, she'll always be on her side."

Phoebe nodded. "And even though I never really knew Mom, I always loved her no matter what. So if she's arguing with Grams—even if she's furious with her—she'll still love her and be on her side."

"Then there's nothing to worry about," Paige said. "They're just having normal mother-daughter stuff, but they're both willing to give their hearts."

"Yeah," Piper said softly. "It's what family does." She reached for her sisters' hands just as Astarte burst through the door once again. "Here we go," Piper said. And she, Paige, and Phoebe recited the spell as Paige hurled the potion at Astarte:

> *Earth, water, fire, air,*
> *See Astarte standing there.*
> *Heed our will, and not our words,*
> *Her name ignored, her essence heard.*
> *Draw our power to do your work,*
> *Vanquish her forever from this earth.*

Astarte's bull head shrunk and turned in on itself to form the stunningly beautiful face of her womanly form. Then that face began to crackle with electric lightning, tiny blue lines of fire tracing over the perfect milky skin. Astarte wasn't laughing now—she was screaming, a sound loud and terrifying like the roar of an oncoming freight train. The blue fire spread from her face down her body, and then her entire form collapsed inward, disappearing in a final flash of lightning.

Piper stood, breathing hard. Somewhere in the distance she heard a ticking sound . . . and she heard it stop. Paige gave a little gasp and held up her wrist. Prudence Warren's amulet dangled from the bracelet she wore.

Then Wyatt let out a wail. Piper whirled to see her beautiful baby in his playpen in the corner. And even though he was crying, all she could do was laugh. The time line was back to normal. They'd vanquished Astarte.

• • •

"If you can get another Indochine tektite crystal, we could do that conference call through time again," Phoebe said as Paige leafed through the Book of Shadows.

Paige shook her head. "They're incredibly rare. It took me six months to track that one down." Finally she found what she'd been searching for. "But we don't need a magical conference call when we have the book!"

She waved her two sisters over to look at the page she'd opened to. "It's a history of the demon Astarte, telling how she was vanquished in 1684, 1860, 1923, and 1967." Paige ran her finger lovingly over the page filled with the handwriting of five different witches.

"Look," Piper said. "Melinda is the one who wrote this: 'My mother's courage in the face of the fearsome demon taught me the true power of any witch: Trust in one's own ability to do good. For even if you are killed in the battle against evil, you will die well, knowing you have done your utmost on the side of good.'"

Paige smiled. "That's how Melinda had the courage to let herself die in the witch trials. She knew she was saving her daughter's life so that her daughter would continue the fight against evil."

"Look at Mom and Grams," Phoebe pointed out. "Mom wrote the whole story and then Grams went through and corrected it!"

"They probably had a huge fight about it afterward," Paige joked.

Piper nudged her in the arm. "I think you should write our part of the Astarte story," she said. "Because when Posie gets around to adding her part in 2049, she'll want to know how much you enjoyed meeting your granddaughter."

"My pleasure," Paige said. As her sisters played with baby Wyatt in the light slanting through the stained-glass window, she added her storyline to the family history.

About the Authors

LAURA J. BURNS has been a writer for years. But what she mostly likes to do is sit on her couch and watch TV. So writing for the Charmed book series is a perfect marriage of her two great loves! She lives in California with her husband, one dog, and four cats.

CAMERON DOKEY is delighted to be back spending time with the Warren witches. Her other Charmed titles include *Haunted by Desire, Truth and Consequences,* and the upcoming *Picture Perfect.* She lives in Seattle with one husband and more cats than she feels comfortable revealing in public.

Primarily known as a television writer, GREG ELLIOT was one of the original writers on the series *Charmed.* He also teaches writing for the UCLA Extension Writers Program. In his spare time he writes short stories, and is working on his first novel.

DIANA G. GALLAGHER dabbled in fantasy art before becoming a full-time author. Best known for her doglike character in *Woof: The House Dragon,* she won a Hugo for Best Fan Artist in 1988. Since her first science-fiction novel was published, *The Alien Dark* (TSR 1990), she has written moe than fifty novels for adults, teens, and young readers in several series, including: Charmed, Buffy the Vampire Slayer, Smallville, American Dreams, Star Trek, and Sabrina the Teenage Witch.

MICOL OSTOW is an editor and writer of books for children, tweens, and teens. She lives and works in New York City, and has written for such series as Fearless, Charmed, Buffy the Vampire Slayer, and American Dreams. In her spare time she enjoys running, snacking, and napping, though not usually at the same time. Though she loves all of the Halliwell sisters equally, she kind of thinks Phoebe kicks butt.

ERICA PASS is currently a doctoral candidate in clinical psychology at the Graduate School of Applied and Professional Psychology at Rutgers University. It is a career switch for her; she was formerly an editorial manager at Nickelodeon for eight years. She has written several books for Simon Spotlight, most recently two for the Survivor series. Her car is named Piper, after her favorite witch.

PAUL RUDITIS started his Hollywood career as a tour guide at Paramount pictures and slowly worked his way up the studio ranks. Eventually he realized that he much prefers to work in his pajamas and left the studio to pursue a writing career. His is the author of Charmed: *The Brewing Storm* and Charmed: *The Book of Three,* the official episode guide for the series.

"We all need to believe that magic exists."

–Phoebe Halliwell, "Trial by Magic"

When Phoebe Halliwell returned to San Francisco to live with her older sisters, Prue and Piper, in Halliwell Manor, she had no idea the turn her life – *all* their lives – would take. Because when Phoebe found the Book of Shadows in the Manor's attic, she learned that she and her sisters were the Charmed Ones, the most powerful witches of all time. Battling demons, warlocks, and other black-magic baddies, Piper and Phoebe lost Prue but discovered their long-lost half-Whitelighter, half-witch sister, Paige Matthews. The Power of Three was reborn.

Look for a new Charmed novel every other month!

Published by Simon & Schuster
TM & © 2004 Spelling Television Inc. All Rights Reserved.

The Queen's Curse

Paige has finally met her Prince Charming. Funny, clever, sweet and absolutely gorgeous, Colin is fantastic, and not at all evil, which is definitely a plus! Paige is completely smitten, so when Colin asks her to marry him she accepts. But love never runs smoothly, and when Paige discovers that Colin is not only a real Prince – of a magical kingdom no less – but also, that he's already engaged, she begins to wonder what else Prince Perfect might be hiding?

ISBN 1416901248

"We're the protectors of the innocent.
We're known as the Charmed Ones."
–Phoebe Halliwell, "Something Wicca This Way Comes"

Go behind the scenes of television's sexiest supernatural thriller with *The Book of Three*, the *only* fully authorized companion to the witty, witchy world of *Charmed*!

Published by Simon & Schuster
TM & © 2004 Spelling Television Inc. All Rights Reserved.

Seasons of the Witch: Vol, One

Discover three of the seasons in a witch's calendar in this great Charmed story collection.

Samhain: 31/10 ~ traditionally known as Halloween. A time to reflect, a time of divination, and most of all a time to honour the ancients. This is Phoebe's season.

Yule: 22/12 ~ the winter solstice. The longest night of the year brings a time of great darkness that looks towards the celebration of the returning sun. This is Paige's season.

Imbolc: 1/2 ~ A time when the earliest hopes for spring are fostered and seeds of dreams are planted for the coming summer months. This is Piper's season.

ISBN 0689872712